ONE BAD APPLE

BLAKE VALENTINE

Published by CRED PRODUCTIONS, 2024.

This is a work of fiction. Similarities to real people, places, or events are entirely coincidental.

ONE BAD APPLE

First edition. March 5, 2024.

Copyright © 2024 BLAKE VALENTINE.

Written by BLAKE VALENTINE.

Chapter 1.

It was the sea spray that woke her. Her eyes opened wide and she jolted into consciousness as if someone had held a defibrillator to her heart. Squinting against the wildcat-like spitting of the surf, she was suspended for a second between sleep and wakefulness. A cloud covered the moon.

Another wave hit. The boat lurched unsteadily on the crow-black sea before it righted itself, creaking.

Involuntarily, she screamed. Or tried to. But they'd used duct tape to seal her mouth. Her desperate breathing was loud in her ears.

They?

He?

She couldn't remember. All she recalled was waiting in the quiet street behind the bank with a notebook in her hand and a head full of questions. It had been a promising tip-off. She sniffed a story. A scoop. Waiting in out-of-the-way places was par for the course in her line of work – it wasn't like every source could be vouched for. She'd stood there for a few minutes until a car – sleek and somehow menacing - pulled up; she'd approached it.

And then, nothing.

It must have been a knockout blow. Someone had crept up and hit her - *surely*? The jackhammer pounding in her head was proof of that. There was a blank shadow clinging to the edge of her vision; in spite of the scythe-like crescent of moon, it stubbornly refused to shift. She grimaced, willing her brain to shake off the cobwebs and start working again.

But daggers of pain drilled at her temples. The pale moonlight showed strands of her hair matted together with dried blood. The tousled hanks scraped at her cheeks as they fluttered in the wind and felt strangely alien to her. She explored the inside of her mouth with her tongue and felt a gap where a tooth had been. Her gum throbbed and the faint metallic taste of her own blood made her nauseous.

Her hands were tied, her fingers numb. When she shifted position, she felt the garrotte-like tightness of cable-ties. Her wrists were raw - the sharp plastic cutting into her flesh in time with the pitching and rolling of the vessel. There was pain elsewhere, too. It came in waves. She shifted position uncomfortably, not daring to think of what else might have transpired when she was unconscious; she was all too conscious of how bare her legs were.

As another salvo of spray whipped at her face, she kicked out her legs in an attempt to free herself. But they remained rooted to the spot. She gyrated violently in a vain effort to free them, but there was no movement - it was as if they'd been nailed in position. Twisting desperately, she tried to place one foot before the other, but merely managed a metallic scraping sound.

A steel bucket.

Looking down, the ghostly lunar light showed her legs disappearing into it from knee height. Confused, she tried to move them once more, but the bucket was filled with concrete that didn't yield to any of her efforts. With a sick feeling that caused her to moan and tears to start in her eyes, she realised her ankles and feet were encased.

The mixture was set fast.

Panicking, she flailed wildly, screaming silently, the tape tearing at her lips; she achieved nothing more than a slight swaying motion. Horrified, she realised she was tied to a sack trolley; the motion was simply its wheels shifting a little against the ties that made it secure. Beyond the bows, the sky was lightening slightly, the horizon was etched with a purple-hued line. She wondered where her press pass was, and her driving licence. Was there a chance they were still in the car? That someone might be able to trace her last movements if they were found?

Crying desperate tears, her eyes opened wide in alarm. The cabin door was pushed ajar. It was wedged open, and a lamp cast its light over the deck. A large figure approached, his pace leisurely - jaunty, almost. At first, he ignored her, walking over to the gunwale to relieve himself, his lack of concern at her presence somehow even more disturbing.

* * * * *

'Woken up then, have we, bitch?' the voice rasped above the noise of the wind. The man spoke from the side of his mouth, an unlit cigar gripped between his teeth. Grabbing his crotch, he leered at her. 'Ready for round two then, are you?' He laughed – the timbre of his chuckle sounding as sharp as shards of broken beer bottles.

The woman emitted a guttural sound, her mouth still muffled by the tape. She writhed from side to side in revulsion. The man raised an eyebrow in mild amusement and tutted. He fidgeted with one of the ropes that bound her.

'You want to calm down, love. You'll do yourself an injury. Then nobody'll want to shag you any more. Well - not *again*.' His eyes were cold, his voice bitter and disinterested.

She continued her protests, emitting a gargling sound.

'Oh, you want to say something?' He looked hard at her and a smile played across his face. He put his cigar down carefully. Then, in a single, vicious motion, he tore the strip of duct tape from her mouth. It made a sound like ripping paper. She howled in agony, her lips and cheeks burning. He watched, steadying himself for a moment as another wave struck the prow.

'You won't get away with this, you know!' she spluttered, spitting blood. The sea air felt suddenly icy against the patch of tender flesh left by the duct tape's removal.

'Yes, we will,' the man assured her calmly.

'I'm a journalist,' she hissed. 'People know who I am. They know *where* I am.'

The man paused. 'No, they don't.' He laughed drily. 'We've had fucking hacks like you sniffing around before, causing problems. We got rid of them, too. *All* of them. So fuck you and your jumped up little ideas.' He paused and rubbed a callused finger down her cheek, laughing as she reeled away. 'There's only one person who makes the rules in this town... and it's not you.'

'But...' she began shaking her head in disbelief.

'Yeah,' he continued smugly. 'You're not the first, sweetheart. Although...' he paused, looking her up and down in the half light. 'You're a bit prettier than some of the others. Nice legs - I kind of fancy having them wrapped around my neck. Well, when they're not dressed in concrete!' He laughed heartily.

'You're fucking crazy!' she cried, and then turned her head to the side of the boat. She began screaming for help. Her captor shook his head. He reached over and pulled a lever. The hydraulics of a motor whirred into action. At the stern of the vessel, a steel tailgate for loading and unloading the day's catch began to lower with a grinding of gears. The sound cut short the woman's protestations. Her heartbeat quickened to a point where it felt like a constant fluttering. A captive butterfly whirled its wings in her chest. 'I'm not a threat!' she cried out. 'I just looked at your accounts - that's all!'

He laughed again, bitterly. 'You bit off more than you can chew here, didn't you?' He began untying the ropes that were fastened to the sack trolley. 'We pay tax... sometimes. But it's the rest of the business that brings in the bread. And who knows what you'd have discovered if you'd carried on rooting around like a little bitch? No - we can't have nosy little bastards like you messing things up! It wouldn't be fair... wouldn't be cricket.' He smirked at his own cleverness, plainly enjoying the fear he was creating.

'But...' she whimpered, a rising tide of hopelessness taking over. 'There must be something we can do. An arrangement? A...'

'No.' He shook his head. 'It's too late for anything like that I'm afraid, darling. We're nearly done here anyway - you're just collateral damage. Anyway – I had what I wanted when you were out for the count. There's nothing more you can offer me now.' He paused. 'You weren't even that good – it was like banging a bag of potatoes. But pussy's pussy, right?' He merely grinned at her gasp of shock.

The wind dropped, and for a moment, the sea was eerily quiet, lapping gently against the hull.

'But you can *help* me!' she pleaded. 'You don't have to... I won't say anything. I'll move away... I'll... I'll do anything you want... You can do...'

The man didn't answer. He simply clipped the cable-ties from where her wrists had been attached to the metal frame. They snapped with a high-pitched twanging noise. For one delightful moment, she thought he was going to free her. For a split-second she was seduced by humanity's endless capacity for denial; she was an optimist walking gamely towards the gas chamber. But, in almost the same motion, he grabbed her wrists with his rough hands and twisted them behind her back. As she yelped, he tied them together, drawing the cord so tight the plastic squeaked.

'Don't! Please!' she begged.

'Nice and easy now,' he cooed softly. 'I bet you used to like being tied up, no?'

The man grabbed the handles of the cart and tilted it towards him, shifting its weight. She leaned back against him, involuntarily, feeling herself fall back against the steel frame. As the woman pleaded, he calmly pushed her towards the dark stern of the boat. The pitch of her screams increased as she approached the edge. But he was resolute. His cocky smirk returned.

Once the wheels hit the steel gutters, the cart stopped dead. The woman's momentum, meanwhile, tipped her forwards, sending her plummeting through the open tailgate and down towards the surface.

She disappeared beneath the waves, the weight of the concrete wrenching her downwards. The splash was large, flinging spray up onto the deck for an instant, abruptly silencing her scream of terror.

And then she was gone.

For a moment, the man stared at the blackness of the sea. He looked absent-mindedly at the thumbnail of dawn now creeping in a violet tinge across the horizon. Then he turned and walked back across the deck, pausing only to collect his cigar. Stepping through the door of the cabin, he nodded at his two companions. Both held a hand of cards. A stack of poker chips was piled on the surface next to each of them, with a half empty bottle of whiskey in the middle of the table. With a smile, he sat down and re-joined the game, lighting his cigar and exhaling contentedly.

Chapter 2.

Trent Rivera walked with a relaxed stride, confident of his own physicality. Dust from the dry earth of the lane wisped with his footfall. Insects flitted in the grass. A gentle wind blew in from the sea, swishing through the branches of trees and carrying the sound of birdsong.

The town of Saltmarsh Cove was nestled in a valley; the walk back up to the campsite had taken him on a steep, chalk path that wound its way through several fields of livestock. It was the kind of path that left hikers red-faced, huffing and puffing.

Rivera hadn't broken a sweat. He wasn't at full strength, though. The energetic blonde who'd ended up back at his campervan had seen to that. She was one of the sun-bleached-sea-kissed creatures the town seemed to sport in abundance – the girls who wandered the promenade with wetsuits hanging open at the waist revealing tight bodies. Rivera had asked her for the time. He didn't recall what she'd said, but it hadn't taken a psychologist to work out what was on his mind. She was fresh and enthusiastic. Come morning, though, he'd been surprised by just how young she looked; she claimed she'd finished university. If they got much younger – he mused to himself – he'd have to start checking passports. Or wearing a condom.

He breathed out contentedly. The sun was shining, and he was a free man. It finally felt like the Army was losing its hold on him. He paused, gazing out beyond the cliff top, and looked down at the sunlight, sparkling as it danced across the brilliant blue of the Channel. Far below him, a fishing boat floated, looking for all the world as if it had been painted on a canvas. Way out in the distance, it was difficult to tell where the sea finished and the sky began. Rivera squinted at a solitary cloud on the horizon for a moment and then walked on.

He was a rugged man in his early forties with sun-tanned skin. Unkempt brown hair spilled down to his shoulders, and he had piercing blue eyes. He wore a red short-sleeved shirt, cut-off denim shorts, and flip-flops. His neck was laced with hippie beads and a shark tooth chain, while his hands and wrists featured an assortment of rings and bracelets which would distract the casual observer from his lithe, toned torso.

Just another happy hippie camper heading out to the countryside to reconnect with nature and smoke a load of dope. Where he was, he fitted right in.

* * * * *

Moving away from the reception area, Rivera followed a gravel path meandering through a small copse of trees. From there, he emerged onto a magnificent green vista stretching all the way to the cliffs. The campsite advertised itself as having direct beach access. He wasn't bothered; he wasn't intending to surf or build sandcastles. His vices, instead, were keeping himself to himself, reading books, having a beer or two in the evening, and smoking the two hand-rolled cigarettes he permitted himself each day. That and his nocturnal pursuits. When he'd left the military, he'd been a heavy smoker and an enthusiastic drinker. He'd also had the libido of a horny teenager. The first two afflictions he'd brought under control. The third... not so much. He'd made concessions, though. He limited his phone usage and had a mobile contract with the least data possible. He was – he reflected – glad the internet wasn't really in existence when he was an adolescent. He'd have ended up with an over-developed right arm and failing vision.

When he arrived, he was pleased to note there were plenty of empty pitches. Having an element of privacy suited him just fine.

The sound of a rattling engine grew in volume as he approached his pitch. His path was cut off by a woman driving up to him on a sit-on lawnmower. Her skin looked to have the leathery texture of an old handbag; she sported an embarrassment of piercings and, as she spoke, a mouth full of crooked teeth was revealed - yellowing stains suggesting she'd stayed faithful to king tobacco. Whatever soft femininity that might once have been there had been buried under smoke and hard living.

She cut the engine.

'Well...' she wheezed in a tone that further suggested a committed nicotine habit. 'You're a bit of alright, aren't you?'

'Excuse me?' he frowned, weighing her up.

'Only kidding!' She cackled as a smile played across her face. 'Mind you...'

'Can I help you?' Rivera enquired, trying not to let his irritation show. He'd had plenty of run-ins with women who were worn around the edges. His charity shop psychology take on it was that it was a reaction to combat. Having spent so long trying to kill people, he was sure that some part of him craved the comfort of human contact; of human affection – however ragged.

But the woman before him was more ragged than most.

'No, love - I'm Janine. Any problems and you give me a shout, alright? Gas. Water. Electric. I'm your girl.'

Rivera nodded and then followed the woman's gaze. There, fifty yards away, glittering in the sun, was a 1979 Volkswagen T2 - a Silverfish campervan. *His* Silverfish. It had a sprig of purple and yellow flowers painted on the driver's side door.

'She yours?' Janine enquired, nodding at the vehicle approvingly.

'She is,' Rivera nodded.

'What do you call her?'

'Iris.'

'Well... she's a beauty. You're a lucky man.' She turned and looked at him, crows' feet puckering the skin around her eyes as she smiled broadly. 'Good work, sir! You've got yourself a good deal there...'

Chapter 3.

'...you've got yourself a good deal there!' The mechanic wiped an oily palm on her overalls before proffering a handshake to the pasty-faced, emaciated man who stood before her. Rivera had returned from Afghanistan three months before. Ever since, his world had steadily fallen apart. All he had left was a khaki duffle bag slung across his shoulder and a haunted look in his eye.

But the card payment had cleared.

That was good enough.

Rivera nodded as he shook the woman's hand. A train rumbled overhead; the garage was situated beneath a couple of railway arches. *Mick's Motors* looked like something straight out of a Seventies sitcom; corrugated iron and barbed wire enclosed a tiny square of Hammersmith back street, untroubled by gentrification. The only other cars on sale were a 1980s Ford Capri Ghia and a Toyota Carina from a decade later - *£150 ONO*. The light rain made them gleam a little – it was enough to cover the rust patches. Almost.

'Nice little runner that one,' the mechanic nodded in the gloom of her office. 'My old man always said she'd go to a good home one of these days.' She sipped at a cup of tea and then placed it back on a gnarled workbench, pushing a rusted spanner out of the way with the back of her hand. The room was bedecked with cobwebs. Stacks of mechanics' manuals for cars long since defunct towered precipitously, almost reaching the roof. 'She won't let you down... go forever...' She licked the tip of a pencil and filled out a chit in her receipt book. Nodding, the mechanic then tore out a carbon copy, which she handed over to the customer. Rivera took it and absent-mindedly thrust it into his pocket, eager to put his past behind him.

* * * * *

The pint of milk had just been an excuse. It wasn't her fault. Shirley. His girlfriend of three years. They'd been serious for a while - moved in together. Even talked of children.

But that had been before.

Rivera didn't blame his girlfriend for losing patience. He'd lost patience with himself a long time before. She'd turned a blind eye to his first couple of illicit liaisons since coming home. There'd been a hunger about him. A desperation. It had been that which had led to him making advances on most of her friends. Sometimes he'd succeeded; other times, he hadn't. But word had got back. He knew it would, and – in a moment of self-loathing - he'd come face-to-face with the regrets that sent him into a drunken spree.

Two days later, he'd put his fist through a section of drywall and smashed up the kitchen of their flat. A pair of military liaison officers paid him a visit soon afterwards. They'd talked with Shirley already - that much had been clear. She'd told them about the drinking. That he wasn't sleeping. Wasn't eating. Told them she heard him chattering to himself in the night. Then, she'd told them she was scared...

That's what did it.

Of course, they'd used words like 'choice,' but Rivera knew the decision had already been made. They offered him a way out on medical grounds. His only other route was a dishonourable discharge. Pale, anaemic, and suddenly scared, the soon-to-be ex-soldier had simply nodded, cracking his knuckles, wondering how the hell things had gone so wrong.

'Travel a bit. Get some fresh air,' the first officer advised. 'You're still young enough - it'll do you good.'

'With what?' Rivera had muttered. 'Last time I checked, I was skint...'

'Draw on your pension,' the second officer instructed, twiddling the end of his moustache. He consulted his notes again before continuing. 'You've done eighteen years and three months, and you've just turned forty. It's yours to spend...'

Rivera had frowned.

'Usually we'd recommend holding off until you're fifty-five,' his colleague added. 'But what have you got to lose?'

* * * * *

He'd seen Shirley on the staircase that morning, coming in as he was going out. She was wearing the same clothes she'd been wearing the night before. Her hair was unkempt. Her make-up smudged. He knew where she'd been – she was little more loyal than him in that regard. She still looked good, though. He felt a stirring and then steadied himself against the bannisters – the last remnants of his hangover surfacing for a second.

'Where are you going?' she'd frowned.

'Milk,' he'd replied bluntly. She'd looked at his packed duffel bag and nodded, in unspoken acknowledgement of all it implied.

Turning, she continued up the staircase while he stepped out into the morning. He paused for a moment on the pavement outside, debating which way to turn. None of the directions available to him promised much.

But a refuse truck pulled to a halt on his right-hand side.

So he turned left.

A short while later, Rivera walked down a side alley and emerged on a down-at-heel street filled with lock-ups. Pigeons pecked at scraps of food spilling from industrial waste containers, and oil-streaked water was pooled in puddles on the broken ground. He picked his way through patches of broken glass and piles of dog shit. Three doors down was a halal butcher, and next to that was a tiny forecourt. It was here that his eye snagged on the purple and yellow flower painted on the driver's side of the T2.

It was love at first sight, and he felt he could be faithful to this partner at least.

Chapter 4.

'You fucked up, Rusty.' The man's voice wasn't angry. More matter-of-fact. Cold.

'Yeah, I know.' The man standing before him looked drawn and uneasy, nervously moving his head to work out the kinks in his neck. He wore a blue trucker's shirt; his name was embossed across a patch in red thread. The sun beating down on the flat roof of the scrapyard office had heated the room like a furnace. The man's forehead was damp with sweat. Across the desk from him, three men lounged on plastic chairs with metal frames. Humourless. In spite of the heat, they were all dressed in black leather jackets. One was bald - one had black hair, and one sported a beanie hat pulled down low on his brow.

There was no doubting the balance of power in the room.

'Listen, you prick,' the dark-haired man announced. The metal leg of his chair scraped as he stood up. He walked over to Rusty and patted him on the shoulder. 'We're not unreasonable. You're young – we know that. Everybody makes mistakes. But this... this was a big one. *Really* fucking big.' As he spoke, he pulled a fresh cigar out of his pocket, calmly clipped it, lit it, and wedged it into the corner of his mouth. 'This isn't just about us, you know? We're only a link in the chain - there'll be other people who're properly pissed off about this.' He paused. 'It doesn't look good. We have to protect things. Protect ourselves. You get me?'

Rusty nodded slowly, uncertain, as the man with the cigar wandered over to the window. 'I'm sorry. OK?'

'It's a lot of money we lost on that shipment, son,' the man with dark hair continued. 'A *lot* of fucking money. And it was *your* fault.' He sighed. 'The cargo's fucked.'

'I know... I...' the man in the blue shirt nodded and then frowned. 'Really?' he began.

'Dammit, Rusty!' The bald man, who'd been silent until now, slammed at the table in frustration. He hit it with such force the whole of the flimsy fibreglass cabin shook; the grates protecting the windows rattled hard. It took a moment before calm returned. 'You know the bosses won't be pleased. And that's a fucking understatement. Someone'll have to take the rap for this...'

Silence hung in the room for a moment before he spoke again, his tone softer this time. He looked hard at Rusty. The younger man squirmed on the spot. 'What went on, anyway? You need to tell us - then we can figure a way out of this. We want to help you - you know that. You've been good for us, but we can't do anything if we don't know what happened.'

'And tell us the truth, for fuck's sake,' urged the man by the window.

A tear rolled down Rusty's face and his voice choked. 'I fucked up. Alright? I told you that.' His lip wobbled slightly before he recovered his poise a little. His words then came in a wheezing torrent. 'I got drunk and fell asleep. And when I woke up and got to the layby, the truck was still there. That's when I called in.'

The bald man nodded sagely, his lips pursed. 'Well - you've been honest with us, so we'll be honest with you.' He paused. 'They found the truck.'

Rusty puffed his cheeks out and sighed heavily.

The bald man continued. 'The Big Man sent a message. He wasn't very fucking happy.'

'I'm not surprised.' Rusty grimaced.

'Yeah,' the man nodded. 'But I told you - he's a reasonable man. Come here and read what he wrote.' He reached over and lifted the vacant chair around to the other side of the table. 'Sit,' he instructed.

'I'm fine,' Rusty shrugged.

'No, you're not fucking fine.' The bald man's words were barbs – the hint of menace ever present. 'Now do as you're fucking told and sit your arse *down*.'

The blue-shirted driver obeyed, lowering himself a little hesitantly into the chair. As he did, the bald man pulled his phone from the inside pocket of his jacket and laid it on the table. He ran a hand over it to wake up the screen, rattling the table a little as he did. 'There,' he rasped, pushing it across the surface and glancing at his watch. 'Have a fucking read of that.'

It was as Rusty leaned forward that the man in the beanie hat stepped silently away from the window and slipped the loop of piano wire he'd removed from his pocket around the driver's neck. He yanked it viciously, drawing it tight and pulling his quarry backwards in a violent motion that sent the chair clattering across the room. Still with the cigar gripped tightly in his mouth, he braced himself as Rusty flailed his legs in a macabre dance, hammering and chiselling at the floor with the rubber soles of his work boots. His hands, meanwhile, clawed desperately, helplessly plucking at the taut metal wire for purchase, frantically seeking to gouge the eyes of his attacker. But the garrotter, as if executing a judo move, spun his torso and shoved his shoulder into the small of the driver's back. He lifted him until his feet were well off the floor. Rusty began frothing at the mouth. His eyes bulged, and the veins in his neck swelled like dammed streams, turning purple at the points where the wire cut into them, trails of blood streaming and soaking into his collar.

Before him, the two seated men looked on impassively. The black-haired man casually lifted his plastic cup when it looked like Rusty's leg might reach the table. He blew at the steam rising from his drink as he regarded the dying man's head turning a beetroot tint. Sipping at his beverage, he watched the driver weaken and returned the cup to the table. 'He always was a useless prick, this one,' he announced to the bald man. 'I told you that when we hired him.'

'Yeah, well – he's not our problem now,' the other man replied.

Rusty gave a few more jerks and spasms, and then emitted a long, low sigh. Then, with a final roll of his eyes, the driver was still, bloody foam flecking his lips.

'One minute and twenty-seven seconds,' announced the bald man, looking up from his watch. 'Not bad.'

'I've done better,' the garrotter smirked. 'Usual drill for this useless sack of shit?'

'Yeah,' nodded the black-haired man. 'I'll tell Wozza to warm up the crusher.'

Chapter 5.

Rivera yawned, looking at his copy of *The Custodian* newspaper.

20 SUSPECTED MIGRANTS FOUND DEAD IN LANCASHIRE LAYBY.

Police are appealing for witnesses after the bodies of 20 suspected illegal migrants were discovered in a layby close to Blackburn in the early hours of yesterday morning. Emergency services were onsite minutes after the alarm was raised, but all casualties were pronounced dead at the scene.

The truck itself was reported stolen on Tuesday night, while the trailer - a tanker - has yet to be traced. Initial investigations suggest the deceased perished from suffocation; the shortage of air within the container would likely have been worsened by the remnants of whichever industrial chemicals were transported in it previously.

Inspector John Harries spoke at an emergency press conference hosted shortly after the discovery: 'Our thoughts at a time like this are naturally with the families of the victims - whoever they may be. They are all the daughters of somebody, somewhere. The Lancashire Constabulary is determined to exhaustively follow all leads going forward.'

'We hereby appeal to the wider public. If anyone has any information that will help us uncover the perpetrators of this dreadful tragedy, then I urge you to come forward immediately. We know there must be people out there who will know details of what has happened. We are talking about the deaths of twenty young women. The nature of the transportation leads us to strongly believe they were being trafficked, and that whoever was driving them was part of a much wider network. If you have any information or know any names, please call the dedicated hotline.'

With the closure of more and more migrant routes, and the tightening of border restrictions across northern France and southern Britain, *traffickers are turning to more ingenious - increasingly risky - tactics to move people across the Channel.*

The so-called Tunis Railroad, which was uncovered 3 months ago, staggered investigators with its complexity. Indeed, the resources the organisation had at its disposal almost outstripped those of the authorities trying to uncover its existence.

'The issue,' claims Professor Lucas Scott, Oxford University - an expert in economic migration from - 'is that once a route is closed, another one simply opens up.'

Autopsies will be carried out on the deceased to confirm causes of death. Should any identities be discovered, the consulates of the relevant nations will be notified immediately.

Rivera yawned again. He'd seen something similar years before; he'd been dressed in combat green back then and had been summoned to an oil tanker trying to cross into Iran just east of Herat. His squad had drawn lots, and he'd been the one who had to clamber inside. The truck had been parked there for days – the aroma of baked bodies caked in excrement and swollen blue in oxygen-starved lifelessness was something he still saw in dreams. He didn't envy the officers who'd made the find. 'Poor bastards,' he muttered to himself.

Flipping the paper over, he began to read the sports section. Fulham were pushing for promotion again. It had been years since he'd been to a game. The last time he'd seen them, they'd beaten United. He'd been there with his brother. Back when his brother was still alive. He looked at the table - they stood a chance. A yo-yo team these days. Shadows of their former selves.

The ex-soldier grinned sadly. He'd grown up so close to Craven Cottage that the floodlights used to shine in through the curtains of his bedroom window. That seemed like an eternity ago. But he still had a soft spot for them. They played how he felt. His perfect club. Anyway, he shrugged, he was tied to them forever - his brother had messily tattooed their badge on Rivera's forearm at age fourteen using a compass and a jar of India ink. The wound had become horrendously infected and, after a course of strong antibiotics, he was left with a smudge of a badge whose lines had all bled into one another. After something like that, there was no way he'd ever switch allegiance. Occasionally, a woman commented on it, tracing its lines with her fingernails in a post-coital embrace. Such was the deterioration of the outline, though, that the last girl had thought it was a war wound.

Chapter 6.

It was a banker in Tripoli that started the ball rolling. Achmed was one of Safia's many bookkeepers. He didn't get to take on extra work - he was employed by her exclusively. It was all accounting that was strictly off the books, of course. The kind of money he was moving called for enormous discretion. But he was an expert in the washing, cleaning, and laundering of funds. And he was meticulous – the last money man hadn't been; his life had ended in the midst of a luxurious soiree. He'd been invited to a party and then, in front of the other guests, ushered into a children's play area at gunpoint. Those present had been made to watch as a sack had been placed over his head, and – moments later – his throat had been cut. Safia then invited those assembled to continue enjoying their evening. The brief silence preceding her announcement was disturbed only by the sprinkler-like sound of the dying man's blood; it spattered onto the sand beneath the monkey bars.

When it came to money, Safia didn't fool around.

Going through columns of figures one night in his apartment in a middle class area of the city, Achmed had noticed an anomaly. And, after checking and checking again, he'd realised there was a problem.

It was quite a significant anomaly. Which meant that, somewhere along the line, there was an even bigger problem.

Safia didn't care for problems. For a moment, Achmed considered hushing it up. But then, the image of his predecessor sinking slowly onto the sand as Safia's guests turned back to the poolside bar came to him.

He placed a call.

* * * * *

When Safia had picked up the call, she'd sucked her teeth in frustration. She'd been in Paris, halfway through a four-hour makeover, sharing a spa with the wives of bankers and lawyers. They emerged from such treatments wearing lustrous sheens of tight-skinned perfection. Safia had politely excused herself in French, before switching to an acerbic form of Street-Arabic as she spoke into her mobile away from any would-be listeners. Naturally, she was used to setbacks in her line of work, and was familiar with having to figure out solutions for herself. After all, it was hardly like she could go to the authorities for help. But this was *big*. This was the sale of an entire cargo that had somehow turned into a black hole.

The gap in the take could mean only one thing: the cargo hadn't been delivered.

Someone had screwed up.

And she didn't tolerate screw-ups. She tersely thanked the banker, ended the call, and turned, looking out across the Paris skyline. Safia dealt with failure the only way she knew – she punished it. Viciously.

Her apartment in Montmartre was enormous. Lavishly decorated with glittering mod-cons, it was one manifestation of her ill-gotten-gains. For someone who'd grown up in the squalid poverty she'd experienced as a child, her old life almost seemed like a distant dream. But it was her memories of what had come before that made her guard the trappings of her new life so jealously. Nobody had ever given her anything freely in her life. She'd learned to take. To grab. To seize. To keep. And once she realised how inherently weak most humans were, there was no stopping her. Enlisting the help of her extended family, she began to rule her neighbourhood. Then, aged twelve, she all but took over the town. Torturing and killing the man who'd raped her three years before was one thing. Posting photographs of his demise around the town was something else.

No one in the town crossed Safia after that.

The girls she traded in never saw Montmartre. Usually, they saw her for only the briefest moment as she ran her monthly online auction. Hassan - her computer expert - set the whole thing up on the dark web. He'd sit in the corner of her finely-decorated lounge, scratching at his eczema-covered cheek, and regarding an electronic screen through thick glasses; his fingers continually typing with a feather-light touch on a keyboard. The channel he used was heavily encrypted and routed through Manila.

It was the Philippines where the banking transfers were processed.

Safia hated the auctions. But she knew it was their existence that kept her in her apartment. Kept her in golden jewellery, fine dining, and fast cars. It wasn't the parade of human flesh that bothered her, nor the objectification of women. It was the rich, fat, old, white men on screen who were making the purchases. 15% deposit. The balance was kept in escrow until the goods were delivered. Their wealth was vetted in advance - they always paid. She looked at them sometimes; pasty-skinned, sludgy masses of lecherous perversion. They watched the girls, drooling, their hands out of sight, their eyes hooded in anticipation of the pleasures they would purchase.

During the auctions, the men leered and sweated as she barked orders at her scantily clad cargo, forcing them to smile and parade for the camera. The girls cowered at her acerbic tone, but she had no sympathy. The way she saw it, if they were stupid enough to end up in the situation they were in, they deserved to be there.

Not her problem. She knew she could have ended up in a similar state had she not had the wherewithal to change her stars.

Anyway, business was booming. It didn't matter how many girls she sold. There was always demand for more. Those fat slobs with big bank accounts and boring lives bought her wares as readily as they might buy golf club memberships or holiday homes on Lanzarote. Clearly, they all told their friends. Because, each time she imported a cargo, she could have sold it three times over. Hassan once jokingly suggested she should offer Viagra with each transaction. He doubted any of the old men could get it up unassisted – the commission would be huge.

Hassan had set up a mailing list. It made her laugh - it was the kind of thing reputable companies who dealt in landscape gardening did. This one, though, was buried deep in the dark web. Its front page presented it as being a business for selling wool and crochet equipment. Occasionally, and most mysteriously, they even received legitimate enquiries from old ladies wanting to buy sewing patterns. But, by and large, they had between fifteen and twenty contacts a week. Each one would bring her upwards of seventy grand so long as the goods delivered matched their descriptions. She had the girls checked out for clean bills of health. It was part of the deal; part of the pricing structure. Of course, the certifications were counterfeit, but it wasn't like any of the buyers had any real comeback.

And whatever price she set in reserve, it was almost always met.

Trade was good. So good, in fact, that Safia was interested in expanding. The boys she dealt with in England were reliable, but stupid. She regarded their poor English with disdain whenever they communicated with her - and English was her *third* language... She felt they lacked ambition. She thought they seemed like guys who'd just got lucky. No spine. The kind of operators who'd settle for second-best. Safia had started to think that as long as the money rolled in, there was no reason why they couldn't make more. Everything was up for grabs, as long as the payments cleared.

But the payments hadn't cleared.

The cargo hadn't been delivered.

* * * * *

Safia sighed. Here, in Montmartre, she was far removed from the apartments in which the girls were currently being held. But they were there - out beyond the Périphérique - housed in a large, concrete tower. When she'd first arrived in Paris, it was the place where she'd lived. Little by little, along with the help of her brothers, sisters, and cousins, she'd taken it over, until she controlled the whole block. It hadn't taken too long. The police had ruled the deaths of her three competitors as being the result of a suicide pact. Late one night, each of them had jumped from the roof. It was plenty high enough that the damage done by the impact masked the marks of the cattle prod Safia had used to usher them off the edge. Two of them had been little more than mangled, bloody messes when the police arrived. The third was fat - watching him plummet, Safia had wondered if he might simply burst upon hitting the ground. As it was, the emergency services practically had to scrape his broken carcass into the ambulance.

She'd risen to the top of the pile by being ruthless; by being systematic; by leaving no loose threads for the curious to pull at. If someone wronged them, they felt the wrath of the whole of the family. Word got around, but she wasn't naïve enough to think she could ever lower her guard.

No challenge could be ignored. No matter how small.

There was no Plan B. If they let up, someone else would move in. Safia knew that - it was exactly the kind of thing she'd do herself. And she was not prepared to be on the receiving end.

She pressed a burner phone out from its plastic packaging and powered it up.

The number she dialled was one she knew by heart. It was answered after two rings.

At the other end of the line, the voice was deep and sonorous. 'Yes?'

'Hakeem. I have a job for you.'

'The usual?'

'Yes.'

She hung up.

Chapter 7.

It was late night in Lampedusa when Gamba's mobile rang. He had four phones. The first was the kind that his mother called him on, or that his friends reached him on to banter about football results. The second was one Bianchi had given him. He very rarely let that one go to voicemail. It was the same with the third – a line that alerted him of good-looking female migrants boarding boats in North Africa. He would monitor their estimated times of arrival to see if his views tallied with those of his contact. If he could have dealt oil, he'd have done so. The same with drugs. Gamba saw his road to riches as trading whatever was in plentiful supply. And here, that meant people. Commodities. Whenever the fourth phone rang, it was in this regard.

He answered it immediately. But when the fourth phone rang, he always did.

No matter what.

It was sitting on the table in his quarters.

Gamba picked it up, muting the volume of the football match playing on television. He slid the porn magazine he'd been leafing through across the table. In its place, he put a notepad. He then reached into his pocket for a pen and assumed the earnest expression of the businessman he imagined himself to be.

'Hello.'
'Gamba?'
'Yes.'
'I need to double my order.'
The immigration official paused for a moment.
'Same date?'
'Yes - double the pay.'
Gamba punched the air in gleeful celebration. 'I...'

Safia didn't waste time on people like him. The line was already dead.

Chapter 8.

Rivera lay hooked in the notch of a tree branch, nearly twenty feet above the ground. He was halfway up the hillside above Saltmarsh Cove. As he lay, he breathed out slowly in a calm, measured rhythm. A sniper scope was pressed against his eye and he stared through its crosshairs, focusing on a distant hedgerow. High above, faint silhouettes of swallows were visible, soaring against the ceiling of sky. As he gazed, he heard the sound of engines drifting on the breeze - motorcycle engines revving with full-blooded snarls. He shifted position slightly and adjusted the angle of his scope.

Half a minute later, they came roaring into view. They were - the numbered crosshairs told him - at a distance of about a thousand yards. Three bikes. He zoned in on the lead one. A tough shot. Squinting slightly, he panned the scope, tracking it as it faded in and out of view. It passed behind trees and bushes before emerging again, crossing the undulating ground.

At five hundred yards, the bikes hit open ground. As the track cut across a fallow field, he had a clear, unrestricted view. The perfect kill zone.

A sniper's dream.

Rivera grinned to himself. Old habits died hard. He turned away as the sound of the engines receded. Then, a movement caught his eye against the treeline. He sighted a buzzard flapping its wings and rising from its perch. He followed it, fluttering - ungainly at first against the cloudless cornflower blue - but then soaring gracefully, rising higher and higher. When it was motionless - gliding on the thermals - he looked back down.

The scope was one of his few remaining Army souvenirs. It had come home in a kitbag from a blood-scorched desert somewhere and not been returned to the quartermaster. So, when the time came, it simply walked off base with him, along with an inventory of scars that ached when the weather grew colder. Bird-watching, along with reading, was something he'd committed to with zeal. Sometimes, the ex-soldier wondered if he had an addictive personality. Whatever piqued his interest became an all-consuming passion. He believed bird-watching to be a positive distraction, though - it took his mind off the tom cat feelings that all too frequently flooded his thoughts.

Rivera yawned widely and lowered himself down, branch by branch until he reached the ground. Slipping his flip-flops back on and picking a thorn out of his toe, he stretched, rotated his shoulders, and sniffed the air.

Town beckoned.

* * * * *

Saltmarsh Cove's seafront had a pebble beach that banked steeply up to the promenade and its wrought-iron fence. A variety of old-world hotels overlooked the water. It was still a prosperous place - not a ghost town of yesteryear like many resort towns further north. It was nestled in a valley with steep hills rising up to cliffs in each direction. One side led up towards his campsite and, from the hilltop in the other direction, people claimed Cornwall was just about visible on a clear day.

The town was busy with a blend of locals and tourists. Cafés and bars bustled, and a collection of shops sold buckets, spades and postcards. The cliffs were of red sandstone and, on the seafront, a woman had set up a stall selling tea towels with etchings of local buildings imprinted on each side. A busker was playing a Celtic reel and, at the water's edge, a barefoot lifeguard surveyed body surfers and swimmers through dark glasses. Rivera cast his eye along the beach, wondering if last night's liaison might be in the water.

* * * * *

It was when he was walking back up the hill, the seafront far below him, that Rivera heard the engines again. A Harley Davidson has a distinctive, guttural roar that's hard to mistake. Three of them together sound like rolling thunder. There was something animalistic about them. Predatory.

As Rivera climbed further, the engines grew louder. He looked back down into the valley at the picturesque regency town.

The bikes didn't fit.

The riders weren't tourists. Day trippers on motorcycles would buzz through and continue. These weren't the kind of weekend hell raisers who gathered for rallies, either. Every town has garages and workshops where petrolheads congregate; every city has a bar with *Live to Ride; Ride to Live* banners and bandanas tacked to the wall, but this was something different. The way they'd ridden earlier - in formation - had been hostile. It was like a statement. Like a way of letting people know who ruled the town.

As he walked on the pavement, back up the hill, the bikes flashed past; the riders opened their throttles. It was a sound so loud it felt like a physical thing – it drowned out everything else; it was powerful enough to rattle the fillings between teeth. He watched the sun shining on their black leather outlines until they passed around a bend and out of sight. Their decals were faded: a Joker; an Ace of Spades, and a Jack of Diamonds.

The sound of their engines faded away.

He'd expected that. Expected they were patrolling their perimeter. Marking out their territory. It was like a West Country version of the Wild West - these would have been the kind of guys who'd have raised posses and deputised marshals once upon whenever: cowboys born out of their time. Of course, they wouldn't have been on the side of law and order; it would have taken a strong man to keep them in line.

What he *hadn't* expected was that they'd come back. Growling ever closer in a crescendo of angry Harley Davidson, they fanned out across the road three abreast. Mirrored goggles caught the sun beneath their open-faced helmets.

They were making straight for him in a hostile line.

Rivera was no stranger to trouble. He seemed to have a knack for attracting it. He could live with that - he'd spent time in places where a wrong glance would get you sliced open. When he'd been in war zones, trouble followed him round. But that was par for the course. Here, though... here he'd been watching buzzards in flight. Here, he was a flip-flop wearing tourist minding his own business, and keeping an eye out for any women who fancied a fling.

That was it.

* * * * *

'What the fuck are you looking at?' the first of the bikers snarled. The three of them had cut their engines, drawing to a halt in front of him. Ticking noises of cooling engines sounded out, and the chorus of crickets suddenly swelled.

Rivera frowned and then smiled a little. 'Excuse me?' He spoke cordially.

'You heard,' black leather number two answered. 'What the fuck are you doing here?'

Rivera sighed. 'Look guys. I don't want any trouble here. I'm just taking a walk - I'm on holiday, for fuck's sake!'

'Do you kiss your mother with that filthy mouth?' black leather number three asked.

'What?'

'Answer the fucking question!' black leather number one insisted.

'Three questions.'

'What?' the first biker growled.

'Three questions,' Rivera explained. 'You asked me what I was looking at, and then you asked me what I'm doing here. And *then* you asked me if I kiss my mother with my filthy mouth.' He paused. 'I hate to be pedantic, but that's three questions.' He paused. 'You *can* count, can't you – you dumb shit?' The hint of a smile played across his face; he'd deliberately raised the stakes with his choice of insult, and the results were instant.

Black leather number three stepped off his bike. As he tried to engage the kickstand, he stubbed his boot against the ground. Rivera smirked. Approaching, the man's breath smelled of beer. His eyes, hidden beneath goggles, doubtless burned with hatred. 'Here's another number, dickhead,' he hissed. 'Three against one. You like those odds?'

Rivera shrugged, his smile fixed. 'I've known worse.'

The three bikers were looking directly at him from behind their goggles. For a silent moment, he returned their gazes, his icy blue eyes emitting a stare that could have sliced through sheet metal. In attempts to diffuse tension, people are sometimes instructed to retreat to their happy place; to breathe deeply and imagine good things. Rivera had no such place in mind. Instead, he slowed his breathing and switched to his sniper mind-set. The Death Zone. The Killing Floor.

'Look gents,' he chuckled, holding up his hands as if in surrender. 'I've got places to be. The sun's shining, the surf's up, and I'm just passing through. You've clearly got the wrong end of the stick. I don't know how, but...' He smiled again and then raised an eyebrow, more menacing now. 'But I'm a fair guy... if you want to do this, then we'll do it.' He paused, looking at each of them in turn. 'You really want to?'

Silence reigned for a moment before the sound of crickets rose again from the long grass at the roadside. It was clear that Rivera's refusal to be intimidated had rattled the three riders - they'd had time to look beyond the tourist outfit and had taken in his wiry, muscled leanness.

'You're a cocky fucker for someone in flip-flops,' black leather number two snarled. 'If I see you again, you're a dead man.'

Rivera nodded. 'We'll see,' he said quietly and began walking up the hill once more. As he drew away from the Harleys, he called back over his shoulder. 'You guys have a great day.'

He counted a full twenty seconds before the engines roared into life and the trio sped back down the hill.

Chapter 9.

'You think they'll still want to deal with us?' Grizzly sighed the worried sigh of a world-weary man. His eyes blinked a couple of times in quick succession.

Spice nodded his head. He was a small man; twitchy, with cold, mean eyes and a look of contempt. 'It's a show of faith,' he reported, raising his hand to his mouth and using a nail to pick at the place where a morsel of food was trapped in his teeth. 'It's all about the money, but if we fuck it up, you know what they're like...'

The man behind the desk nodded glumly. Where Spice was small, he was huge, with bulky shoulders and giant forearms. It was because of his appearance that he'd gained his nickname: Grizzly.

Three years separated the half-brothers. Ever since he could remember, Grizzly had been a giant to him. Any time Spice had an issue, his older sibling would wade in and sort it out. Before long, he'd earned such a reputation as a fighter his mere presence was enough to persuade someone round to an alternative point of view. And that was long before he was fully grown.

Through it all, though, the younger sibling had been the brains of the operation. And he knew what his brother had done aged fourteen. It was a secret big enough to buy his loyalty forever. Spice always had a sharpness - an intelligence that meant he saw things before other people; he reacted sooner. He could be just as vicious as any of the other hard men they grew up around - it was just that people very rarely saw that side of him. Grizzly's appearance told people everything they needed to know about it. Spice, though, preferred to hide his thoughts and intentions behind a blank, impassive impression. He was bright enough to have aced school, but smart enough to know there wasn't any point.

It was his half-brother's brains that Grizzly needed that afternoon. Strategic planning wasn't his strong suit. Anything requiring more finesse than tearing someone's head off and shitting down their neck lined his face with deep furrows.

* * * * *

The office was a strange mix of austere and opulent. It was located on a gantry overlooking the loading bay of Denton Laine Transportation – the company where Grizzly was the boss. It had plasterboard walls with shipping manifests and schedules tacked to them. However, the furniture and the men themselves looked too wealthy to belong. They *were* too wealthy to belong.

Grizzly's chair was built from carved mahogany - it was handmade and upholstered with expensive fabric; his desk was constructed in a similarly impressive fashion - sturdy and topped with a baize covering and golden ornaments. Both men wore expensive jewellery, and each sported a glittering Rolex. They had an array of gold chains, and Spice wore solid silver cufflinks in the shape of naked ladies.

'So...' the big man sighed. 'What do you suggest?'

'You need to take care of Rusty. He's a fucking liability,' Spice replied.

'It's done,' Grizzly reported bluntly.

'Well, that's a start,' Spice nodded. 'Who did you use? Popeye.'

'Yeah.'

The smaller man's brow furrowed. 'You know he's a dumbass, don't you?' His tone grew bitter. 'What have I told you before? He's careless, and he's all fucking talk. It's because of him that people like that bitch journalist come sniffing around. I thought he was going to tell those two mates of his to keep a low profile too, but I'm still seeing them gallivanting around on their bikes like a bunch of big bull queers.' He shook his head, irritated. 'What's going on? Haven't you told them?' He narrowed his eyes. 'You haven't turned pussy on me or something, have you?'

Grizzly threw up his hands in frustration. 'What can *I* do? They're the three fucking musketeers. Always have been - I just pay their wages. Anyway – they've been useful before. When they're not dicking about, I mean.'

'They're *your* Navy buddies, though.' Spice shrugged. 'Tell them to stop. Get them to keep a lower profile.'

'But it's *because* they're my Navy buddies that I *can't* tell them to stop. We went to war together. Remember?'

Spice shook his head, scoffing. 'War? Bullshit! You went through *whores* together, more like. I'm surprised all those doses of VD didn't end up making your dick drop off. When you came back from the tropics you were a disaster area - a walking case of crotch rot.' He chuckled almost warmly. 'You need to sort it, though. They're going round picking fights with any fucker who looks at them funny.' He sighed. 'If he wasn't so good at tying up loose ends, that prick would become a loose end himself. And you know what would have to happen then...'

The threat hung in the air for a moment.

'I'm on it,' the bigger man nodded.

'I mean it,' Spice insisted, fixing him with an unblinking stare. 'It's bad for business.'

* * * * *

Half an hour later, the two men were sitting at the same side of the desk, hunched over a laptop screen. In side profile, their shared genes were evident. Each man frowned in the same way. Both sat awkwardly, squinting at the rows of figures on the spreadsheet.

'We're five hundred short,' Grizzly sniffed, looking up.

Spice nodded. He'd switched his attention to scrolling on his phone.

'You knew?'

'Yeah – of course I fucking knew.' Spice nodded, his lips pursed. 'But if the cargo's ruined, then we can't sell the cargo. And if we can't sell the cargo, then...'

'... we get no money,' his older sibling interrupted. He wore his worry in the lines on his face.

Spice nodded. 'But we still owe the difference. And we're not dealing with good guys here, remember? They don't fuck about. They're going to demand their pound of flesh. And, one way or another, they're going to get it.'

'So, what do we do?' Grizzly's brow creased further as he turned to look at his sibling.

'We carry on, bro,' Spice announced confidently. 'Don't worry your ugly old head about it. There's another shipment on the way. I've sorted it already. Double or quits. But we do this one right. Clear it and take the hit. Otherwise...' he sighed. 'Otherwise, we've got problems.'

Grizzly nodded. 'How far along the chain are we with it - the next one? Have the people in Salerno been told?'

'They're getting ready for them in Paris, mate. They're on it. This whole thing's well underway.'

'Paris?' The bigger man frowned again. 'But that means...'

'... that we need to get a fucking wriggle on,' Spice cut in. 'But don't worry - I'm way ahead of you.' At this, he rose, pushing himself up off the solid desk and patting his half-brother on the shoulder. 'Just leave the thinking to me - remember?'

Grizzly leaned back, fidgeting with the heavy gold bracelet that adorned his tattooed arm. He chewed his lip and nodded. Then he looked back at the spreadsheet. By the time he raised his head again, Spice was gone.

Chapter 10.

Rivera sighed, marvelling at one of the most incredible sunsets he'd ever witnessed. Above the cliffs, the entire sky seemed to be aflame. The sun dipped below the horizon like an overflowing bucket of liquid gold. And the sea's surface had taken on the appearance of liquid mercury; the water was suddenly a mass moving as one body.

The ex-soldier watched as bats began to appear. He toyed with the idea of photographing the dying embers of the day, but reasoned no camera could ever do such a view justice. Instead, he drank it all in. In the military, he'd spent years wishing he could be anywhere other than where he was. Now, though, he simply revelled in the knowledge that he was alive and that this was happening. Now.

Unfortunately for him, the glorious sunset wasn't all that was happening. From the clubhouse across the field, the tinny whine of the bingo caller rolled out across the grass, inescapable. While the sun had been dipping down across the water, Rivera had been able to shut out the not-so-hilarious stream of bawdy rhymes and sexual innuendo emanating from the speakers. Now, though, he'd reached his limit. He stood, stretched, folded his chair and leaned it against Iris' side. The T2 formed a perfect privacy barrier against other campers and allowed him to sit beneath its awning undisturbed. She was, however, no match for the noise. The bingo caller announced he was taking a short break and pressed play on a compilation of cheesy disco hits.

Then, the DJ played Gloria Gaynor. That was the final straw. Since he'd been on the road, Rivera knew his standards had slipped. Yes, he maintained a military liking for early mornings and a sense of order – but when it came to women, he'd become less discerning. At times, he felt like a sailor on shore leave. He knew the disco would be stuffed with soft-bodied, hard-eyed women. But he still had some self-respect.

*****

Rivera opted for a walk. He'd already smoked the second of the hand-rolled cigarettes he permitted himself each day. He knew if he stayed put, his resolve would be broken. Instead, he thought he might try to find out where the surfer girls congregated of an evening.

Reaching out to Iris' silver wing mirror, he lifted a fresh shirt from where it had been drying. It featured a garishly bright Hawaiian design. He pulled it on over a black vest he'd been wearing all day. Rolling the sleeve down, he covered his tattoo of the Black Flag logo. The 80s Hard-core Punk band formed in Hermosa Beach had always been one of his favourites - having their badge inked onto his shoulder hadn't been a well-thought-out decision, though. Years previously, he and a group of recruits had been out on the town, celebrating their completion of basic training. They'd drunkenly spilled into a tattoo parlour where most of them had proceeded to scar themselves with the regimental crest. Rivera, though, had opted to follow in the footsteps of Henry Rollins, emerging back onto the street with four vertical black rectangles emblazoned on his arm; the second and fourth lower than the first and third, to give the impression of a flag waving in the breeze.

Reaching up, he propped open the small window at the rear of the camper. Rosie - his tabby cat lay on the table where it had been warmed by the setting sun. She would doubtless depart for a rodent hunt at some point soon. Rivera left the Hawaiian shirt open, with chains and necklaces spilling over the neckline of his vest. His wardrobe was completed by a woven straw fedora. There was just enough light left for him to check his look in the wing mirror before he wandered off in search of a little more solitude.

After a lifetime in fatigues, some ex-servicemen develop a profound sartorial sense once they begin to dress in civvies.

Others don't. Rivera had given up on such niceties. He was toned enough, and ballsy enough to approach almost anyone – that had served him well so far.

* * * * *

Walking into Saltmarsh Cove was pleasant. The evening was sultry, and the soporific sound of the surf breaking below the cliffs floated to him on the breeze. Few cars passed him. Rivera was in no hurry. After years of other people telling him where he needed to be and when, the freedom to make such decisions for himself was still a novelty.

As he walked, his mind wandered. Afghanistan. Hammersmith. Shirley. The breakdown. The split. The girl last night. Looking back, he remembered how it was only five minutes after purchasing Iris the crushing realisation hit him: he was entirely alone in the world. The thought had all but slayed him. After years of having a coterie of companions with him at all times, he felt suddenly cast adrift on an ocean of uncertainty.

He'd parked the brand-new eighth-hand van on a quiet street not far from the Westway, removed his seat belt and rubbed at his eyes. Patting at the pockets of his leather jacket, he'd run through his list of essentials. Passport. Driving licence. Bank card. That was all he needed, he'd reasoned to himself, unconvinced. He had no clue where he was going; he just knew he had to go somewhere.

Then, he'd caught a glimpse of himself in the rear-view mirror. He was - he had to admit - a mess; a shadow of his former self. Stubble; bags under the eyes; grey complexion. Looking away from his own reflection, he'd then peered further behind him at the campervan's interior: bench seating; folding bed; table; miniature kitchen. He'd nodded with approval. Though the worry over his place in the world had made him feel light-headed, he realised the T2 had everything he needed.

It was just as well.

It was all he had.

And then, he saw the cat. It gazed back at him imperiously from the edge of his field of vision and seemed quite at home. Arching its back, it stood on the fold-down table, stretched, yawned, and settled back down onto the bench seat to sleep. Rivera's first impression of Rosie was that she didn't give a toss.

He liked that.

Since then, he'd spent three months on the road. He'd moved from place to place and watched as spring turned into early summer. Some mornings he'd awoken in the snow and on others, he'd been roused from slumber by sunlight pouring through the windows of the vehicle, or by rain hammering on the roof. He'd talked to people when necessary, but he'd mainly kept himself to himself. After all, there were enough ghosts to keep him company without other people intruding.

And he'd healed. At least on the outside. His pasty complexion had grown tanned once more from outdoor living. His physique - which had veered on the precipice of resembling that of a puffy booze hound - had reverted to the trim, wiry state it had been throughout his years of service. He had a beer now and again, but usually limited himself to just one. And the clean living had lent him a healthy glow. Proof came with a litany of ladies who'd suddenly started to pay him attention. It was a relief – he worried he was getting too old. Worried he'd have to get used to Rosie's disapproving glances as he resorted to seeking distraction on his phone.

It was only late on the nights he was alone that his demons returned. Occasionally, he'd awake, cloaked in cold sweat, wondering where he was. At such times, he'd step outside and breathe clean air, thankful to be wherever he was; grateful to be alive. Mindful of the fact he had a cat that needed feeding and watering - an entity that actually valued his continued existence.

When he'd first come home from Helmand, the trauma had overwhelmed him. It was as if a darkness had enveloped him. He'd wanted to tear it out; eviscerate it; wrench it from himself like an unwanted limb. Now, though, he was less naïve. For better or worse, he was stuck with his memories, and they were stuck with him. They would - he reckoned - simply have to learn to live with one another. After all, they were dug in; entrenched.

He slept fitfully. Sometimes, he couldn't sleep at all. And other times he wanted only to lose himself in the fleeting love of a woman. Any woman who made him feel alive enough to outrun the death he saw when he closed his eyes.

* * * * *

The Royal George looked like Rivera's kind of place. He suddenly felt tired. Old. A quiet drink would do – anything that wasn't bingo. By the time he reached town, the night had grown dark; the streets were lit up and twinkling. Rivera had given The Duck and Goose a wide berth - it was karaoke night; The Clock Tavern had a quiz, and The Smugglers' Inn was filled with people who looked stuffed full of their own self-importance. He wasn't sure his Hawaiian attire would fit in with their sports jackets and tweeds. So, he'd approached the last pub on the high street. It had looked just about down-at-heel enough to be unpretentious - the kind of bad-side-of-the-good-side-of-town establishment that would welcome him. It had a chalkboard outside listing the football matches it would be screening, and a door that opened straight onto the street.

It was through that door which the stranger was flung. He moved at such speed that he ran headlong into Rivera, who caught him, stopping him from falling. He was tall; thin; gangly - certainly much lighter than his tormentor. Rivera didn't recognise the man on the threshold. But he recognised his black leather jacket.

'And fucking stay out - otherwise I'll break your legs, cocksucker!' the big man in the leather jacket bawled after the drinker he'd just ejected. From inside the pub, the braying sound of drunken laughter sounded. The man was on the verge of stepping back inside when he sighted Rivera - his hand still on the stranger's arm to steady him. The ex-soldier nodded, smiled, and raised a hand in a jovial wave.

The man in the doorway swayed a little drunkenly, unsteady. He adjusted the unlit cigar wedged in the corner of his mouth and narrowed his eyes, squinting at the two men in the street. Frowning, he let the door close behind him. He folded his arms and then leaned on the railing outside the door.

'You,' he hissed, staring at Rivera, recognising him finally. 'What are you? Some kind of retard or something? I fucking told you to get out of town.'

'And yet here I am,' he shrugged. The ex-soldier was a loner. He had no wish to involve himself with matters that didn't concern him. If he did, he knew there would be consequences. Rivera reasoned he could simply walk away. It was a split-second decision: he opted to stick around.

The tormentor turned to the man he'd punched. 'And you,' he sneered, his teeth barred. 'Who's he? Your boyfriend?'

The injured man shook his head and wiped at his nose. It was bleeding from where he'd been punched. His white shirt now bore a Jackson Pollock-like design of red splatters. He looked from one man to the other, worried.

'Oh well,' sighed the big man. 'Don't say I didn't warn you.' He removed his jacket, hanging it over a bollard, and then approached the pair, cracking his knuckles. 'I've got a lager inside,' he grumbled. 'It had better not get warm.'

'Yeah,' scoffed Rivera. 'Good luck with that.'

'You're a jumped-up fucker for a drag queen,' the big man said hatefully. 'Elton John would have dressed up less flash than you.' He spat on his palms and rubbed them together. 'Right then. How long do you think this is going to take? I've got a girl guarding my drink, so I'm not in the mood for this shit. And...'

'...about five seconds,' announced Rivera calmly.

'What?' chuckled the tormentor, a little confused. 'How do you figure? You're wearing flip-flops. This'll be over in two. I'm going to deck you, and then I'm going to flatten your fucking head until it looks like a Frisbee.' He chuckled. 'Five seconds!'

'Well... anything more than five seconds is a waste.' Rivera shrugged.

'I bet that's what you tell all the boys,' the man huffed. 'What line to you use with them anyway – just pretend you're drowning and my bollocks are full of oxygen. Something like that?' He paused and laughed drily. 'Oh, I see – you were talking about you winning,' he scoffed. 'Well, good luck with that.'

'Queensbury Rules?'

'You what?' the big man frowned.

'I mean – are we going to keep it sporting? No biting; no gouging; no rabbit punches.'

'You do what you want, petal,' the big man growled. 'I'm going to knock your fucking head off. And I'm going to film it too, to give me and my buddies a laugh.' He took his phone out of his pocket, pressed the screen, and set it on the pub's window sill.

'But this is a game!' Rivera smiled cordially. 'Here. I'll even let you go first.'

The other man frowned, pausing for a second; then he laughed, uncertainly. When he moved, he moved fast for a big man. But he was out of shape. Slow. For too long, he'd got his own way through intimidation. Through reputation. Through trading on past glories and having frightening friends. His wheezing intake of breath, his laboured second step, and the giant swing of his haymaker meant Rivera almost had time to roll a cigarette before the punch arrived.

Rivera simply watched the man's fist approach, whipping out of the way at the last instant and bringing the heel of his foot smashing into the middle of the big man's leg where his knee cap exploded. Above the crunching sound of bone, he howled in agony. The sound, though, was cut short by Rivera's elbow driving upwards into the bridge of his nose, snapping his head back and sending him sprawling onto the ground, unconscious.

The tall, thin man turned in stunned silence, both horrified and impressed. He pressed his hands together, wringing them as he looked at Rivera. 'You don't need to fight me now, do you?' he enquired, his voice little more than a plaintive whimper.

'No.' Rivera shook his head, frowning.

'Good.'

The pair regarded each other for a moment. Evidently the thin man was a little disbelieving of what the ex-soldier had said.

'Do you want to go and get a beer?' Rivera asked - almost apologetically.

'Oh, I couldn't let you do that...' the man protested.

'It's alright,' Rivera announced, walking over to the prone tormentor and drawing a roll of banknotes from out of the man's pocket. 'Our friend here is buying.'

The other man grinned. 'Listen,' he sighed, gesturing at his bloodied shirt. 'You're very kind, but nowhere will let me in if I look like this.'

Rivera frowned for a moment before sauntering over to the bollard. He removed the big man's black leather jacket and threw it to his new acquaintance.

'With his compliments!' he grinned, nodding at the man on the ground. 'Can't promise it'll fit, but it'll cover up the claret!'

'Are you sure?' the other man questioned, hurrying after Rivera. 'Won't his mates be after us?'

The reply was blunt. 'All the more reason to get a beer, then. Surely?' Rivera walked over to the windowsill and picked up the phone. 'It doesn't look like he was live-streaming,' the ex-soldier shrugged. He stopped the video and switched the phone off. Then he dropped it between the slats of a drain grate. 'Ready?' he enquired.

Chapter 11.

Evening in Lampedusa. A warm wind blew all the way from the Sahara. Beyond a bank of searchlights, the blackness of the Mediterranean loomed. It felt like a floating vessel anchored offshore. There was something at once beautiful and malevolent about it. Come night time, though, the darkness surrounding it was complete. It was like a single tooth remaining in a rotten mouth. A pinprick of light in an ocean of blackness. There was nothing between the outcrop and the shores of Africa.

It was from that coastline the migrants poured.

Libya. Tunisia. Anywhere unscrupulous traffickers could put them on boats. Of course, their journeys in most cases commenced many miles away from Tripoli or Tunis, but it was those places they invariably passed though. The arrivals all wore the same masks of desperation. For a brief instant, sighting land buoyed their spirits; the sickening swell of the sea and the putrid stench of the noxious engine fumes were side-lined for the briefest of moments.

Hope is a powerful thing.

The despair they'd carried for thousands of miles, though, was swiftly recovered as they made landfall. Once there, the hopes and dreams they'd been sold by traffickers and gangsters were exposed as a façade; a thin veneer of lies and deceit. The reality was a bright orange life vest and a view down the barrel of a Beretta ARX160. Pepper spray and billy clubs were deployed liberally, and the promised land suddenly looked like a confidence trick. Guard dogs strained at leashes, and angry, uniformed voices ordered the newcomers into separate lines. Were the scene to have been rendered in monochrome and squinted at, it wouldn't have looked too dissimilar to Oświęcim at mid-century.

It was in this fashion, following their precarious journeys across violent lands and a treacherous sea, that the migrants who didn't die along the way reached Lampedusa. They were cold. Tired. Hungry. Afraid.

Intensely vulnerable.

That suited Valentino Gamba just fine.

From a guard tower overlooking the migrant camp, he gazed down upon the latest group of arrivals being marched onto his side of the wire. Those welcoming them were none too welcoming - kicks and punches were dispensed to hurry the newcomers along. Had Gamba ever thought deeply about it, he might have noticed the irony: most of the officials were from right wing regions. Most saw Italy as being under attack. And most were hugely resentful – hateful, even – of the new arrivals. Yet it was they who were responsible for their welfare. Gamba rarely thought deeply, though.

As the most recent boat load moved out of the evening gloom, they entered a patch of brightly lit concrete where they were made to stand in single file.

Gamba cast his eyes discerningly.

He'd been on Lampedusa for nearly two years. Officially, he was a customs officer with responsibility for organising transports to the mainland. Once there, asylum claims to stay in Europe might be processed. Frequently, though, claimants would languish for months - years, maybe - under lock and key.

Not his problem.

His youthful affiliation with the Lords of Italia had led to him being briefly imprisoned. That was nearly five years ago. It had been his criminal record which had barred him from securing a job while on parole. After myriad rejections and closed doors, he'd been surprised when he was eventually called for interview. It was only when he arrived on Lampedusa that he realised he was in good company - many of the men he'd called colleagues ever since had followed similar paths to the island.

Bianchi had explained all that to him when he'd arrived. 'You know,' he'd begun, 'here, we're like God.'

'How come?' a naïve Gamba had asked.

The older man smiled. 'We get to decide who lives and who dies.'

It had been Bianchi who'd enlisted him into his side-line business. With the money on offer, it hadn't been a difficult decision. All Gamba had to do was pluck out any female migrants who looked passably pretty and make sure they got on the next transport. Usually, a burner phone in his pocket would vibrate with a message if it looked likely that a newly departed boat held promising passengers. The chain stretched back to North Africa and then all the way out through western Europe. Once they reached the mainland, the women were whisked away to whichever life they were to be sold into.

Not his problem. All he was interested in was the fat fee he received each month by way of a retainer. That, and the fact the girls stayed in his quarters for twenty-four hours before he dispatched them. Bianchi's words still echoed: 'shag as many of them as you can as often as you can. It makes them more obedient – you'll be doing a favour to whichever rich bastard ends up owning them. They'll have been softened up for them.' There was – so Gamba believed - a similar arrangement further along the chain near Salerno.

There, the cargo got more of the same.

Bianchi had justified such liaisons by declaring himself a child of Rome. The old empire had slaves, and so, therefore, should he. Gamba had been sceptical at first, but soon fell into line. After all, the ebony princesses that emerged onto the island were only too glad to escape the clutches of fellow migrants, gangsters and traffickers. It made rich pickings for a man like him. Most of them had been continually goaded and groped and much, much worse ever since setting out from whichever warzone or brutal regime they'd decided to flee. The way he saw it, it was a simple choice: they could either sleep beneath a tarpaulin sheet on the hard ground, forever at risk of being violated, or they could sleep in his bed and do what he told them to. He had a growing shelf of VHS tapes where he'd filmed his exploits on a couple of old cameras – they'd grown more depraved as time moved on. Gamba hadn't upgraded to digital film – Bianchi had warned him about electronic footprints. His mentor had even appeared on some of the films himself. 'Don't trust anything that can't be burned,' he'd counselled.

Gamba had a scar running right down one cheek. It was a souvenir of incarceration that made him instantly recognisable. While he wasn't a big man, he was strong - his arms and neck were covered with prison tattoos. Despite his hostile appearance, the migrant women saw him as a ticket out of the barbed-wire encased squalor of the camp. It was a role he played up to with theatrical flourish. Bianchi had eventually been moved on. He now ran things in Salerno, so Gamba was entirely free to pry the hard-earned savings from any of the girls that still had them to hand. Many of their families had scrimped and saved for years to send them on to what they prayed was a better life. The cash Gamba took in return for the speedy promise of granting them asylum was all they had. He spent it on jewellery, booze and cocaine and sent them on their way, leaving them with the legacy of his lies.

Not his problem. And the beauty was that he was still remunerated as a state employee all the while.

He looked down once more at the line of new arrivals and proffered a leery grin with his yellowed teeth. Lighting a cigarette with one hand, he scratched at his crotch with the other. After having a particularly bad batch of warts burned off with liquid nitrogen, the end of his cock had scars resembling craters on the moon. Some of the migrants he took care of were riddled with disease even before they reached him. But – he reasoned – porn stars didn't use protection. So nor would he.

His eyes locked onto a group of new arrivals.

A good day was when he saw two prospects. A great day was when he saw three. But today, stepping gingerly across the broken ground, picking her pathway carefully like a frightened lamb, was prospect number four.

And behind her came number five.

Chapter 12.

'So what the hell was that all about?' Rivera asked, frowning.

The two men had walked silently through the town, turning down a couple of side streets until they reached a small, old-world pub called The Ship. Bright lights burned through its lattice windows. It was quiet and, as the two men entered, nobody paid them much attention. Two old men were playing chess in a corner, and another drinker was playing darts by himself – he was engaged in a seemingly endless loop of retrieving the darts from the board, and then tramping back to the oche.

It was – Rivera figured – not the kind of place the biker's friends were likely to frequent. Buying two pints of lager, he'd joined the other man in a corner booth where he'd sat down and asked him about the fight.

'You really want to know?' The other man looked pale. He glanced around the room, furtively.

'Sure,' he shrugged.

'Eddie Lomas.' He offered a handshake.

'Trent Rivera.'

* * * * *

'So, you want to tell me or not?' Rivera pressed.

Lomas stared down at his phone and checked it for messages. He shook his head. 'Not really,' he answered, uncomfortably.

His opposite number grimaced and scratched at the stubble on his chin. 'Well, you're going to have to tell someone, mate. In a town like this, word gets around. You don't end up putting one of their guys on the ground without facing some kind of comeback. Know what I mean?' Rivera paused. 'It might have escaped your notice, but they didn't look like very nice people.'

Lomas shrugged. 'Hey - I wasn't the one who put him on the ground!' His tone was defensive.

'You're welcome.' The response was terse.

Lomas grinned ruefully. 'Yeah - thanks... I guess. He looked like a cross between Goliath and the Grim Reaper.'

Rivera chuckled.

'What about you, though?' Lomas pressed. 'I mean, what *are* you? I've never seen anyone fight like that before. You a cop? A soldier?'

Sighing, Rivera shook his head. 'Long time ago,' he began, evasively. 'Not any more, though. These days I'm just trying to keep myself out of trouble.'

'Well, you're not doing a very good job of it.' Lomas smiled thinly.

'You're a fine one to talk!'

'Yeah, you're right enough there,' Lomas sniffed. 'Anyway...'

Rivera held up his hands. '*Mea culpa*. I smashed up a motorcycle man out there *and* I don't regret it. They're going to want payback, I reckon. That's on me. But they're not going to leave you alone either.' He looked hard at Lomas. 'You know that, right? Blokes like that are bullies. Cowards. They hunt in packs. I don't know *who* they are, but I know *what* they are. I've seen them around.'

Lomas nodded. 'So what will you do if they find you?'

Rivera shrugged. He opened his mouth to speak and then closed it again for a moment, opting to sanitise his response. The ex-soldier was a chameleon – when it came to conversation, he was adept at moulding himself to fit his audience. So, he stopped short of explaining how he'd exact his vengeance. He was – he reminded himself – not talking to a squaddie, or a gangster. Lomas was strictly white collar. He'd sussed that from shaking his hand. And from listening to the man's Received Pronunciation. 'I can handle myself,' he announced. 'But, listen - there's no point worrying about things we can't control. That's the future. How about telling me what's going on with you now? What prompted the whole thing? The fight. I mean?'

The man across the table sighed. 'My sister.'

* * * * *

'I'll get you another,' Rivera reported when Lomas was done. Wandering over to the bar, he weighed up what his new acquaintance had told him. Half of him was intrigued. The other half wished he'd simply walked away from the fight – he could feel himself being roped in. He already regretted telling Lomas about his years as a military investigator. Sometimes, he wondered if living alone was destroying his filter. When he'd started confiding, part of him had been screaming out, urging him to stop.

But then Lomas had shown him a photograph of his sister.

She was simply stunning – she glowed with the kind of clean-cut Californian sheen beloved by the makers of soda pop advertisements. At that point, common sense had gone out of the window. Rivera had, instead, been consumed by the idea that if he were to rescue her - a damsel-in-distress - she might be keen to reward him for his trouble. It wasn't logical, and he was almost irritated that he thought that way, but he was hypnotised by her. Blinkered by her beauty.

Katie Lomas – the man's sister - was two years older than her brother. As an economic journalist, her writing had been in reasonable demand and a variety of publications had flown her around the world. It was usually to report on tax havens. Oil wells. Money laundering. Short selling. She was no stranger to greed and corruption and had had to deal with the kind of sleazy underworld characters who tended to go along with it.

Lomas had arrived in Saltmarsh Cove because this was the last place his sister had been seen. She'd been sent on assignment, but the details were scarce.

All her brother knew was that she'd seemingly vanished off the face of the earth. Her last correspondence was a text message sent to him:

DENTON LAINE TRANSPORTATION.
RUSTY AND SPICE.

That was all. Lomas couldn't make head nor tail of it. He doubted it was cryptic, but the first time he'd started asking questions, he'd ended up with a bloody nose and a narrow escape. So, there was clearly something behind it. And people weren't taking kindly to him sniffing around.

* * * * *

'Well?' Lomas enquired as Rivera returned with two fresh pints. 'Any bright ideas? You ever encounter anything like this when you were investigating things in the military?'

Rivera sat down and spoke heavily. 'Listen...' he began. 'Just so we're clear, I'm simply a guy on holiday. Understand?'

Lomas nodded.

'I'm not the police, and I probably won't be much help. I've done a little investigating before, but I was never really more than a soldier.' He paused. 'You'll have as much luck looking through that phone of yours, I should think. What did the police say?'

'You've already listened to me more than the police,' Lomas answered.

Silence.

'May I speak bluntly?' Rivera asked.

'Yes.'

'OK. Worst-case scenario. Katie's dead.'

Lomas gave a start.

'Listen - I'm being candid here. The police won't say she's dead until they have proof. Probable cause – that kind of thing.' He sipped at his beer. 'They haven't got that yet, but these are bad people - it's pretty obvious. I told you that already.'

'So?' Lomas' tone was a little riled.

'So? Why would they kill her - a journalist? It's because she found something out that they wanted to keep secret - that's what I imagine. And, if she's dead, then it's a pretty big thing. Otherwise, why go to the trouble?'

Lomas shrugged. 'But this is Saltmarsh Cove! We're in Devon. It's a peaceful little backwater.'

'How do you know?'

'Because... well, have you seen the place? It's glorious!'

'Exactly,' Rivera nodded. 'What better place to set up camp? Who would suspect you were up to no good around here?'

Lomas paused for a moment. 'And you think that's what's happening?'

'Possibly. Possibly not. It's maybe a bit too small for a big operation.' Rivera sipped at his drink. 'I'll tell you what I think. I think you stumbled across some brainless goons who freaked out when you started asking questions. They're small fry - hired muscle. Nobody who makes decisions or wields any power needs to act like they do. But if she'd been kidnapped, then you'd likely have heard something. Ransom demands or the like. The fact you haven't means it might not be that.' He let the statement hang in the air.

Lomas nodded.

'Whatever the neanderthals riding round on bikes do, they're only the tip of the iceberg. If your sister was - *is* - a threat to someone or something, then she's going to have dirt on people higher up the chain. That's what I think. Because people like that don't go snatching journalists. They don't have the brainpower to make links like that. That's why I reckon she was on to something bigger.'

'You're not making much sense.' Lomas shook his head.

'Alright, let me put it like this,' Rivera sighed. 'Let's say, for the sake of argument, your sister got lucky and discovered there's something going on here which is part of a huge illegal operation.'

'Like what?'

Rivera shrugged. 'Something profitable enough you'd go to any length to protect it. Drugs. Diamonds. Weapons. Something like that.'

Lomas frowned. 'But what have they done to my sister?'

'I think you're asking the wrong question. Better to ask what she did to them? What was it that made her such a threat?' Rivera scratched a little at his elbow. 'If you can figure that out, then maybe you can work backwards.'

'And what do you think?'

'Well... killing a journalist for sniffing around is a pretty nuclear option. So, hopefully I'm wrong on that front. This must be big news, though – whatever she's found. But what it is – who knows?'

'So what do we do? Can I pay you? Can you help?' The other man's tone was earnest. Hopeful.

'No.' Rivera shook his head and watched as Lomas' shoulders sank. 'Look,' he continued, chewing his lip. He ignored the voice in his head: it informed him he was interfering; that he didn't need this; that he was a prick; that the sister probably wouldn't be as good in the sack as she was in his head. 'I'm going to dig around a bit. I'm curious - that's all, but I'm making no promises. I'm sorry about your sister. I mean, if something's happened. But – to be honest – I'm more interested in figuring out if I'm likely to have to fight any more cavemen.'

'Where will you start?'

'Denton Laine, right?' Rivera shrugged. 'Whatever happened, we've got to assume they had something to do with it. And if they don't, then maybe they'll lead to something else. It might be nothing, but it's all we've got. Right?'

Lomas nodded. 'I'm going back to that pub if you find nothing, though. Someone in there knows something - I'm sure of it.'

Rivera raised his eyebrows. 'Listen. Pardon my French, but they'll kick the shit out of you if you do. Fair warning and all that, but I think it's a dreadful idea.'

'I don't care,' Lomas insisted. 'I'm going.'

'Well,' the ex-soldier continued calmly, 'before you do, you might want to call the local constabulary.'

'What?' The man across the table frowned, sitting up straight. 'I thought you said you were going to look into things yourself? What the hell are you on about?'

'There are two men in black leather jackets standing across the street,' Rivera reported in a low voice. 'You walk out of here, and they'll pulverise you. You won't get a chance to get back to that pub. So your whole plan of striding in there will be dead in the water before you even start.'

Lomas' eyes widened, and a sick feeling rose from the pit of his stomach.

Rivera grinned. 'Don't worry. I've seen them three times today. I've only been in town a couple of days, and their bikes have been like a constant soundtrack. Whoever they work for clearly needs them to be out and about and acting as a visible presence. They've only got a couple of brain cells to rub together, but I'm betting that even they're not so stupid, they'll risk getting arrested if a patrol car comes rolling past.' He paused. 'Look on the bright side. At the very least, they'll probably offer you a lift back to wherever you're staying.' He paused. 'Where are you staying?'

'The Cliffside Hotel.'

'Well, there you go - this is a tourist town in tourist season. The Chamber of Commerce won't want visitors getting scared - they know which side their bread's buttered on. Anyway, show them your nose - that way they'll have to take a statement. And they'll have to log the fact you've actually been attacked. They do that, and they'll disrupt the biker boys when they eventually catch up with them and start asking questions. Understand?'

Lomas nodded, picking up his phone from the tabletop. He held his thumbprint to the screen and, seconds later, dialled 999.

Chapter 13.

Eddie Lomas was awake long before the sun rose. He'd alternated between lying in his vastly overpriced hotel bed and pacing around the rooms of his suite, but sleep had not come. Instead, he'd been haunted by visions of his sister – things she'd said to him years before; images of her being tortured; her lying in a shallow grave somewhere, calling out to unhearing ears. His mind was a blur as he churned over details, worrying. He'd obsessively searched for her name online. Her many articles were present, and there was a short piece about her disappearance. But nothing more. No matter how he tried to banish them, the questions kept coming. Where was his sister? What the hell had she found out? What did they want with her?

And, more than anything, he was bothered by the thought of the bizarre stranger he'd met the night before. The hippie who'd seemed far more hate and war than peace and love. He felt like he could trust him, but it didn't make him feel any better about his situation.

Trent Rivera - if that really was his name - had been right about the police, though. As soon as the patrol car rolled to a halt, the black leather-jacketed figures of his welcoming committee had melted into the night. Then, just as the ex-soldier had predicted, the officers gave him a lift back to his hotel. He'd sat in the rear of the car, the row of illuminated dials at the front casting a glow through the rest of the vehicle. The radio had crackled continually, almost incomprehensibly.

At around three in the morning, he'd gingerly stepped out onto his balcony to cast an eye along the promenade. Part of him felt sure they'd be watching. The paranoid part of his brain even thought there'd be a sniper somewhere on the shore, just waiting to bring the beads of his crosshairs to bear. And then his mind was awhirl once more. He saw himself in grainy 8mm Kodachrome – a figure in the

Zapruder film before Kennedy's head explodes in a watermelon-like smear. Lomas had hastily moved back inside to a safer vantage point. But he'd seen nothing.

And why the hell would Rivera want to help him, anyway? What was he? *Who* was he? Some kind of crusading hero? As he went over his thoughts, it felt like things weren't adding up. Still, he reasoned, any lead was better than no lead, and someone willing to help him was better than him being alone. He'd drawn a blank with the police, so any assistance was welcome.

He sighed and pushed away an empty cup of instant coffee. Deep down, he knew he could have gone down to the dining room in search of better, but he was worried about who might be down there waiting. He'd been scared enough when his strange bodyguard had been walking the streets alongside him last night. Without him, he was sure he'd be terrified. There was something sinister about Saltmarsh Cove. He'd been an outsider before, but here he felt even further removed. There was something almost hostile about the town.

Lomas picked up his phone. Had he been given Rivera's number, he'd have called him. But the number hadn't been forthcoming. So he called the police - just as he'd been instructed. The officer who'd driven him home had seen the bloodied shirt and urged him to follow up on it.

* * * * *

Detective Inspector Lois Christie was slim and olive-skinned. Her dark hair was cut in a bob; her eyes sparkled and her teeth shone white. She'd arrived at the hotel twenty minutes after Lomas' call, and had gone through all the usual protocols, speaking into a Dictaphone, and getting the hotel guest to describe his attacker. Her manner was efficient. She was brusque. Blunt even. But not impolite, and she seemed genuinely concerned by his experience.

'Well, thank you, Mr Lomas,' she announced, closing the band on her notebook. 'You've been a great help.'

'You're welcome,' he nodded. 'What now?'

The officer raised her eyebrows. 'Now, I put out an identikit photo and we'll see if anyone comes forward.'

'But they won't...'

She raised her eyebrows. 'You seem pretty sure of that. For a tourist...'

Lomas shrugged. 'I've seen the way things work around here already. My sister saw it too - there are people pulling strings, and it's guys like the ones who charge around on motorcycles who do their bidding.' He sighed in exasperation.

She looked back hard.

'Are you from here?' Lomas continued. 'Originally, I mean.'

'No. But I don't see why that makes any difference.'

'You must have seen it. You're the law, but... it's like they're the law too.' He spoke seriously. 'Thank you for taking my statement, officer, but you and I both know that nothing will happen. Don't we?'

Lomas sank into his chair. Deflated. Defeated.

'Mr Lomas...' she sighed. 'Look. Saltmarsh Cove isn't paradise, that's for sure. We have bad people here, just like everywhere else. But we've got some good officers. They work hard.'

Lomas shrugged.

Christie glared at him and stood with a hand on her hip. 'I *said* I'll look into it. I know you're the victim here and I'm not naïve about what happens in this town, no matter what you may think. But I'll be damned if a member of the public – whose statement I've just taken, I might add – stands there and criticises me for it.' She paused, her eyes blazing. 'We all choose our battles in this life. We all choose sides - even if we don't want to. That's why I chose to uphold law and order.'

'But you're not, though, are you?' he argued. 'I mean...'

'...you mean, why am I not charging you as an accomplice to an assault that took place outside The Royal George last night? Is that what you mean?' The pitch of her voice rose slightly; her tone took on an acerbic edge, and her eyes narrowed as she continued. 'Why am I not looking too hard for the person who put a known associate of some very bad people in hospital? Is that what you're saying?' she tilted her head sharply, looking at him in expectation.

'No... I... I'm sorry,' Lomas shook his head.

'Good. Keep your ears open.' She handed him a card. 'You hear anything, then call the number on this. It comes straight to me.' She hesitated. 'Don't call the station. Understand?'

Chapter 14.

Gamba watched from the dock as the boat left Lampedusa. The cargo had been a bumper one, and he looked forward to his remuneration, licking his lips slightly. A warm wind blew across the harbour, sending ripples across the surface of the water. He ground a cigarette butt into the stone of the dock with his heel and sent a brief message on burner phone number four.

FULL CARGO DEPARTED.

A minute later, Safia replied.

MESSAGE RECEIVED.

Gamba knew that was all the communication he'd get. He also knew that, once the girls arrived in Salerno, he'd be paid. His only regret was that, with so many girls required, he hadn't been able to keep any back for his own amusement. He yawned, lit another cigarette, and started picking his nose. Pondering the rest of the day, he reasoned he might cross the wire and have a look around – see if there were any likely candidates he might want to make promises to. He cleared his throat and hacked a globule of phlegm into the water.

* * * * *

The riot three nights before had played right into his hands. He knew Safia wouldn't accept the order being short. He also knew that his position was always precarious; if he didn't deliver girls of a suitable quality, she'd simply find someone else to organise her supply. Bianchi had always been clear about that. Government men were no less commodities in Safia's eyes than were the cargoes of flesh – they were easily replaceable.

As it was, he'd needed three more migrant women to fulfil his quota, and time was running low.

But then, the riot started.

Riots were not unknown on Lampedusa. Bianchi used to run a sweepstake on them breaking out when he lived on the island. Each of the immigration employees would pay five euros and indicate when they thought the next fracas would occur. The winner would claim all the cash. There was a bonus paid in the event that anyone correctly guessed the body-count.

They were usually prompted by something small: an argument; a rain storm; bad food; a broken shelter. This time, it had been a fire in an oil drum which had grown out of control. The panic caused a ruckus, and a crowd of migrants attempted to overrun the guards at one of the gates.

Wielding billy clubs and pepper spray, the body-armour clad immigration police, protected by shields, and accompanied by guard dogs, rushed back. As they were hailed with rocks, stones, and bottles, a full-scale battle broke out. The fire spread, and a handful of young men climbed to the top of a security fence where they sat, sneering and spitting at the guards below. Benito was in charge of operations that night, though. He simply ordered his subordinates to slice through the metal fence posts with a reciprocating saw. At first, those atop the fence thought he was bluffing.

He wasn't.

Any of those who weren't killed by the eighteen foot fall onto concrete were despatched with billy clubs.

Fortunately for Gamba, he won the body-count sweepstake that night. It was also lucky the authorities opted to separate the men from the women in the name of safety and security. Shorn of their male protectors, and severed from the ties of extended family bonds in the case of those migrants who'd travelled en masse, female detainees were easy to procure. So he'd waded right in.

Gamba simply syphoned off any of the ones he wanted, pocketing their pathetic piles of greasy banknotes. They looked at him wide-eyed against the raging backdrop of tangerine flames. He smirked - it was as if he was their guardian angel. He thought he might write that moniker on the spine of his next VHS tape.

By the end of the evening, he could have filled his quota three times over. After eventually returning those that didn't pass his selection process to the compound, he'd collected his winnings. Safia – he mused – would be delighted with the quality he'd provided this time around. He smiled with satisfaction, scrolling through the naked photographs of the cargo he'd snapped on his phone, and replaying the memories in his head.

Chapter 15.

Rivera hit town early. He'd left Iris soon after first light, leaving food out for Rosie. The events of the previous evening had troubled him. As much as anything, he was bothered by the thought he seemed to have embroiled himself in something best avoided. On reaching town, the dawn lit seafront had been deserted save for a few dedicated swimmers. Rivera joined them, swimming far out beyond the rock islands with slow, but powerful strokes before turning, floating, and regarding the town and its cliffs. Despite his caution yesterday, he instinctively knew he needed to maintain fitness, and so started swimming back to shore, pushing his muscles hard.

After drying in the sun, he set off in search of a coffee shop. Rivera loved towns and cities early in the morning - the hustle and bustle of delivery trucks and street sweepers; the shouts of market traders; the air of buildings shaking off the blanket of night. It was those moments before everyone else was fully awake, which he enjoyed the most. Saltmarsh Cove was quaint – it was a place that still possessed civic pride. The ex-soldier watched as a dedicated team of enthusiasts went around watering communal flower displays.

Chewing on a croissant and sipping at takeaway coffee in a paper cup, Rivera picked his way through the melee. By the time he'd got back to Iris and climbed into the back of the T2 to sleep, he'd formulated a plan. He'd half-expected the shady figures from outside the pub to turn their attentions to him, but he hadn't crossed their path. Rivera had no real reason for helping Lomas - he knew that much. But something was tugging at his conscience. Something bothered him about a town where people like the neanderthals they'd encountered felt untouchable. He also knew that, without a body, the police would be able to do little to assist in a search for the man's sister.

In truth, he felt sorry for his new acquaintance. Besides, it wasn't like he had anything else to do. There was only so much time he could spend birdwatching, reading, and sitting around waiting to get laid before he got bored.

* * * * *

The library was just about to open when Rivera reached it. He finished the last of his coffee and placed it in a bin. From a bench outside the building, a raggedly-attired man looked hard at him. His skin was weatherbeaten and worn; he'd clearly been sleeping rough for some time.

'What the fuck are you looking at?' he spat.

Rivera shrugged, strolled over, and lowered himself onto the man's bench. He'd learned long ago that showing fear was a surefire way of becoming a victim. So he showed none. As he sat, he noticed the man wasn't quite as old as he'd first thought.

'Best place I've slept in years,' the man shrugged, indicating his makeshift camp. His tone this time was almost hesitant. On a little lawn before the library, a tree spilled its long, leaf-laden branches down onto the ground, forming a canopy. The man had rigged up a blue tarpaulin that was attached to it, and a camp bed and cooking equipment had been installed beneath it. Rivera was quietly impressed; while rough and ready, there was a certain precision to the way the shelter had been constructed.

'And they're OK with you sleeping there? The library?'

'They must be,' he sniffed. 'For now, at least. They'll move me on after a while. Anyway,' he began, looking Rivera up and down. 'You don't look like the scholarly type. What brings you here?'

'Information,' Rivera replied bluntly. 'I need to know a little about some of the people in town.'

The derelict gave him a sidelong glance. 'Oh, information is it? Well... I'm not sure you'll have much luck in the library. You want to ask me instead – the name's Fraser - I know everything.'

Rivera looked at the man, frowning. 'That so?'

'Damn right, chief. You want information, you come and ask old Fraser here. I'll see you right.' He paused. 'Now... forgive me for asking, but have you got a smoke?'

The ex-soldier nodded, reached into his pocket and rolled a cigarette for each of them. As he did, the homeless man opened a can of strong cider that had been secreted inside his shirt, took a drink, and belched contentedly.

* * * * *

Belinda, the librarian, was a brisk, dark-haired lady in her mid-fifties. She wore thick glasses and had just finished setting up a table with complementary coffee and biscuits. Rivera was beginning to understand why Fraser was so taken with the place. The librarian showed the ex-soldier to the reference section he required, instructed him about how to use the online catalogue system, and then encouraged him to ask for help if he required it. He smiled pleasantly in return and thanked her.

Two hours' worth of trawling through records and archives didn't reveal much. Rivera was a believer in paper, though. Sometimes, an internet search - though much speedier - would wrap the user up in knots. People could be taken down blind alleys and dead ends without even realising it. It could happen so quickly that it wrong-footed researchers and didn't give them the time to process what they were seeing.

Rivera was not a stranger to investigating. The night before, he'd not given Lomas any real details when pressed, but he knew how to look for clues. In the Army, he'd trained as a sniper, but then he'd been seconded to a specialist department. As part of a research team, he'd worked to trace the ways terrorists were diverting funds through legitimate channels and using them to buy weapons. It was office-based, but it was off the books. And he was attached to a team that was peopled by clever, competent operatives. He'd enjoyed the work.

It had been his best year in uniform and, had he remained there, he may never have returned to civilian life.

But then he was given new orders. His rifle skills were required once more.

And that was that.

One day he was in an office poring over documents about shell companies and off-shore accounting. The next, he was in Afghanistan. It was back around then that he'd started to think seriously about his future. And whether he might even *have* a future. Having to travel to the hostile other side of the world on the back end of someone else's order had started to lose its appeal.

* * * * *

Rivera didn't find much of use in the library, but what he did see were certain similarities with work he'd done before. Spread out across the table, the documents and archives he possessed told him small parts of what he suspected was a much, much bigger story. He'd eventually coupled his book work with some internet research and had printed out a selection of records from Companies House.

Denton Laine Transportation looked like a moderately successful local haulage firm. But it seemed to subtly change its name every six months or so. One moment it was Denton Laine Transportation. Next, it was DL Transportation. Then, DL Haulage. No company needed to do that unless it had something to hide. It was an old trick, designed to make the money harder to follow. In this case, though, it hadn't been done very well.

Rivera frowned. If Katie Lomas had followed the same dead ends, then her journalistic instincts would have been firing on all cylinders.

Maybe there was something in what Lomas suspected after all.

He bundled the books and archives back together and placed them on the trolley, thanking Belinda on his way out. The ex-soldier had decided to purchase some more data for his phone. If he was disciplined, he told himself that he could use it for research only – not for any extracurricular purposes.

'I'll see you around Skipper!' Fraser hollered, deliriously from his bench. Rivera gave him a slight wave. The homeless man had evidently consumed a few more cans of cider while the ex-soldier had been in the reading room.

Rivera headed for The Cliffside Hotel.

Chapter 16.

'Well?' Grizzly asked.

'Well fucking what?' Spice frowned at his half-brother. His stance was defensive. Combative.

'How come you didn't fucking tell me the cargo was twice the size of the last one?' Grizzly's knuckles whitened as he gripped at the edge of the table. It felt as though the temperature in the room had risen for an instant. As if the big man's inhalation had sucked the cool air away. His teeth were gritted. 'I just got the manifest.'

'You did?' Spice narrowed his eyes. 'But it's encrypted.'

'Yeah, well, I'm not completely stupid. Prick.'

He paused.

'You're not turning pussy on me now, are you?' Spice grinned. 'Remember - this is what we do. This is what puts bread on the table. This is how we get the shit.'

'Listen,' the bigger man argued, a rasping timbre entering his voice. 'We always had bread on the table before... And we've got more useless shit we don't need now than you can shake a stick at.' He rattled his Rolex in irritation.

'Alright.' Spice shrugged. 'So that was a bad example. Have it your way. How about this? It's the little side-line that put that watch on your wrist. The extra job that means you'll retire at fifty if you want. You ain't gonna get that from driving white goods up and down the M5 for the next five years. Know what I mean?'

Grizzly sighed.

'You've got as much blood on your hands as the next man, anyway,' Spice went on. 'You knew what you were getting into. You knew what the fucking risks were. These aren't people – they're just poor men's slags who'll become rich men's slags once they're sold on.' His eyes hardened. 'Most of these bitches love it, I bet. Three meals a day and a good gang-banging every once in a while. What's not to like?'

'Oh, what?' the big man frowned. 'They tell you that, did they?'

'Course not, dumbass.' Spice was indignant. 'I don't speak African or whatever the fuck language they talk in. But I know a horny-looking bitch when I see one. And I see plenty.'

'But...!' his older half-brother protested.

'But I've never heard you complaining when the dough rolled in!' Spice interrupted, his voice rising.

The younger man was wearing a cotton shirt in salmon pink with chinos and deck shoes. His hair was gelled back and his face was clean-shaven. He looked every inch the socially mobile entrepreneur ready to spend a day shopping for yachts. He'd swiftly bounced back from the setback of the lost cargo. But Spice always bounced back. The contrast with his half-sibling couldn't have been more marked; Grizzly wore faded blue jeans and steel toe capped boots. His stained T-shirt was covered by a sleeveless fleece jacket that hung open. He wasn't exactly overweight – he carried himself well enough to conceal his paunch. But time was starting to show; TV dinners and takeaways were taking their toll. He had bags beneath his eyes and rubbed at the stubble on his chin in irritation.

'I know.' Grizzly's reply was blunt. 'But I guess I'm not so sure anymore.'

'Woah!' Spice held his hands up, the tone of his voice rising, echoing from the thin walls of the office. 'Well, it's not like you can bloody back out now. You know that, don't you? You start fucking about with this stuff, and we're all fucked!'

The big man frowned and looked hard across the desk. He'd sunk down into his chair, looking drained. Spice, meanwhile, paced the floor energetically. Light on his feet. Eyes bright. He'd suspected the meeting might be tense, so he'd had a quick bump beforehand, just to take the edge off.

'Why?' Grizzly demanded again. 'Why can't we just cut the fucking ties?'

'You know that phrase, *in too deep?*' the smaller man enquired. His question was met with a nod.

'Well, you're in too fucking deep... We all are. It's a one-way street from now on.'

Grizzly slammed his fist down onto the table. 'This one's the last one - this cargo. I fucking mean it!'

'But then the money dries up.' Spice raised his eyebrows. 'You want to go back to old-fashioned haulage? If so, you're a mug. You remember what the profit margins were like? That thing I said about fridges and freezers – it's all true. So, why mess with a good thing?'

'This isn't a good thing - this cargo. It's not right. I've been thinking that for a while.'

'See, that's another thing,' his half-brother sighed. 'Why do you always call it a cargo? Does it make you feel better or something? Does it make you think we're just hauling crates instead of truckloads of slags?' He shook his head. 'You need to fucking man up, sunshine.'

'I...'

'You knew what we were moving when we first got involved in this. You can't undo that. Don't tell me you've got a conscience now all of a sudden?' He laughed. 'Fuck me! Mr Morality now, are you?'

Grizzly glared back at him.

'We carry on,' Spice announced bluntly. 'Because if it's not us, then it'll be someone else. And we've already fucked up one shipment. That's why I doubled the numbers this time. Remember, we're dealing with warlords here. Mafia men. They don't take prisoners - you know that. They're not going to have any kind of Geneva Convention if they get their hands on you.' He raised his eyebrows. 'You remember that film they sent us of that kid who grassed?'

The big man nodded.

'Yeah – well, there was no putting all the pieces of him back together, was there? And if they think you've shafted them, they won't think twice before pulling the trigger. We have to keep our end of the bargain. Understand?'

'Or else what?'

'Or else we wind up poor. Or dead... like Rusty. Got it?'

Grizzly drummed nervously on the surface of his desk and then gave his half-brother the finger.

'Anyway, I'm taking the Head of the Coastguard out for lunch,' Spice announced. 'You know why.' He looked hard at the seated man, and then his tone softened somewhat. 'Just don't overthink things. Leave the figuring out to me. You just concentrate on acting normal and keeping your mouth shut. OK?'

Chapter 17.

Rivera sighed.

There was evidently something going on, but he wasn't figuring out anything fast.

The ex-soldier walked past The Cliffside Hotel. Seeing a police car parked in the entrance, though, he'd reasoned it was better for him to keep a low profile. After all, if he dropped in on a neighbourhood officer taking a statement from Lomas, they might start asking questions about last night's fight. His knuckles weren't too bruised, but they were bruised enough. And if he was in custody, he wouldn't be able to look into anything. The ex-soldier looked away as a police officer exited the hotel.

That was a conversation Rivera wasn't yet ready to have. He had no doubt someone in uniform would come asking him about it at some point. If they didn't figure it out for themselves, then someone from Denton Laine would probably despatch them - if only to get the ex-soldier out of the way and temporarily into a holding cell. The fact he had no fixed abode put him only one step above Fraser – the derelict – in the eyes of the law.

Rivera returned to Iris for the afternoon. The daytime nap was one of the perks of his not having a job. He reasoned he'd find Lomas later on. In the meantime, he bedded down in the back of the T2 and was quickly dead to the world. He tended to sleep better in the daylight hours - it was with night-time when the darkness really came down upon him.

*****

The squealing noise that tore him out of his sleep was piercing and continual. One moment he was snoring, and the next he'd leaped into a fighting stance beside the table in the rear of the campervan, thinking he was under attack. He frowned; the van's door was still closed – he wasn't being invaded.

Looking down, he saw the source of the sound was an enormous, half-dead rat. Rosie had deposited it as a gift on the floor of the Volkswagen. She'd somehow carried it through the small window he left open for her. It ran around in desperate circles, trailing blood. Rivera frowned at the cat who, he swore, raised her eyebrows at what she doubtless considered a benevolent gesture. She settled herself down, as if to suggest the rat was now his problem.

'If you're going to do a job, Rosie,' he began, 'then at least finish it.'

The cat mewed in response. Such libations were becoming more frequent; summer had clearly brought an abundance of available prey.

* * * * *

Half an hour later, the floor of the T2 had been cleaned and disinfected. The rat - dispatched with a swift blow from a spanner - had been deposited in the refuse, wrapped in a discarded poster which had previously advertised the campsite's bingo evening.

Rosie, of course, had been forgiven and rewarded with a fresh pouch of food. The ex-soldier left her sleeping peacefully.

Rivera looked down at the shoreline from the high ground of the campsite. Before the town was a large harbour. But on either side of it were several small coves. While he could see them from where he was, he realised they would be all but invisible to anyone at sea-level. He pulled out his sniper scope and studied them in more detail. Each had a small beach that would allow a boat to land - or, at least, to unload a cargo. They looked postcard-perfect in the sun; their pebbles shone, and the water surrounding them was bright blue.

He thought again about Denton Laine. What were they trying to protect? If it was drugs, then any of these coves would be a perfect place to land them - if they were brought in by sea. The trucks of the transport company could then be used to transport them incognito all over the country.

But why? He mused.

Why land anything here? Alright, so it was an out-of-the-way place, but there were hundreds of locations that would be easier to use if they wanted to import something in secret. It made little sense.

Rivera decided to do the only thing he could think of. He'd had little success in town, and Lomas hadn't been able to tell him a great deal of useful information either. All he knew was that the neanderthals were involved somehow.

So, he resolved to find out more. Despite no longer being in the military, there was part of him that still longed for a mission. A focus.

* * * * *

Nobody who'd been inside The Royal George the night before had witnessed Rivera's intervention. They'd seen Lomas being manhandled out of the bar, of course, but the ex-soldier figured that similar random acts of violence would be par for the course in such an establishment. It had a pool table. And it had a chalkboard with 3D writing – they were always dead giveaways.

Either way, nobody paid him much attention as he walked in. The pub was not busy. A pair of punters were playing darts in the corner. A fat man was half-asleep at the bar, and a group of heavily tattooed twenty somethings were playing pool. Beside them, two drunken girls were laughing shrilly and applauding their shots, swaying a little. Rivera studied them for a second – they weren't surfers. That was certain.

Rivera sidled up to the bar and ordered a lager. He nodded his thanks to the barmaid. She looked to be in her early twenties, but had the skin of a seasoned drinker and cold, defeated eyes. Her gaze locked on to his for a moment, and then moved off – any warmth flickered away like the dying embers of a fire. Taking his drink, he retired to a corner table in the shadows where he sat with his back to the wall, a clear view of the door before him. Next to the table was a partition which separated the bar from the bathrooms. From his back pocket, the ex-soldier withdrew a paperback book and, with one eye on the entrance, began to read.

* * * * *

Reading a book in a pub in central London is a perfectly acceptable pastime. Reading a book in many of the establishments in Saltmarsh Cove would have raised few eyebrows. However, reading a book in The Royal George was *not* a normal occurrence. Rivera looked up as an oddly mismatched pair of men walked in. The smaller of the two was well-dressed, with sharp-eyes that darted around the room, lingering on the ex-soldier's table. The larger of the two was enormous, with forearms like sides of ham. He resembled a miserable gorilla.

'What are you reading for?' he demanded.

Rivera frowned. 'Do you mean what am I reading, or what am I reading for?'

'You fucking heard,' the huge man rasped, his expression clouding.

The ex-soldier held up the book. 'Does that answer your question?'

Opening his mouth to speak, the big man closed it again in incomprehension. His eyes went through various phases of bewilderment as he looked at the cover. The ex-soldier had picked *The Naked Civil Servant* up in a second-hand shop. Its tatty cover showed it to be an edition reprinted to accompany the TV adaptation; it featured a scantily-clad John Hurt as Quentin Crisp. 'What fucking filth is that?' Rivera's accuser hissed, his teeth gritted.

'Come on now, mate,' the younger man urged, grabbing the arm of the other. 'Let's leave the bloke in peace, shall we?'

Rivera held eye contact with the big man for a moment, then shook his head in puzzlement and returned to his book. But he listened carefully and discerned footsteps as the aggressor walked away, following the other new arrival.

The pair walked over to the pool table. Immediately, the group playing on it put down their cues and reverently greeted the newcomers, before retreating to a respectful distance. They took seats at a booth between the pool table and the bar, and watched the two new players, smiling and nodding from time to time.

As the pair racked up the balls and broke, they stole occasional glances at Rivera. Other than that, the bar was reasonably quiet. The jukebox was turned down low, but it pumped out enough noise to drown out the men's conversation. Cracks from the pool balls occasionally cut through the background noise. The drunken group at the booth was more subdued. And the barmaid had moved to the far end of the bar where she was now seated, awaiting any orders from the two most recent arrivals. She made a show of leaning over while polishing glasses, exposing cleavage to the pool players. The bigger man noticed and stared, drooling a little. He elbowed the other man and nodded towards the bar, grinning. The barmaid made an exaggerated show of surprise and became suddenly coy.

* * * * *

Lomas entered around eight, just as Rivera had expected. He caught his acquaintance's eye, but Rivera gave an almost imperceptible shake of his head. The journalist's brother was savvy enough to notice it and kept walking. Behind him trooped the remaining two bikers. Build-wise, they looked like carbon copies of the man Rivera had dealt with the night before. In spite of the warm evening, each of them wore a black leather jacket. The ex-soldier noticed the second man's lack of fitness – it was manifested in his heavy, rattling breaths.

The ex-soldier had expected they'd notice him, but they went straight past, eyes fixed on the pool table. He noticed they both walked with a spring in their step - a sense of pride no doubt at bringing in the upstart they saw as their target man. The pecking order was becoming clear: the recent arrivals, though clearly men of respect in the town, were foot soldiers.

The pair at the table were higher up the food chain – it was they to whom the new arrivals looked for instruction.

Unnoticed, Rivera slipped into the shadows and stood outside the door of the bathroom, peering through a crack in the partition that screened the toilets from the bar. As he did, Lomas approached the neon lights by the pool table. The smaller player smiled warmly, while the larger one regarded him with a haggard expression, his jowls resembling those of a disgruntled bloodhound. He couldn't hear the exchange of words above the noise of the jukebox, but through studying body language, he was able to guess how it was playing out.

In the tableau before him, Lomas was being open – clearly presenting himself as a reasonable man who just wanted to find out what happened to his sister. The smaller man responded to him cordially, but with an undercurrent of threat. The bigger man, meanwhile, simply glared. Rivera, though, was sure he read a hint of uncertainty in his expression. When he did eventually begin speaking, his voice was raised in a torrent of effing and blinding. What was said was unclear, but he began to gesture more angrily. It was at this point that all three turned and regarded the empty table where Rivera had been sitting previously. Lomas' brow furrowed when he noticed the now vacant seat.

Seconds later, the smaller pool player turned back to the table to take a shot, seemingly bored by proceedings. The giant looked at the two bikers and gave a nod. They walked up behind Lomas and, each taking an arm, conveyed him towards the partition where Rivera stood. The tall, thin man wore an expression of alarm, his feet not quite touching the ground. He kicked his legs a little, scrabbling unsuccessfully for purchase. The rest of the pub was a study in not paying attention.

The ex-soldier ducked into the ladies' toilets and listened through the door. He knew the goons had two options: either take Lomas out through the fire escape, or - more likely - force him into the gents' toilets. As he expected, they took the second option. With the police already aware of last night's violence, the pair would be unwilling to risk administering a beating to a man out on the street. It was much better to contain their activities to a place where nobody would claim to have seen anything.

Hearing the door shut, Rivera stepped back outside. The partition hid him from the rest of the pub goers. He noticed the barmaid had bolted the front door, evidently the result of an unspoken order that had been dispensed more than once before; she was returning to her seat at the bar. He pressed himself into the shadows and peered again through the crack. The two men were still at the pool table while the other group remained at their table. The sleeping drunk snored on, oblivious.

Rivera entered the gents' toilet.

* * * * *

Voices echoed from the tiled walls, and a cistern hissed noisily. The lighting was dim – a single glass fixture was attached to the ceiling; it was filled with dead insects silhouetted in profile. Twelve-inch high graffiti was scrawled along the near wall: *KAREN LUVS KOK.*

'And your fucking mate put Popeye in the hospital last night,' leather jacket number one growled. 'So Pluto here is going to break your fingers.' He scoffed disdainfully. 'Dickhead.'

'And Pugwash is going to break your toes,' the other man added. Lomas' eyes widened in disbelief, but the threat was real. 'All of them. And you're gonna like it. Because you're a little bitch. And if we get any more trouble...'

'Then it'll be fucking curtains for you. I'll throw you off the cliff and cut your fucking head off. Understand?'

'Will you cut my head off before the fall or after?' Lomas asked, his tone one of innocence.

'Don't get fucking loud!' The man slapped the captive across the face.

Lomas tried hard to suppress a whimper.

Rivera clicked the door shut. The three men turned.

'You do know,' began Rivera, 'that kids in the schoolyard have better imaginations when it comes to nicknames? I've been standing here listening, and the only way I can think to describe you lot is... fucking stupid.'

'I'm gonna fucking kill you,' replied the one who'd been referred to as Pugwash. He spoke with calm assuredness, unmoved by the new man's presence. It was the voice of a man used to making threats. Used to being feared.

'You reckon?' Rivera raised his eyebrows. 'How so?'

'I used to be in the Navy,' the big man bristled, removing a claw hammer from his jacket. His face wore the hint of a frown; he couldn't quite compute the lack of fear on the other man's features.

'That figures,' the new arrival shrugged. 'Thanks to Churchill, we all know about Naval traditions.' There was a silence, broken only by a stifled snigger from the obviously more literate Lomas. 'Really? Not ringing any bells? Rum, sodomy and the lash?'

The big man approached him, his face a mark of twisted contempt, while his friend looked on, relishing the encounter.

Rivera didn't hesitate. He feinted left and then jabbed the man full in the throat. As he clutched at his crushed larynx, Rivera kicked him in the groin so hard it looked like the man's eyes were about to fly out of their sockets. Pluto, meanwhile, hesitated. He'd never seen Pugwash fail, let alone fail in such spectacular fashion. He simply stared, mystified.

This hesitation was his undoing. Rivera launched a flying kick that caught him full on the chin. It sent his head reeling back, smashing into the mirror on the wall, shattering it. Clutching at the washbasin with one hand, he clawed at his bloodied face with the other. The ex-soldier grabbed him by the collar, swung him round and wrenched his hand, drawing the leather-jacketed man's arm involuntarily straight. From there, he delivered a side kick that broke a series of ribs and sent his head sprawling into the overflowing trough of the urinal.

'What are you, some kind of ninja?' Lomas hissed. He paused. His voice was steady, but his eyes were wide in bewilderment. 'Thanks... again.'

'Get the door.' Rivera replied.

'What?'

'Block it. We're going to send a proper message this time. No more fucking about. These guys are nobodies – they're starting to piss me off. We need to move up the chain for answers.'

'So?' Lomas' brow was furrowed.

'So... do unto others as they would do to you.'

Lomas frowned, backing against the door to block it. It had a bolt on the frame, which he slid across quietly. Looking on, he gasped as Rivera reached down and methodically broke each of Popeye's fingers, wrenching every one back until it cracked. He then shook his head in disbelief as he watched his acquaintance progress further. Rivera removed the prone man's shoes and then calmly shattered each of his toes with the hammer that had been dropped in the fracas. With each blow, the man twitched slightly. Rivera then repeated the procedure with Pluto, incapacitating him in the same way.

'You do know that you've started a war now?' Lomas frowned from his position by the door.

Rivera straightened himself up. 'Listen,' he whispered. 'They were going to do the same to you. So ask yourself this question: would you rather it was you sprawled out on the floor there with no working digits and a face full of piss?'

'No.' Lomas shook his head.

'First rule of combat,' Rivera continued. 'Leave the enemy in a worse state than yourself. Got it?'

'Yes.'

'And there's no way these guys are going to be any use when things get more interesting. Everything else we can figure out as we go.' He tapped at the man's arm. 'You OK?'

Lomas nodded.

'Good.' The ex-soldier held the other man's gaze for a moment. 'Follow me.'

Rivera killed the bathroom light and, as the door swung open, he ushered Lomas out behind him. Peering through the crack in the partition, he surveyed the bar once more. All was as before, with the various parties still in their same positions. The ex-soldier had only entered the bathroom a couple of minutes before; it would likely be the same amount of time again before a search party was sent in, he reasoned. He paused for a moment, grabbing the bar of the fire door, hoping it wouldn't trigger an alarm. Breathing a sigh of relief when it opened silently, he stepped through it into a dark, deserted side alley.

'What now?' Lomas frowned when they were a safe distance from the pub. The streets were quiet; the ex-soldier had checked there was nobody watching as they exited the building.

'Let's get you back to your hotel. You need to give me your number and then hang a *do-not-disturb* sign on the door. Bolt it. Put a chair or a cabinet against it. And don't open it to anybody.' He looked hard at the other man. 'And I bloody mean it. Anybody. That officer you were talking to today – did you trust her?'

'Yes,' Lomas nodded. 'I believed her – she said she wanted to help.'

'Good. Tell her that you're in fear for your life, so they'll put the word out about you. I'm going to do some digging - I'll come and find you when I know more, but I'll call if I'm outside. Otherwise...'

'Don't open the door,' Lomas cut in.

Rivera nodded. 'And don't worry - we haven't started a war. I think these guys were already at war - that's why they're so jumpy. Your sister just stumbled on something that must have really spooked them. That's all. At least that's what I think.' He paused. 'I can't promise I'll be able to work it out, but I might at least be able to find some kind of reason for why things around here are happening in the way they are.'

Lomas nodded, grimacing slightly. 'Did it bother you? Breaking those blokes' bones, I mean.'

'No,' Rivera shrugged. 'Why?'

'It's just...'

'Listen. This thing here – I didn't ask to get involved in it, right? But now it seems I am. I don't know who this lot are that we're up against. All I know is they're not good people.'

'So?'

'So, fuck them.' Rivera winked.

Lomas laughed a little uncertainly.

Chapter 18.

Genteel surface impressions aside, Saltmarsh Cove had always had a lawless element. Centuries before, the coves had been the preserve of smugglers landing casks of bootleg liquor and using dark lanterns to evade the customs men. Then, there had been the usual litany of ne'er-do-wells who used isolated barns and old outhouses for their nefarious purposes. That much hadn't changed, despite the gradual transformation of the backwater fishing port into a thriving tourist destination. These days, though, you were as likely to find a mini meth-lab as an illegal liquor still. But as long as the pictures of the sunlit seafront were plastered on advertising paraphernalia, people could turn blind eyes to such activities.

The police remained relatively powerless. Naturally, if they caught someone red-handed, they'd send them to jail. And for larger crimes, they'd draft in reserves from the rest of the county. But, for the most part, they were under-resourced and stretched to breaking point. Pretending they could cover the hundreds of miles of roads and tracks around the town would have raised a smile at any of the local alehouses. Their approach was as much hope-for-the-best as anything else; just about keeping a lid on things was just about good enough. They were a useful visible presence, but any lawbreaker knew that time and distance would usually be on their side; wrong-doers would be long gone before the cavalry arrived. So it was that low-level misdemeanours kept occurring in the ways they always had.

More recently, there had been county lines. The moving of drugs from inner cities to rural communities had caught on quickly: fresh markets meant new users; new users meant larger incomes. The unscrupulous overlords who dispatched needy adolescents on trains and buses didn't care about how picture-perfect the towns were they were moving their trade into. If there were properties they could cuckoo and street corners where they could shift their wares, they were happy to take on all comers.

And so they did.

That had been the fate of Saltmarsh Cove for a period of around six months. In the very Caucasian world of the Devon town, the sudden proliferation of teenagers from minority ethnic groups was never going to go unnoticed. One moment, they simply seemed to appear, running errands on mopeds and scooters. Tearing up and down the seafront at night. Kicking people out of their homes. Hooking the local users on their particular brand of pills and powders. And then, once they had their claws into them, bleeding them dry. They were notable for their utter lawlessness. Boundaries for them simply didn't exist. And, in a land of corn-fed country boys, their often weasel-like appearances adhered strongly to the phrenologists' code. But they were dangerous; it wasn't that they didn't play by the rules – more that they didn't even know there were rules in the first place.

Of course, the elderly population wrote letters of complaint to *The Saltmarsh Herald*. They badgered the Town Council and begged the police to act. But it was all to no avail: any time a youngster was arrested, they rarely had any form of identification on them. And if they were sent away, ready replacements appeared to take their places. The police knew they would never lay their hands on any of the big players. It was the street rats huddled under their hoodies who they'd ship back to Croydon or Birmingham, Manchester or Liverpool that were the beating heart of the operation. And they were untouchable.

Social Services would get involved. They'd even arrange for the delinquents to be escorted elsewhere.

But they invariably returned. Slipping out of care homes and juvenile detention centres, they would find their way back. They had little choice; when orders were dispensed at the business end of a shotgun, they followed them, rolling back into town like bad pennies.

Until one day they didn't.

* * * * *

Nobody knew for certain what had happened. They just knew the problem seemed to disappear overnight. One day there were mopeds terrorising the sea front. The next, there were slow, almost regal parades of Harley Davidsons patrolling the promenade in twos and threes. The huddles of youngsters hidden beneath their hoods and glued to their phones had evaporated.

Compared to what had come before, the new masters - with their black leather jackets and pot bellies - seemed almost civilised. And when presented with a safer alternative to the antisocial behaviour that had preceded it, the town's people tended not to ask questions. They just shrugged their shoulders, bowed their heads, and gave thanks things were getting better.

Of course, rumours abounded over what the bikers had done to defeat the county lines troops. There were those who suggested murder, while others believed there was a payoff somewhere along the chain. Either way, the outsiders had been scared into submission. To all intents and purposes, they'd been banished.

That was good enough.

* * * * *

'Good bloody riddance, I say.' Janine suppressed a belch. 'If you ask me, they should've hanged the lot of them. And drawn them. And quartered them.'

Rivera nodded. The groundswoman had drunkenly availed herself of a spare chair beside Iris. He'd been about to feign tiredness, but then Rosie emerged from the shadows and sat on Janine's lap. The woman had fussed over the cat while giving the ex-soldier a potted history of the town. All the while, she'd swigged at a bottle of rosé liberated from the campsite clubhouse. Rivera was unsure whether it was the booze that had loosened her tongue or whether people in this part of the world were always so indiscreet. He simply listened as she held forth, interjecting with occasional questions.

'And what do *you* think it was?' he enquired, his interest piqued by the sudden shift of power to the men in motorcycle jackets. He knew his standards were sometimes questionable, but surely he wasn't so desperate he could overlook the crooked teeth and the flesh partially protruding beneath the ill-advised crop top? He decided to stay focused on his questions. His eyes, though, kept snagging on her chest – inwardly, he noted how hard her top was working to contain it.

'You what?' Janine frowned.

'The bikers - you think they're just vigilantes or something?'

'No.' She shook her head. 'I think they're proper bad men. I reckon they've just moved in and taken over the drug trade for themselves.' She shrugged. 'People round here seem to think of them as some kind of Robin Hood figures, but that's bollocks – for sure.'

Rivera nodded again, pensive. He then frowned as Janine's hand began working its way up his leg. He bit his lip, careful to give no reaction. She looked at him appraisingly; her touch taking in the taut physique beneath his casual clothes.

'How about it then?' she asked, raising her eyebrows and flashing a drunken smile. 'I won't tell if you won't.' She raised her eyebrows and batted her lashes, her eyes blurrily sparkling with mischief. 'There isn't a Mrs Muscles around, is there?'

'You're - er - very nice, Janine,' he said hesitantly. 'Really. It's just...'

She stood up abruptly, handing him the cat. 'Well,' she sighed. 'If you change your mind, then you know where to find me.'

He smiled sadly.

'You ever done it on a sit-on lawnmower?' she enquired, turning back to look at him.

'I can't say I have.'

'Shame.' She turned and walked slowly back across the field. Her sauntering pace sent out a message Rivera strove to ignore.

Chapter 19.

Rivera blinked himself awake and then regarded his surroundings with distaste. He was in a caravan that looked like it had time-travelled from the late-1980s. A large *Athena* print adorned one wall.

Janine stared at him adoringly.

'Morning sleepyhead,' she purred, making a vicious grab for his groin. He rolled over, shielding himself slightly.

'What's the matter? You don't want to play any more?' The woman raised her eyebrows. Suddenly, the events of the previous evening came barrelling back to him. After Janine's departure, he'd sat, trying to read. Then, he'd shifted his attention to the clock, watching its second hand tick lethargically from number to number. He'd eventually offered himself an ultimatum: drink; smoke, or shag.

He'd chosen the latter.

She hadn't been surprised.

'Told you!' she smiled as she opened the door of her caravan.

* * * * *

'That thing you got me to do...' Rivera began hesitantly.

'Yeah, it's kind of my thing.' Janine shrugged.

The ex-soldier frowned.

'A fair used to come to my hometown once a year,' Janine announced.

'Yeah?'

'Yeah,' she nodded. 'And once, when I was fourteen, a bloke from the dodgems tempted me back to his van.' She paused and lit a cigarette, blowing the smoke towards Rivera. 'The first time it was barely consensual, but I guess I must have liked it well enough – when the fair came back to town the next year, I let him do it again.'

Silence.

'Mind you,' she mused. 'He was a wily one. One year he did it so hard I ended up in hospital for three days. Anyway,' she paused. 'You want breakfast?'

'No.' He shook his head, both in response, and also in an attempt to clear the images arising in his mind. 'Thanks. I've got things to do today.'

'Yeah?'

He nodded. Rivera had never paid for it. But, over the years, he felt he'd paid for it plenty in a whole host of ways. Had he been given to talking to himself, he'd have admonished his behaviour, and ridiculed his reflection for the fact he'd fallen into the same trap that always snared him. Instead, he simply ambled on with a sense of amused resignation. Stepping into the campervan, Rosie seemed to regard him with a disappointed, judging expression.

'Don't you bloody start,' Rivera began, taking a pouch of cat food out of the cupboard. 'She made me do it!' The cat's impassive stare merely served to emphasise what a piece of self-deceit that remark had been.

Chapter 20.

The truth of Saltmarsh Cove's dismissal of the county lines brigades was a closely guarded secret. Old man Laine had been in business for many years and had a near monopoly on all haulage in the area. Lucrative contracts came his way, and he was - according to most - a decent employer who paid wages on time and looked after people he trusted. He was wealthy – not in an oligarch sense – but certainly more moneyed than many of his peers.

While his sons were away serving in the forces, he'd watched the town change like everyone else. It didn't make him happy, but it didn't affect him so much that he wanted to get involved. He'd seen and heard the moped couriers blazing up and down the seafront. It had irritated him when he'd been night fishing, and he'd been livid for a week after their wheels ruined the green on the seventeenth hole of the golf course, but - other than that – he'd stayed locked within the confines of his gated property. The trials and tribulations of the town were something that happened outside. Not in his backyard. Not his problem.

Until things changed.

It was a small enough thing. He'd been out having a steak dinner at King's restaurant with his wife. After several glasses of wine, and pleasantries exchanged with fellow members of the Royal Saltmarsh Links Course, the two opted for a stroll along the promenade.

The boys who'd emerged from one of the shelters and jeered at them were just that. Boys. But they said some extremely insulting things about his wife. They'd called her fat. Old. Ugly. The usual. Then, when they got no reaction, their rhetoric was stepped up. Laine had been about to go after them, but she'd held him back.

Then they'd said something else, and it had been her that lost her cool instead, slapping one of them around the face and mouthing off at him. She may have been part of respectable society, but she'd clawed her way up. Her language – when she reverted to her previous persona - was sharp and direct. It usually cut people to shreds. But instead of moving away, the boy had simply laughed in her face.

That lack of respect was something Denton Laine wouldn't usually have tolerated. But he bit his tongue and narrowed his eyes. He weighed up whether to hit the youngster, but he restrained himself. It was what the boy said afterwards that made him turn. It was a cuss and a challenge all rolled into one:

'You've got no balls.'

He hadn't done much. He'd just calmly advised the kid with the scouse accent to mend his ways, and then walked away with his wife. Inwardly, he was seething; as he turned his head to give them a mouthful, his wife had clutched tight to him, steering him away.

The kid had imitated the sound of a clucking chicken. His friends had joined him, their laughter echoing out of the shelter. Walking away, old man Laine felt suddenly calm. Reconciled. He wasn't the toughest guy in the world. And he definitely wasn't the strongest – or the youngest. But, when it came to getting even, he had a one-track mind. By letting him walk away, the yobs had left open the path for revenge.

* * * * *

What happened next was like a beer hall putsch; dominos fell one after another until there was no longer any doubting who was in charge.

First of all, Spice and Grizzly - Denton Laine's sons by different mothers - returned. They'd both left the forces and had come home, intending to spend time pondering their futures. Grizzly - always the more amicable of the two - had brought three friends in tow: Popeye; Pluto, and Pugwash. Idiots in the eyes of Laine, but loyal. They were all tough, strong men, and all were in need of employment.

Laine realised that, with them on his side, he had the makings of an army.

It was just as well, because what happened next was tantamount to a declaration of war. Battle lines were drawn in the sand.

That truckers love their trucks is an axiom few would dispute. Laine was no exception. But this was a special case. He'd spent three years restoring an imported Kenworth W900 to its former glory. It was immaculate. Perfect. A safe bet to win a rosette at the Big Truck Festival South West. It had been parked in gleaming perfection; it had pride of place in one of Laine's warehouses.

But the scally who'd bad-mouthed him stole it.

And crashed it, writing it off.

That - for Denton Laine - was the final straw. That he'd bad-mouthed him was trouble enough. Old man Laine had the kid marked down for a knee-capping. But the truck took things to a whole new level. In a first test of their allegiance, Grizzly's Navy buddies had been sent out to find the culprit. They were big, mean, and frightening. And even the nothing-to-lose street kids who were usually so full of front lost their nerve at seeing the leather-jacketed bikers bearing down upon them. They confiscated some of the boys' mopeds and torched them, thrusting burning rolls of newspaper into their fuel tanks. Another youngster was tied naked to a street lamp on the front. The bikers prevented any would-be Samaritans from approaching during the evening, and disconnected any nearby CCTV. As night fell and a storm blew in, they threw stones at the shivering wretch, jeering. Shortly before first light – according to local rumours that nobody could corroborate – they cast him into a riptide. He might have made it out of the water. But if he did, nobody saw him again.

Then, with the dispensing of a few more broken bones, they extracted a name: Kyson Francis.

*****

Before he removed his balls with a pair of bolt cutters, Laine shone a flashlight in Francis' face so he could be sure he was the one. The old man's expression was impassive.

'So... you stole my truck?'

'No.' The youth was defiant in response. 'Fuck you!'

Popeye gripped his neck with one hand and used a pair of pliers to extract a tooth. It was wrenched out with a sound like a tree being ripped from the ground. The adolescent's howls were swallowed by the winds that blew on the deserted path high above the town. He began begging for mercy.

'I asked you a question, son,' Laine continued calmly.

'Yes,' the boy spluttered, spitting scarlet dribbles of blood down his chin.

Laine nodded before continuing. 'See – the problem here is that you're basically sub-human.' He paused. 'Do you know what an Apex predator is?'

The kid shook his head.

'An Apex predator is me,' Laine chuckled. 'But you – you're just a useless piece of shit that barely registers on the food chain. If we remove you, then some other useless fucker will just move in to take your place. You've basically got no balls.' The old man frowned. 'And didn't you tell me I had no balls once upon a time?'

The boy nodded again, his eyes widening.

'Well... two can play at that game,' Laine announced, raising the steel handles before him. He took his time, examining the blades carefully, before lowering them, ready to put them to purpose. 'I wouldn't worry,' he announced. 'Your dick probably doesn't work, anyway. It's not like any girl's gonna let you fuck her, you ugly bastard.' He paused. 'Or any boy, for that matter.'

He moved the handles hard together.

A scream arose.

*****

Laine's anonymous leaking of the horrific details of the torture to the press was meant as a warning. The neutered male who'd been found at the base of the cliffs had had his mouth roughly stitched up. When the coroner unpicked the stitches on the face of the corpse, they discovered the young man's severed manhood had been placed in his mouth. Such a find should have been kept quiet, but it was almost immediately plastered over the front pages of tabloids up and down the country.

Saltmarsh Cove was suddenly big news. And the press claimed dark forces were running the place, showing no mercy. The lurid details of the dismemberment were widely circulated – there were even visitors who came to see the cliff for themselves, driven by morbid curiosity.

Letting the word out was a gamble - Laine knew that much. But he was through with being tolerant. He wanted his town back, and he wanted blood. The haulier knew the county lines organisation would either send in their best and brightest, or they'd withdraw.

They chose the former.

Which was a mistake.

Back then, Laine's sons and their friends were still combat-ready. Their muscles were hard and their wits were sharp. And they knew how to use weapons. More than that, though, they were still hungry – they hadn't yet developed drug-addled complacency. A war for them was just the kind of challenge they still thrived on. It didn't matter that their opponents were killers; their trade had been learned ad hoc in concrete canyons and pub car parks. Laine's men had been trained to kill for a living.

The committee sent down from the Midlands was ruthless. They didn't come to town to take prisoners. But they hit the depot. Which was a mistake. Denton Laine was a veteran of several conflicts, and a big fan of the writings of Von Clausewitz. One of the Prussian general's first rules is that the enemy should only ever be engaged after careful thought about terrain.

One point to Laine.

Another, according to *The Principles of War*, is that the enemy should – wherever possible – be cut off from his lines of retreat.

Two points to Laine.

A third rule - make sure firepower is always concentrated on a decisive position.

Make that three points.

And the fourth: less Von Clausewitz and more an old street fighting adage: if fighting is necessary, then be tougher, meaner and more ruthless than any adversary.

Denton Laine knew his men would be able to defeat most of the hard cases sent their way. He also knew that the county lines boys didn't possess infinite resources. Much like the Roman Empire, their business plan only worked if they kept expanding into new territories. For that, they needed manpower. And they lost a lot of that at the depot. Their expansion stalled, which left them in a quandary.

All of a sudden, their leaders feared being faced with Visigoths at the gates. They could either send in more troops and risk annihilation, or they could retreat.

They chose the latter.

Which made sense - especially after what had happened.

* * * * *

It's tough to make people disappear. It happens in movies, but it's really far more difficult than people think. Ghosts tend to leave footprints. Trails. Clues.

But the squad dispatched to the depot effectively vanished off the face of the earth.

Six men knew the truth. Confiscation of mobile phones; destruction of mobile phones and SIM cards; removal of hands, feet and teeth; transportation to Wozza's scrap yard; crushing of corpses in cars; loading of metal cubes into a fishing boat; dumping of the metal cargo far out at sea; the truck being burnt out and then reported as stolen.

The only casualty was found nearly twenty miles away. There was no doubting who it was, though. Or the intended audience. A bag of heroin had been stuffed in the corpse's mouth, and an Aston Villa scarf had been tied around his neck. The press were tipped off first, so grisly photographs of the scene made their way into the national dailies and were plastered all over the internet. The kid had been buried up to the shoulders. As far as the pile of rocks surrounding the freshly turned earth suggested, he'd then been stoned to death. The press blamed it all on a gang-related conflict. Nobody suspected the respectable local businessman.

There was a brief phoney war as Laine waited for retaliation. But none came.

And then Laine died.

* * * * *

After his sudden, untimely passing, Spice and Grizzly took over. Laine's final wife was not their mother; they had no interest in her, so they paid her off and gifted her the family's villa near Torremolinos. She argued briefly, but the sons made it clear that it wasn't a choice she was being offered.

In their more romantic moments, they enjoyed imagining themselves being like the Kray twins - keeping their neighbourhood safe through the fear they exercised on the people of the town. For a time, they'd even employed a tailor to cut them suits like Ronnie and Reggie. But their size difference made them look less like Bethnal Green and more like a mismatched BBC comedy duo from the 1980s. In truth, it didn't matter how they dressed; people accepted the new order.

The streets were safe. The drugs were less visible. And the town had its veneer of respectability again.

But then they got greedy.

Chapter 21.

'What can I do you for then, chief?'

Fraser was hunched over on his regular bench. His eyes seemed to be pirouetting, independent of each other.

'Started early today then, did you?' Rivera enquired, nodding at the pile of crushed empty cider cans at his feet. Upon seeing him, the ex-soldier had attempted to divert, but the homeless man had honed in on him like a radar beacon.

'Always do, hombré!' the homeless man smiled. 'You know what they say, anyway – the early bird catches the worm and all that...'

Rivera nodded and handed over the cigarette he'd just rolled. He was keen to keep any interaction with the derelict to a minimum. It was simply pity which had led to him sitting down. That, and the fact the library hadn't opened yet.

'You never told me your name, chief.' Fraser frowned.

The ex-soldier shrugged.

'Enigmatic!' The homeless man's chuckle turned into the guttural wrench of a hacking cough as he spluttered on the smoke of the cigarette that had just been lit for him. He looked hard at his visitor. 'Anyway, chief – you didn't answer me.'

'What do you mean?'

'I mean, I'm a drunken derelict who sleeps in front of a library. A good day for me is a day when I'm not feeding myself out of the bins. A good night's when I'm not getting pissed on by local hoodlums. People usually do their best to avoid me. And yet here you are. Again. We'll be sending each other Christmas cards at this rate!'

Rivera grinned. 'Call it coincidence,' he shrugged. The homeless man had a mealy fragrance that mixed with his residual aroma of alcohol and tobacco. It was an essence to which most people would have turned up their noses. It reminded Rivera of travelling in troop transports.

'I'm looking for someone,' the ex-soldier began. He was loath to share such information with Fraser, but he reasoned it couldn't do much harm – he'd drawn a blank everywhere else. Besides, these days he knew what it was like to live on the margins of society; to be judged as semi-criminal simply due to a lack of conformity. Part of him felt sorry for the cider-ravaged figure sat beside him.

'Who?' the tramp questioned.

'A woman.'

'Aren't we all?' Fraser chuckled. 'Name?'

'Katie Lomas.'

The homeless man shook his head. 'Never heard of her. What's she done?'

'Disappeared.' The ex-soldier spoke bluntly.

'And?'

'And I think it's got something to do with the local chapter of the Hell's Angels.'

'Ah!' Fraser nodded. 'Those leather jacketed twats. Well, they're a bunch of fucking idiots. They come around here from time to time – I think having a beer inside them and dishing out kickings is the only thing that makes them feel like men.' He paused. 'I can't imagine they treat women much better. So, what? Do you want me to keep my ear to the ground or something?' He smiled. 'I'm not exactly a sleuth.'

Rivera rose and patted him on the shoulder. As he did, he realised the homeless man was stronger than he'd expected him to be. Though he hid behind a cloak of booze, there was something sharp about him, as if he was more aware than he was letting on. 'Any information is good information,' he announced. 'I appreciate it.'

'Of course you do.' He paused. 'You know what really shows appreciation, though, don't you?' His eyes hardened.

'Enlighten me,' Rivera replied, his tone neutral.

'Cider and cigarettes, sir. The Romulus and Remus of the modern world.'

Rivera nodded. He strongly suspected the homeless man was someone who veered between lucidity and an abstract, alcoholic version of the world. The man's vacant smile suggested he'd now moved into the latter state.

Chapter 22.

After the passing of Denton Laine, his two sons set about stabilising their trade. They buried him with pomp and ceremony; funeral notices were put in all the papers, and the *Herald* all but deified him for his civic contributions. The Chamber of Commerce commissioned a marble bust of him for the town hall. But, once the mourning period was over, Laine's sons resumed their work with a laser-like focus. They knew that a peaceful town would mean prosperity for them, so they set about keeping the law functioning in a way that suited everyone. The place looked orderly, but it permitted them to commit infractions whenever they pleased. The police may have patrolled the streets, but it was clear who was pulling their strings.

Their business swiftly became more and more profitable. And soon, the sons, plus the three musketeers who'd joined Grizzly for the ride, were living high on the hog. The Denton Laine mansion became a fun house where the new lords of the manor partied late with whichever girls they chose to invite. Their new lives were fuelled by champagne and complacency. Prostitutes were taxied in and then kicked out in the morning. Soon, the residents of the Laine mansion began to resemble bloated rock stars who'd long passed their prime and were now on the slippery slope towards full-blown addiction.

Of course, the residents of the town were under no illusions; they knew what happened at the house in the woods, but they also knew Saltmarsh Cove was much safer than it had been before. And so, they turned blind eyes and deaf ears to what they saw and heard, tolerating disturbances here and there for what they believed to be the greater good.

The drugs trade boomed. Alongside their legitimate transportation business, profits increased tenfold. Spice was adept at manipulating the books, and he began enlisting the help of crooked accountants who laundered money through a variety of fronts. When this grew difficult, Spice began to form shell companies to wash their money clean. Where other barons struggled with the logistics of transportation, the Laine organisation already had a network in place. And it was legitimate.

Before long, the Denton Laine organisation had become so moneyed that it was contributing to the construction of public buildings and dedicating significant sums to civic projects. It was because of them that Saltmarsh Cove had a Shakespeare in the Park season each summer. It was due to them that the sailing club held an annual regatta. It was as a result of their benevolence that the library was saved from closure. And the more they gave, the more the people of the town let them operate with impunity. Grizzly grumbled at how he was spending more time in a suit than he was spending in the depot. But his half-brother counselled that such social acceptance was manna from heaven. For a couple of years, it seemed they could do no wrong.

Until Grizzly committed the dealer's ultimate sin and started getting high on his own supply.

It wasn't an issue at first – a taste. A flirtation. A dalliance. As long as the trucking company was operating at full capacity, then the brothers could afford to take their eye off the ball once in a while.

But his judgement went awry. He administered a public assault.

Had the beating been dished out behind closed doors like so many of the others, then people could have been paid off and things might have been hushed up.

But it wasn't. It took place on the promenade, slap-bang in the middle of Folk Music Week. Grizzly pounded the mouthy tourist into the ground in full view of hundreds of festival attendees. The incident was captured on camera; mobile phones recorded the audible gasps of the crowd, and each impact of the big man's fists. His punches landed like the slaps of a steak tenderiser. It was a horrendous mismatch, and a crowd of locals eventually moved in to stop him, fearful there would otherwise have been a murder.

* * * * *

Quite how it was that Spice ended up in court was a mystery to many. He hadn't even been in town on the day the assault happened. But nobody said anything. Nobody came forward. Instead, he calmly proceeded to take the rap and was served with a three-year jail term.

Anyone who knew Grizzly knew he didn't lose his temper very often. But when he lost it, a red mist descended. It had happened before, which was why he had a whole string of previous convictions to his name. For years at a time, he was able to play the part of the roguish colossus with a heart of gold. The bad-man-made-good. But, deep down, he was all brawn and no brains. So, when he lost it, he *really* lost it. And it happened just frequently enough that spent convictions were never quite spent.

If Grizzly had presented himself at the courthouse, he'd have been looking at a ten-year stretch. So it was that, with much bribery and chicanery, and the issuing of a sizeable number of threats, Spice stood in the dock as the accused. The jury of his peers – many of whom knew him personally, or at least knew of him – had no choice but to find him guilty. That much, he'd expected. He'd briefed them all beforehand, looking them in the eye and smiling with a wolfish grin. What came as a surprise to the judge was the way the jurors argued so strongly that the sentence should be reduced for good behaviour and that he should become eligible for parole after only eighteen months.

Grizzly knew that he owed Spice forever, and that he would have to defer to him in future business decisions. So, the older brother decided to turn over a new leaf and do his best for the business while his sibling was incarcerated. He cleaned up. He swore off using drugs himself, and instead, concentrated on moving them around to locations the markets demanded. He knew he'd dodged a prison-shaped bullet and vowed never to lose control again.

Spice, though, was a different story.

In jail, he made various underworld connections. Lying on his cell bunk night after night, he learned of new opportunities; he began to dream big. Bigger than Saltmarsh Cove at any rate. So it was that when the board granted him an early release from his stint in detention, he emerged back into the world with a vaulting ambition, which made the previous Denton Laine operation seem like a minor concern in comparison.

Meeting his half-brother at the prison gate, Grizzly had given him two choices: 'Massage parlour or the racetrack?'

'Neither,' Spice had said, inhaling his first breaths of freedom. He spoke with determined resolve. 'Let's get to work. I have a new plan. We're going to change things around.'

Grizzly had frowned, shrugged, and nodded. 'You're the boss,' he'd replied in a resigned tone.

Sitting silently in the passenger seat of the new Mercedes convertible, Spice had replayed Grizzly's words: *you're the boss.* The phrase rang in his head.

He decided he liked it.

Chapter 23.

Lomas' phone rang. He'd fallen into a fitful sleep in his hotel room and had dreamed of being pursued along the seafront by leather-clad bikers. This had been interspersed with images of his sister. At one point, she rose, howling from beneath a sea of leaves that covered an autumnal clearing. Her eyes were two empty worm-filled cavities. Rolling over, he blinked and looked around, taking a moment to adjust to his surroundings. He looked at the screen of his phone.

R.

'Hello,' he whispered, punching a green icon on the screen.

'I'm outside,' came the voice on the other end of the line.

* * * * *

Entering the room, the visitor took a quick look around, admiring the luxury of the suite. It had a table with a bowl of fresh fruit on it; plush armchairs, and curtained doors that opened onto the balcony. 'Nice digs,' he announced, lowering himself into one of the chairs without being invited. 'Posh enough that you'd have to get out of the bath to take a piss, no?'

'You should have seen it earlier,' Lomas grumbled.

'What?' The ex-soldier raised his eyebrows.

'I had to have Christie back here – she only left an hour ago.'

'Why?' Rivera frowned.

'Because someone broke in.'

'What do you mean, someone broke in?' Rivera paused, uncertain. 'With you in here?'

'No.' Lomas looked uncomfortable. He drummed his hand nervously against his trouser pocket.

Silence.

Rivera shook his head. 'I told you to stay in here and keep the door locked.' He paused. 'I was pretty bloody clear about that, wasn't I, Eddie?'

'Yeah – but I got bored. I went for a swim.' Lomas shrugged. 'I needed to clear my head – I can't hold on to a single thought at the moment. It's driving me nuts.'

Rivera widened his eyes and stood up. Lomas was the taller man, but Rivera's irritation suddenly seemed to make him rise in stature.

'I was climbing up the walls here!' Lomas protested, worried. 'Everything seemed to be quiet. I was feeling lethargic...' he trailed off, apologetically.

'What did they take?' the ex-soldier asked bluntly.

'Nothing – at least I think nothing.' Lomas shrugged. 'My cash is still here. They went through my bags – chucked some stuff about.'

'That all?'

Lomas nodded. 'It might just have been kids.'

'No – it wasn't kids.' Rivera shook his head. 'Phone?'

'I had it with me at the spa. I don't see it's a great problem – they just messed the room up a bit. The Detective Inspector said there wasn't anything much they could do about it, though. It's breaking and entering, but if nothing's been taken...'

'Then they've got nothing, right?' Rivera enquired.

Lomas nodded.

'She asked the hotel for the CCTV, but there was a fault with the camera on this corridor, and nobody had seen anyone coming in or going out. Apparently, one of the fire doors was propped open.'

'Let me guess – nobody was seen near that one either?' The ex-soldier pursed his lips.

'Correct. In her defence, Christie seemed pretty irritated at the staff here. She didn't say they were incompetent in so many words, but it was pretty clear what she was thinking. Oh, and she even asked about you.'

'That so?' Rivera frowned. 'What did you tell her?'

'Just that I'd seen you around, but I didn't know who you were.'

'And she bought that?'

'I think so,' Lomas replied. 'But she said she wants to talk to you. Reckons there's no link between you and the strange spate of violent beatings the bikers have suffered, but she says she's got some questions.'

'Yeah,' nodded Rivera, lowering himself back down into the armchair. 'I bet she has.' He paused. 'What did she look like?'

'Like a police officer,' Lomas shrugged.

'What – six foot five with big bones and stubble?'

'No – she was pretty-ish. Why?'

The ex-soldier said nothing.

'What do you think they were looking for?' Lomas asked, changing the subject.

'Who knows?' the visitor shrugged. 'But you're clearly on their radar.' He leaned back and closed his eyes for a moment. The realisation struck him again – he could just walk away; it would be the easiest thing to simply climb into his campervan and leave. Sitting there, he wondered what the hell he was doing, and how it was he'd become embroiled in something that had so little to do with him.

Nevertheless, he felt something gnawing at him: guilt?

In the past, he'd wanted to involve himself in countering injustices the Army decided not to class as injustices. He'd had to button down his lip and bite his tongue. Events in Saltmarsh Cove, though, felt somehow similar. He didn't want to be involved, but he knew deep down that he didn't want to walk away either.

This was an injustice he didn't have to ignore.

Chapter 24.

The office above the Denton Laine depot was quiet. Grizzly sat, hunkered over the desk, watching his half-brother and picking at scabs on his forearms. His sibling paced the floor, cracking his knuckles and grinding his teeth. He had the motion of a caged animal. The larger man looked on, frowning; his gaze tracked the other man's movements as he traversed the room.

'Are you going to tell me what the fuck's going on?' he enquired, eventually.

Spice continued to pace. He puffed out his cheeks and exhaled slowly.

'Look,' Grizzly continued, his tone one of exasperation. 'You're going to wear a hole in the fucking rug if you don't calm down. And that rug was your idea – I could have had a year's worth of blowjobs off of Lorraine for what that cost me.' He paused. 'And it looks shit.' He grinned, but it did little to lighten the other man's mood.

'We've got a problem,' Spice blurted out.

'What fucking problem?' Grizzly frowned.

'This strange guy. Whoever the fuck he is. Popeye said he looked just like a tourist. But he's the one who's been dishing out the beatings. I'm sure of it,' he seethed. 'So we need to sort the fucker out.'

'Which guy?'

'Have you been asleep or something?' Spice raised his voice, slamming his fist down onto the table. 'Wake up, you fat bastard! Popeye. Pluto. Pugwash. They're all in the hospital. You know that – right?' He paused. 'This guy's trained,' Spice continued. 'He's good. He's hard-as-nails, that's for sure.'

'So what's he got to do with us?' Grizzly shrugged. 'Why not just kick the shit out of him?'

'Not that easy. We don't know who he is or where he's hanging out.'

'So how do we know it was him then?' the big man frowned.

'He was seen. And not long after, Pugwash had his leg broken. Our cop – Beatty – the useless twat on our payroll. He told me he's been hanging around with Lomas.'

'Who? The journalist?'

'No, you tool.'

'Who then?' Grizzly narrowed his eyes, irritated.

Spice looked hard at his brother, folding his arms. 'Not the journalist.' He shook his head. 'She won't be causing us problems any more.'

Grizzly frowned. 'You fucking didn't? You...'

Silence.

'This thing,' Spice announced, gesturing around the room as if to an imaginary audience. 'This thing we do here – we can't have loose ends. Remember? That's how it works.'

The big man folded his hands behind his head and leaned back, sighing. 'Why didn't you tell me?' he enquired, his voice filled with menace. 'Why the fuck didn't you tell me?' His eyes blazed.

'Well, why the fuck didn't you tell me about Rusty?' Spice's voice was cold. 'It's not like it's one rule for you and one for everyone else.' He shook his head. 'I take care of my shit, and you take care of yours.'

'That was different. This, though...'

'...needed to be done,' the smaller man interrupted.

'I wouldn't have signed off on something like that,' Grizzly smouldered. 'And you fucking know it.'

'Which is why I didn't tell you,' Spice sneered, tilting his head to one side and widening his eyes, as if waiting for the penny to drop. 'Otherwise you'd have pussied out.' He laughed as the other man began to rise from his seat. 'What? Are you going to tell me different?'

'Fuck you!' Grizzly hissed. 'I feel like I don't even know you at all sometimes. I...'

'...stayed free.' Spice held his hands up. 'You would've been given ten years. Ten fucking years. You know that. As it was, I did the time for you. And it was no fucking picnic, either. I had to watch my arse in the shower, just like every other bastard in there. You remember what we said when I got out?'

Silence fell.

'We said that I call the shots from now on,' Spice went on. 'And that's what I've been doing. So don't start questioning my methods – if we all acted like you, we'd spend all our time sitting on our hands.'

Grizzly shook his head once more. 'Well, if she's out of the picture, then why the fuck would you bring her name up? What's the problem?'

'Not her.' Spice paused. 'It's her brother. Her no-good, shit-for-brains, posh-twat, needle-dick interfering brother with his hard man mate poking around and breaking bones. He's the problem.'

'But you've been moaning about the three musketeers for months now. I thought you'd be glad to have them out of the picture?' The big man shrugged. He looked at his sibling. 'No?'

Spice raised his hand, pinching the bridge of his nose. 'But now we have no fucking foot soldiers. There's no one left on the ground any more. They're all on bloody hospital wards. Useless bastards.'

'Do we need them?' Grizzly frowned. 'I mean, we can do without them for a while, can't we? We're not that fucking useless, surely?'

'You forget – the cargo's on the way. A double cargo. And it's in motion. I'm not taking any chances with this one. If we fuck it up, we're as good as fucking ruined.'

Grizzly nodded, heavily.

'So, I need troops on the street keeping an eye out and making sure that nothing goes wrong,' Spice explained.

'Who do we have, then?'

'Well,' Spice answered. 'At the present moment... approximately fucking nobody. It's me and it's you. And we can't take the risk of leaving things to get fucked up.' He paused. 'Don't forget, if any of those county lines twats get any silly ideas and show their faces again, we'll have nobody to fight them off, either.'

Grizzly shrugged. 'We'll be fine. People know who we are. You worry too much. The whole town's shit scared of us. A few days won't make any difference.'

'Except they're not scared,' Spice replied, glaring. 'Or at least one of them isn't, and at this very moment in time, he's wandering around town busting heads. It's bad for business. I want him dead – or, at the very least, I want him out of commission, so he stops causing problems.'

'So, what do we do?' Grizzly asked.

'Can you remember how to ride a motorcycle?'

The big man glowered, his tone clipped. 'Of course I fucking can.'

'Then you're going to have to get your arse back out there and ride one. Make sure that people know we're still a presence.'

'What?' the big man slapped the desk in irritation. 'What *is* this? A show of force or something?'

'Precisely.'

'But I look like a twat when I ride a Harley. I'm like a fucking clown in a circus on a miniature bicycle. You know that. I don't even like bikes that much...'

Spice grimaced. 'You'll look like more of a twat if our friends think you've turned pussy on them. Remember the video they sent - of their guy in the camp? You fancy having that happen to you?'

The video to which he referred was of a man's death in a camp near Sangatte. He stood accused of betraying the organisation. The brothers' contact had sent them the footage couched as a show of support. They both knew what the message really was, though. The screaming man's hands had been tied behind his back. As he kneeled in the sand of the dunes close to Calais, a masked trafficker had approached him with a carving knife and cut his throat. Blood spurted onto the sand. The traffickers had laughed as the victim writhed around, dying.

Grizzly nodded slowly.

'Don't lose your head!' Spice spoke with mock jollity, but paused to let his utterance sink in.

'Alright then,' he replied. 'I've still got a jacket. I'll ride the bike. But you've got to ride one too.'

'I will,' Spice nodded. 'We'll take it in turns – keep a lookout.' He stopped. 'You remember that bloke in the George - the one who we'd never seen before?'

'Yes.'

'I think it's him.'

'What?' Grizzly frowned. 'But he was reading a bloody book. You're not telling me that he's a fucking fighter – surely?'

'These are strange times,' Spice shrugged. 'So, if you see him, fucking grab him. Meanwhile, I'm going to call the police.'

'Beatty?'

'No.' Spice shook his head. 'The *real* police.'

'What?' The big man's eyes widened. 'That's not how we operate.'

'I know. But I've had enough of this fool running around bumping off our bikers. I reckon the boys in blue can make themselves useful for once. He's got blood on his hands – three counts of assault. I think they need to launch a manhunt.'

'Are you serious?'

'Why not? If nothing else, it'll slow him down. Hopefully, they'll take him off the streets. And then, once the shipment arrives, we can take care of him properly.'

Chapter 25.

'You're keen, aren't you?' Fraser grinned and then chuckled, a bronchial cough swiftly following. It was early morning, and he'd only just woken up. He stood, stretched, and turned his wrinkled face to the sun.

Rivera nodded, frowning. He was beginning to think that the tramp never moved – he seemed a permanent fixture.

'Excuse me for a moment,' the derelict announced. 'I need to water the plants.'

The visitor shrugged and sat down on the bench while Fraser disappeared behind a screen of trees. He emerged a minute later and sat next to Rivera, automatically accepting the hand-rolled cigarette offered to him.

'So,' Rivera began, releasing his thumb from the wheel on his disposable lighter. 'I was just passing by.'

'Listen,' Fraser began. 'I know I said I'd keep my ear to the ground, but I don't work that quick.' He paused. 'You're not queering me up are you, chief? I mean, I'm flattered and all. But...'

'No,' the ex-soldier said, bluntly.

'Alright.' The other man nodded. 'All I can tell you is that those blokes you're going after - they're not good. They've dished out beatings to me before, like I said. Said they wanted to clean the place up. Told me that if I didn't get out, they'd keep coming back.' He paused. 'If you ask me, the place would be a whole lot cleaner if they were out of the picture.'

Silence.

'I guess I don't scare that easily,' the homeless man went on. 'I bruise though... And I saw them doing the rounds earlier.'

'Who?'

'Your biker boys.'

'Really?'

'Not the usual ones, though.' He wheezed a little. 'This was just one – the big one. I've seen him around before, but this time he was dressed the same as the others. I swear he's twice their size.'

Rivera nodded, wondering how reliable the information was. He realised he wouldn't be surprised if such a sighting were a figment of the other man's imagination.

'Yeah,' Fraser continued. 'He's the head honcho - the guy at the depot. Grizzly – that's what folks around here call him.'

Rivera idly fidgeted with the string of beads around his neck. 'So, did you think it was strange? Seeing him on a bike, I mean.'

Fraser shrugged. 'Well, they usually travel in threes. This bloke was on his own, though. Big ugly fucker.'

'Anything else?'

Fraser shook his head. 'Your guess is as good as mine. I'm only in it for getting pissed, remember?' He paused. 'Maybe he's freaked out or something? Or maybe he just fancied riding his bike?'

The ex-soldier nodded, noticing how the other man's eyes seemed to be glazing over. He ground his cigarette out on the floor.

Fraser turned, eyeing him suspiciously. 'You're a curious one, aren't you?' He shook his head and grinned.

Rivera shrugged.

'It's probably drugs, isn't it?' Fraser continued. 'Isn't that what everyone does to make money?'

'Maybe.'

Silence.

The homeless man sniffed. 'You know their depot, right?'

Rivera shook his head.

'It's up on the hill. You can't miss it – big searchlights everywhere. It's lit up like a fucking Christmas tree at night. Big warehouses and stuff like that.'

Rivera looked hard at him. 'You sure?'

'Definitely.'

'It doesn't sound like the easiest place to get into... with the lights, I mean.'

'Oh, it's not!' Fraser shook his head. 'There's barbed wire fences and all sorts. But that's why you should go there – if you're looking for this girl of yours and you reckon they've got her, then they'll be keeping her there. It's like a fortress. That's what I'd suggest.' He paused. 'I could even tell you how to get in...'

'Bullshit.'

'God's honest, mate. Hobo code.'

'What?' Rivera frowned.

'I lived there for a while.' He shrugged. 'Well – just outside.'

'You're shitting me.'

'Dead serious squire. But before I tell you my secrets, my vocal cords might be in need of a little lubrication. Know what I mean?'

The ex-soldier nodded and lifted a plastic carrier bag up from off the ground. He pulled out a four-pack of cider cans held together with plastic rings. Rivera knew that any transaction of information would come down to booze. He'd arrived prepared.

'Now you're talking my language, chief!' Smiling, he reached over and took hold of them. 'And they're cold – that's a rare treat!'

'So?' enquired Rivera, expectantly.

'So,' whispered Fraser. 'There's a thicket close to the back perimeter of the depot. It's filled with bracken and brambles, but there's a path cut through it. I should know – I used to sleep there. You can get right up to the fence unseen, and there's a tree you can use to get over. It's easy – I used to help myself to groceries when I was there.'

'Sounds ideal....'

'Yeah, but there was never any alcohol.' Fraser looked downcast at the memory for a moment. 'I'm better off here, chief.' He covered one nostril with his thumb and blew hard, snotting onto the floor by the bench.

Rivera stood swiftly. 'Alright then. Thanks. I'll swing by.' He looked at the other man seriously. 'You will let me know if you see anything else, right?'

'I'll keep it all in here!' Fraser beamed, tapping at the side of his head. As he tilted backwards, the ex-soldier noticed how his eyes appeared to flitter from side-to-side for a couple of seconds, before his focus seemed to sharpen once more.

Walking away, Rivera turned. 'You are going to put those dead soldiers in the bin too when you're done, aren't you?' he asked, gesturing at the cans. 'The library will get pissed off with you otherwise.'

'No. Fuck 'em!' Fraser belched. 'I'll put them in recycling, thank you very much.' The homeless man grinned. 'You've got to think about the planet, chief!'

Rivera nodded, sighing as Fraser fell back to picking his nose. As he watched, a pigeon landed by his feet and he threw an empty can at it, screaming incomprehensible curses. As he walked further away, the ex-soldier wondered how much credence he should give to any of the derelict's observations. He might be well-positioned as a witness, but Rivera had his doubts; he worried the homeless man was as likely to see unicorns and fairies as leather-jacketed bikers.

Chapter 26.

By the time Rivera reached the wire of the depot, he'd been scratched and scraped by the brambles that reached all the way up to the fence. Dabbing irritably at the blood that ran down his forearms, he cursed Fraser, but the path the homeless man had spoken of was there. He half expected the clearing would be nothing more than a cider-induced hallucination. But he was wrong – it existed. At least it *had* been there. But it had become overgrown and, in the summer months, the vegetation had flourished. Inch-long thorns bit greedily at him with their angry barbs.

Rivera silently admonished himself for only having a Swiss Army knife with him - he'd used it to hack and saw at the worst of the branches, but it hadn't done much more than add welts to his already grazed and bleeding fingers.

For a clearance task like the thicket demanded, he would have needed a machete. And even then, it would have taken hours.

But he'd reached the wire, and he had the depot in his line of sight.

The tree with the overhanging branch that the homeless man had mentioned was there, too. He paused, looking over at the warehouse. A patch of grass stretched for around thirty yards before the tarmac of the loading area began. A bored looking functionary with a clipboard and hard hat stood on a gantry. He looked in the ex-soldier's direction and then looked away. Rivera, hidden in the foliage, swept him with his sniper scope, but saw nothing unremarkable: the overweight man was sweating, sucking greedily at a cigarette.

The depot itself looked like any other depot. But the ex-soldier knew appearances could be deceptive. He remembered a compound he'd attended near Jelga. From the outside, it looked little different to any of the other buildings surrounding it. Once the squad entered, though, they discovered the remnants of what had essentially been an IED factory; the scale was astonishing. An outwardly innocent-looking depot, therefore, was not something to be taken lightly.

* * * * *

Five minutes later, a truck pulled up. It parked directly across the grass from Rivera's vantage point and its driver climbed out, stretched, and walked off towards the gantry. The ex-soldier took the fact he was now shielded from his watching eyes as a cue.

Looking around with a final glance, he swung over the branch, dropped to the ground on the other side of the fence and rolled over, lying motionless by the foot of the wire. There was no noise other than crickets in the grass and the slow ticking of the truck's engine cooling. Rivera looked in each direction but saw no signs of life. Bees flitted lazily between the dandelions reaching up from the sun-warmed ground.

He rose and sprinted to the trailer of the truck. While surveying the depot thoroughly earlier on, he'd made his way slowly around the whole of its perimeter. As he'd done so, he'd noted the position of each of the CCTV cameras, studying them carefully through his scope. For such a large operation, they were relatively thin on the ground. The main warehouse had them. They also covered the entrance from the road. But there were large gaps that weren't in any field of vision. Rivera wondered if Fraser's interpretation of the place as a fortress was somewhat misplaced. Something didn't feel quite right.

Rivera crawled beneath the trailer, hidden by the wheels of the truck. As he reached the far side of the vehicle, he looked up and saw that the gantry was now empty. Removing the sniper scope once more, he noted that the yard was free of surveillance equipment. The ground-level entrance to the hangar-like warehouse, though, was not. He squinted for a moment and sniffed at the air before launching himself from beneath the truck and sprinting across the tarmac.

His heartbeat sounded to him almost as loud as the scuffing of his boots, but his progress went unnoticed.

Reaching the foot of the gantry, he paused, hidden beneath the steps. His stance was that of a fighter, poised to spring into action. Somewhere along the duration of his stay in town, he realised he'd crossed a line. He was no longer going to simply react to violence; he was going to pre-empt it.

Rivera listened for a moment, his pulse slowing to a regular, slow thud in his temples. Hearing nothing from inside the building, he swung himself up onto the steel ladder and swiftly climbed onto the bridge which led into the warehouse. He was at a height of about fifteen feet above the ground. The walkway beneath him was made of intersecting metal plates that shifted slightly when he stepped onto them.

By the edge of the warehouse, Rivera paused and turned, looking back towards the fence. He wanted to check he could still exit the way he'd entered: the coast looked clear. Moving into the shadows of the entrance, he turned to look behind him again, realising suddenly that the barbs at the head of the wire were turned inward.

It made no sense.

Rivera frowned. A drugs empire would have valuable produce awaiting transportation. The wire should have been positioned to keep out anyone aiming to steal it. Viewed from this direction, it almost seemed as if the reverse was true. It looked less set up to stop people getting in, and more designed to prevent them from leaving.

The ex-soldier shrugged, checked for onlookers, and then crossed the threshold.

* * * * *

Rivera had seen drugs in Afghanistan. *Lots* of drugs. One of the things that had led to his disillusionment with the Army's presence there was that - in order to create favourable relations with tribal warlords - the occupying forces had had to turn blind eyes to the opium harvest. He couldn't reconcile himself with that. Indeed, the ex-soldier remembered occasions when he and his colleagues had effectively acted as guards for shipments being taken to the border. It was, he was informed by his superiors, the way things worked. What made it so difficult to swallow was the way the warlords' foot soldiers gave knowing smiles. Armies meant nothing to them. Nor did borders. The only laws they respected were tribal; centuries-old covenants. And if the foreign military was supporting opium transportation for them, then they were winning – and they didn't care who knew about it.

But the opium there was raw. It was unrefined. It was carted about in the rear of pickup trucks.

As his eyes adjusted to the gloom, Rivera realised that he didn't really know what he was looking for. It wasn't; he smiled grimly, as if he were likely to discover a large crate stamped *NARCOTICS*, after all. As a soldier, he'd prided himself on always having an objective - a plan. This, though, was far more speculative. He realised he'd been expecting to find something. But it was only now that he became aware he didn't know what it was. He considered the bikers to be dunces, but they were keeping things better obscured than he'd expected. The issue was what, exactly, those things were.

The interior was remarkably empty; stacks of boxes stood on pallets, but they were all labelled with recognisable brands. Rivera toyed with the idea of slicing some of them open, but thought it pointless; it would raise suspicions. He looked around further, deciding against descending the steps lest he ended up in the field of the CCTV's vision.

It was eerily quiet.

A forklift truck was parked in a corner and, beyond that, a door was marked *NO ENTRY*. The door was very clearly in the line of sight of the security cameras. Other than that, Rivera perceived little of interest. For a profitable shipping concern, there seemed to be a marked lack of merchandise. On the warehouse floor, there was more bare concrete than cargo. And the truck outside remained the sole vehicle present.

In the distance, Rivera heard voices. He watched as the rotund man from the gantry walked towards the stationary truck with the recently arrived driver. The two of them had emerged from a side door which looked like the entrance to a staffing area. The intruder pressed himself against the corrugated iron of the walls and vanished into the shadows.

The pair were too far away for him to catch their words. All he heard was a rasping laugh, and the sound of the driver clearing his throat and spitting on the floor. Neither man seemed in a hurry, and neither seemed to be particularly wary of any overseer keeping an eye on them. It felt - Rivera reflected - like a place that was winding down. Anywhere with managers present would have had a more urgent atmosphere; employees would likely have feared reprimands for shirking. But, as far as the ex-soldier could see, no such nerves were evident in the depot.

From his vantage point, Rivera looked down upon them, unobserved. The place seemed short-staffed. But if this – as Fraser had suggested – was the epicentre of the operation, there must be something about the organisation that he was missing. Clearly, though, the daytime was not when the depot came alive.

He vowed to return at night. Sometimes he saw things more clearly in the dark.

Chapter 27.

'Nice van!' The smile that spread across Detective Inspector Christie's face was one of genuine admiration. The sun caught her eyes as she grinned, and Rivera couldn't help but smile back. She was – he found himself thinking – remarkably pretty for a crime fighter. Lomas had definitely undersold her. He squinted slightly as he looked back at her from beneath the awning on Iris' side.

'Er, thanks,' he replied, a little hesitantly, looking her up and down. He reasoned the police would come asking questions sooner or later, but he'd expected an old, haggard constable. Rivera was used to unpredictable situations, but he realised the olive-skinned officer with coal black hair and a glamorous demeanour had rather wrong-footed him. He peered at her, searching for the glint of gold or silver on her ring finger. There was nothing.

'So, I guess you're the man I've been looking for?' Her tone betrayed little emotion.

'Well... my mother always said I was the best-looking boy in my class, so you'll have to join the queue.' He raised his eyebrows and grinned.

She laughed a little, holding his gaze slightly too long. 'Do we need to talk about the three men in the hospital?'

'I'd rather not.' The seated man shifted position. 'Anyway, we've only just met. Shouldn't I offer to buy you a drink or something?'

'Listen, Mr Rivera,' she sighed. 'I've run the plates of your campervan. So I know who you are. I know all about your military record - the distinguished and the less so.' She flipped over the pages of a notebook, looking down at it. 'What I don't know is why you're here.' She looked up, fixing him in her eye line once more. 'Care to enlighten me?'

The ex-soldier shrugged. 'I heard about you – I thought I might ask you out.'

'Answer the question.'

'I was just out shopping for postcards and buckets and spades. I'm only a tourist, officer,' Rivera continued.

She paused, frowning. 'Except you're not, though, are you? You've come here and embroiled yourself in what's shaping up to be a war.' Unbidden, she reached out, unfolded one of Rivera's chairs that had been leaning against Iris, and sat down beside him. When she spoke again, her tone was even more serious. 'Now, we can either talk here, or we can do it down at the station.' She paused. 'It's your choice. But obstructing an investigation is an offence – no matter how much you try to dress it up as romantic overtures.' She narrowed her eyes.

A light breeze whipped up from the sea as Rivera rolled himself a cigarette. When he finished licking the paper, he offered it to the police officer, who politely declined. For a while, the only sound was the distant sea and Rivera's breathing as he smoked. He knew he could wait.

It was Christie who broke the silence first. 'I've had a complaint against you, you know? I'm supposed to look into it. A claim of aggravated assault.'

Rivera raised his eyebrows. 'But...'

'But what?' Christie frowned.

'But I don't think you believe it - not really, I mean.' The ex-soldier leaned back in his chair and looked straight back at her.

'How so?' she frowned.

He sighed. 'Because of what you told Eddie Lomas.'

She looked hard at him; her face drawn. 'So, you're in cahoots?'

'No.'

'Why help him then?' she paused. 'That's the bit I don't get. You're a free spirit – you can just walk away. It's not like he's paying you. And I know for a fact you didn't know him before. You're hardly a moral crusader, so why the sudden burst of altruism?'

Silence.

'It means...' she began.

'...I know what it means,' Rivera interrupted. He shrugged. 'Sometimes things just seem right. He wanted to find his sister, and everywhere he turned, he was getting no help. Either that or there were hordes of leather-jacketed cavemen trying to bust his skull. I guess I felt sorry for him.'

'So, you thought you'd wade in like a knight in shining armour?' She grinned and then frowned a little. 'You know, I reckoned I'd run into a proper bruiser today. After reading the incident reports, I thought I'd be questioning a thug. Not a philosopher.'

'Sometimes there's not so much difference as you might think.'

'Really?'

'No. And there is no grand plan, but if someone attacks me...'

'... then you'll put them in the hospital,' she interrupted. 'By rights, I should nick you. You realise that, don't you?'

'But you won't.' He paused, drawing on his cigarette and leaning back in the chair. Rivera held her gaze until she looked away, smiling slightly. He thought he saw the faintest hint of blush.

'You seem pretty sure of yourself.' She pursed her lips as she spoke, but her tone was bordering on friendly.

'Listen,' he announced, crushing his cigarette and placing the butt in a sand-filled jam jar upon which he replaced the lid. 'If you were serious about arresting me, you'd have come here with blue lights flashing and brought back up. If you really think I'm a threat, then you wouldn't take any chances. But you clearly don't, because it's just you here.'

'So?'

'So I don't think you're entirely in disagreement with the fact I put three bikers out of action. What's more, I think you're secretly quite glad I did it. Which tells me two things: number one - you don't like the power a certain sector of society wields over this town, and number two - you don't trust all of your colleagues.'

'That's quite an accusation!' She frowned. 'And how did you arrive at that conclusion, pray tell me, Mr Rivera?' She folded her arms and looked hard at him, half in outrage, and half in seeming amusement.

'Because you're looking at me right now as if I've dished out more justice in the past few days than you've managed to in months. That tells me that you're frustrated. You seem like a good officer, miss...'

'Lois is fine.'

'You seem like a good officer, Lois. You've asked all the right questions, but you strike me as being frustrated. My guess is that you've been on to the bad guys for a while now, but you've kept coming up against brick walls placed there by the higher-ups.' He looked sidelong at her. 'Sound familiar?'

She bit her tongue, grimacing slightly.

'It's hardly unique,' the ex-soldier went on. 'They'll have been pieced off just like always happens in cases like this. If you've got police on the payroll, they'll make sure fellow officers don't get too interested in things they don't want them to be interested in.' He paused. 'You think it's drugs?'

She sighed. 'I don't know. They're clearly bringing in some kind of cargo. It's like Prohibition-era Chicago as far as I can see. Everyone knows who the bad guys are and everyone knows that they're transporting something. But nobody ever seems to find out what, and they're all too scared to go looking. The police included. A few people have tried, but they've either been beaten bloody or they've disappeared.'

'You're divulging quite a lot of information, officer,' the ex-soldier said.

She shrugged. 'You used to be an investigator, right?'

'Correct. But I can't offer you any answers.' Rivera sipped at a plastic bottle of mineral water. 'So – that talk of Chicago... you need me to be an Eliot Ness or something?'

She grinned. 'Don't flatter yourself!'

'What?' he smiled. 'I reckon I'd suit a waistcoat and fedora. I might even wear a pocket watch!'

Christie smiled.

'I checked out their depot today,' Rivera announced.

'Really?' Christie raised her eyebrows. 'They wouldn't give me a warrant – unsurprisingly.' She paused. 'Find anything?'

'Nothing much.' He shook his head. 'It didn't look like a drug den, though. And it seemed too quiet to be the centre of something big - at least when I saw it.' He took another sip.

'See anything odd?'

He nodded. 'Yes, as a matter of fact, I did.' He paused. 'It seemed like the fences and the cameras were the wrong way round.'

'How do you mean?'

He sighed, frowning. 'It looked almost as if they'd been built to keep people in, instead of out.'

Christie frowned. 'Well, that would be stupid. Even for the cavemen we have running around here.'

'That's what I thought,' Rivera replied. 'It makes no sense.'

Silence.

'So... any more plans?'

He chewed his lip before answering. 'Are we talking date night or the depot?'

Christie sighed.

'Worth a shot. Anyway, I'm going back tonight,' he announced bluntly. 'Anything you need me to do up there? I guess I'm involved in this thing enough that I want to see it through. So – can I be of any help?'

She shook her head; her face serious. 'I didn't hear that – officially, I mean - but obviously you need to be careful.' She looked directly at him. 'These are bad people. I mean it. Don't take any chances.'

He nodded. 'I know.'

'And keep me informed.' She reached into her pocket and handed him a card.

He looked at it. 'Is this your number, or the station's?'

'Mine.'

He grinned. 'So, if I feel like treating you to dinner later, then this is the number I text you on, right?'

'Don't push it!' Christie frowned. 'I won't be hungry.'

'How do you know?'

'Call it a premonition.'

Rivera shrugged.

'Listen – you find out anything, then tell me straight away. I mean it.'

Rivera nodded. 'Alright then. But you need to keep an eye on Lomas - whatever his sister found out spooked the bikers. If they hushed her up, they'll be willing to do the same to him. And I can't imagine he's much use at looking after himself.'

'I know,' she nodded. 'I've seen him. And it's not down to me there's been no progress on finding the sister.'

'Let me guess,' Rivera interrupted. 'Your superiors put the brakes on?'

Christie frowned, snapping her notebook shut. She ran her fingers through her hair, shaking her head, a little frustrated. 'Yeah - it's almost like there's a pattern here, don't you think?'

He nodded slowly. 'I'll keep you posted. I promise.'

She stood up, folding the chair and leaning it back against the side of the T2. 'Take care, Mr Rivera,' she said, offering a hand. The ex-soldier shook it, maintaining his grip longer than she expected. Her hands were strong and capable. Rivera stared straight at her.

'What?' she frowned, laughing a little uncomfortably.

'I think...' Rivera began, 'that you're very alone here, Lois. I don't mean it as a criticism – far from it. But if you're the one good officer on a rotten force, it can be a lonely place.' He paused. 'And I think I can help you.'

Christie frowned. 'Listen – those lines might work on other girls, but I can look after myself.'

The ex-soldier shrugged. 'Suit yourself.'

'You *can* help me, though.'

'Yeah? How?'

'Simple. Don't get killed and tell me anything you find out.' At this, Christie turned and walked towards her car. She turned momentarily, raising a hand to wave back at him.

As Rivera watched the Detective Inspector drive away, Rosie jumped up to sit in his lap. He looked down lovingly, stroking her. 'What do you reckon, then?' he enquired. Rosie purred in response. 'Yeah,' he nodded. 'I think she likes me too.'

Chapter 28.

'Well?' Spice eyed the new arrival suspiciously.

Officer Beatty shifted uncomfortably as he stood in the middle of the office floor. He was a small man with red hair and freckles; he wore his police uniform and reached up to switch off the radio attached to his shoulder. He then removed his cap and idly turned it around in circles, holding its brim between his fingers.

'You said you wanted information,' the policeman began. He'd parked his car directly outside the depot as he had before. On previous occasions, he'd been plied with beer and wine, and cigars had been pressed upon him. The reception this time, though, was frosty. He squirmed, unsure of himself. Having Grizzly and Spice onside had made him feel like a big part player. Them giving him the cold shoulder was making him feel minute.

'What have you got?' demanded Grizzly, grumpily. He stood up, walked around to the front of his desk, leaning against it with his arms crossed. The solid mahogany frame groaned a little at his bulk. His shadow, cast by the corner light, all but consumed the visiting officer. 'You'd better have something worthwhile, you useless prick.'

Spice stood alongside him, his arms crossed in a similar fashion. Expectant. Both men eyed Beatty coldly.

'It's Christie,' Beatty began.

'Who? The slag?' enquired Grizzly, frowning with disdain.

Beatty nodded.

'What's she got to fucking do with anything?' Spice enquired, his pitch rising.

'She ducked out today - said she was going down to the seafront, but she wasn't there when I checked.'

'Well, that's hardly a fucking showstopper, is it?' Spice scoffed.

'No, but when I checked on her car locator, it was up the hill at the caravan park. We can monitor the cars from the station.' He paused. 'So she was there,' he announced, almost triumphantly.

Grizzly straightened himself. 'If you don't start making sense soon, I'm going to throw you off of that fucking gantry, son,' he announced angrily. 'I don't pay you to come here and spin me yarns. Now get to the fucking point.'

Beatty breathed deeply, recovering his poise. 'She's dodged away from the station a few times - I think she's onto something. I reckon she might have located the mystery street fighter.' He paused. 'My worry is that she should have brought him in. But she hasn't, so I don't know – maybe she's roped him in or something.'

At this, both the siblings tensed.

'She's a better officer than you then,' Grizzly rasped. 'She's managed to find the fucker, at least.'

'But you don't want them teaming up, do you?' Beatty demanded, suddenly aware that his tone sounded too forthright. 'Sorry,' he added, hastily.

'And you're sure she was at the campsite?' Spice pressed.

The policeman nodded.

'Well, maybe she was just there to get her oats?' Spice continued.

'Yeah, once a slag, always a slag,' Grizzly muttered.

'I can't think of any other explanation,' Beatty continued.

'What – other than her shagging him?' Grizzly frowned.

'No. That she's working alongside him,' Beatty replied.

'We'll deal with the street fighter first,' Spice announced.

Silence.

'Why haven't you warned her off anyway?' Grizzly enquired, frowning.

'She's as straight as a die, mate.' Beatty shrugged.

'Mate? Who the fuck are you calling mate?' he spat angrily. 'When you talk to me, you fucking call me sir. Now answer me. Otherwise, I'll take your head off with a shovel and see how far I can fucking punt it.'

'She's a jobsworth... sir,' Beatty said, his breath coming more quickly. 'Truth be told, I think she's on Lomas' side. I know officers are supposed to be impartial, but she's been digging in the kind of files we don't want her digging in. And I don't think she likes how things work around here. I kind of get the - er - crazy idea she might want to change things.'

'So, what are you going to do about it?' Spice pressed. 'Can't you get her reassigned or something?'

'That's what I'd hoped,' the officer nodded.

'Well then, fucking do it,' Grizzly shrugged.

'I can't!' Beatty explained. 'It's not that simple.'

'Why?' Spice hissed.

'Because she's gone upstairs with something she's found,' Beatty announced, a pained expression crossing his face.

'Which is what exactly?' Grizzly tilted his head to one side.

'There's some footage that's come to light,' the officer shrugged.

Silence.

'I'm not liking the fucking sound of this.' Spice looked hard at him. 'Footage of what?'

'That night... the night when... the Lomas woman...'

'Hang on!' Spice's voice raised several decibels. 'You said you'd got all the footage. You said you'd fucking sorted it!'

'I *did*. I *had*,' Beatty protested, backing involuntarily towards the door. 'But there was film on one of those dash cams - private footage.'

'So get rid of it,' Grizzly shrugged once more.

'But it's private footage.'

'Fucking wipe it,' Spice ordered. 'Or kick the shit out of whoever needs the shit kicking out of them. Stop being such a pussy.'

Beatty sighed. 'You see, that's the thing.'

'What – you being a pussy?' Grizzly frowned.

'No. This car - a Ford Focus - was involved in an accident the next day.'

'So?' Grizzly frowned.

A fearful expression crossed Beatty's face. 'So the dash cam footage went off to the insurance brokers. There was nothing I could do about it. And some fucking bright spark in one of their offices played the wrong section. It turns out the camera had a pretty good view of a trussed up body being unloaded from a van and wheeled off on a sack trolley.'

'And?' Spice's whisper seethed with barely concealed rage.

'And, when the call came through, Little Miss Butter-wouldn't-melt-in-her-knickers took it.' He paused. 'She went straight to the bigwigs with it - all bells and whistles.' He grinned helplessly. 'I think she sees herself as the next Chief of Police - running on some kind of anti-corruption ticket. Unbelievable, isn't it? What a shit show!'

'It's your fucking shit show, you useless prick!' Grizzly growled.

Silence descended for a moment.

Spice looked at Grizzly and then looked back at Beatty.

'So...' he began. 'I still haven't had an answer.' He spoke slowly; deliberately. 'What the fuck are you going to do about it?'

'Well, there's not much I *can* do, is there?' the policeman shrugged. 'I wish there was. But if it's gone to the Top Brass, then it's out of my fucking hands. It's above my pay grade. I have no influence there.'

Spice sighed. 'I'm not liking your fucking tone,' he announced, clearing his throat. 'You know, when I was growing up,' he spoke wistfully, 'people always said things like that to me. How things were always someone else's problem. How they had no control.' He shook his head. 'It's a pussy's trick – wimping out and saying it's someone else's responsibility.'

'It's a bitch, isn't it?' Beatty nodded, half smiling.

'They said I'd never amount to anything,' Spice continued, beginning to pace. 'That I was too small.' He sniffed. 'That my accent was all wrong.' He turned to the officer. 'And do you know what happened?'

Beatty, uneasy now, shook his head.

'Well... I proved them wrong,' Spice grinned. 'Wouldn't you agree - I proved them wrong?' He raised his eyebrows, nodding – as if to encourage the other man to do the same.

'Oh yes, er – sir,' Beatty replied, uncomfortably.

Spice nodded. 'And do you know how I did it?'

The man shook his head, frowning. Spice looked hard at him and then glanced briefly in his brother's direction, nodding slightly. At that point, the officer's neck was swallowed up in the older sibling's huge palm. It was held fast in a vice-like grip. The sound of bones being misaligned was audible. Beatty's fear-induced paleness was mixed with a rising tinge of rose as his circulation was restricted.

Spice sauntered around to look at the helpless, uniformed man. 'Well,' he announced. 'One reason I got ahead was by having a brother that could crucify anyone who got in my way. And sometimes, that's all you need. Wouldn't you say so? Officer Beatty?'

A frothing noise emitted from the policeman's throat.

'You see,' Spice went on calmly. 'I don't like you. I don't think I trust you. And frankly, I find you a little disappointing. In truth, I think you're a useless prick. Anyone who becomes a copper has got a defective gene somewhere in their DNA.' He shook his head disdainfully. 'And from where I'm standing, you look pretty fucking defective. You'd do well to remember that I can make your whole career vanish in a puff of smoke with no more than a click of my fingers.' He walked over to the office door and opened it. At this point, his older sibling propelled Beatty out onto the gantry as the officer kicked impotently at the air. Then, the big man shifted position, hoisted his captive over the side rail and dangled him by his ankles.

As the man squirmed, he screamed and regarded the concrete surface directly below him. The blood rushing to his head began colouring his visage in burgundy. The shaving rash on his neck bulged in an angry, mottled scarlet crust. A couple of shift workers on the depot floor peered up briefly and then opted to studiously avoid looking in the direction of the drama.

'You have one more fucking chance, Beatty,' Spice announced above the din. The upended man clutched desperately at the foot of the railings. He looked up in terror; Grizzly grinned down at him, chuckling in gentle glee. 'Fucking sort it,' the younger sibling went on. 'Otherwise, we'll do this at the top of the cliff.'

Chapter 29.

Safia stepped out onto the balcony of the Paris apartment where the auction was to take place. She lit a cigarette, inhaling deeply as she looked out from the tower block. When she'd first moved in, gangs had fought openly in the yard below. On occasion, there had been barbecues: rival dealers burned alive in the trunks of parked cars. It had all been over drugs. The drugs trade still played a big part on the estate – an enormous part. It wasn't as if Safia's minions had stopped it. But what they had done was move it fully underground. The police – she'd learned – were prepared to ignore certain infractions if they happened beneath a veneer of obedience. So that's what she'd arranged. Casting her eyes below, she saw the lack of litter; the absence of unruly, hooded youths on the concourse – surface impressions meant there was no reason for law enforcement to come calling. In the distance, cars passed by on the Périphérique. She checked her phone for messages.

There were none.

She reached into the pocket of her leather overcoat and withdrew another burner phone. This one had only one number in it: Serge Valais – a bent cop on her payroll. He was the one who ensured the safe passage of the cargo to the coast and was about as corruptible as it was possible to be. She texted him a time and waited for him to respond with a location.

Her phone buzzed moments later, and she returned it to her pocket, satisfied with his reply.

* * * * *

When she'd first run an auction, it had taken a long time. It had been a profitable experiment, but she hadn't enjoyed the lack of control. When she walked into a room, she wanted to be the most powerful person there. If not, she felt uncomfortable. So things had changed. Since then, she'd streamlined proceedings. Reserves were placed and customers' credit ratings were analysed in advance. The bids were overseen by Hassan and, as soon as an offer was accepted, a new girl was moved out into the living room and ordered to go through the same gyrations as her predecessor. It was a numbers game: the more commodities shifted, the greater the profit.

The first auction had been open to all of Europe. She had, since tightened the net, though. Although crossing the Channel was a headache and carried with it no small number of risks, Britain was by far her best market. A confidante had told her of their suspicions; that English men of a certain class and disposition were desperate to recapture a sense of the glory days of the Empire. Having a live-in sex doll to subjugate seemed to play into their psyche. It meant they were willing to pay big. And Safia was happy to take their money.

Customers there paid well, and paid on time. They scared easily, and the agreement with Denton Laine meant the cargo was delivered quickly and efficiently.

At least it had been.

Until last time.

Generally, Safia tried to have as little to do with the operation on the ground as possible. However, on this occasion, she'd vowed to accompany the cargo to rendezvous with her contacts on the south coast of England. She couldn't see any other way of achieving what she wanted quickly enough otherwise. Her motivation was straightforward: if you want something to happen, then do it yourself.

Her plan was simple. Get rid of the incompetent fools who were organising things, and take over the running of their operation. The other people on the English end of the chain would soon fall into line, she reasoned. They would have no choice.

That was where Hakeem came in.

*****

She flicked her cigarette butt over the edge of the balcony and watched it fall towards the ground far below. It fluttered and whirled like a sycamore leaf until she lost sight of it against the asphalt. Then she slid open the balcony door and stepped back into the apartment.

'We're good to go,' Hassan announced, looking up from his laptop. 'Five minutes and we're underway.'

Safia nodded.

Chapter 30.

Slipping into the depot under cover of darkness was more difficult than Rivera had imagined. For a start, it was incredibly busy. And then, there were the lights - great arcs of fluorescent beams that played across the no-man's-land between the fence and the buildings. They cast giant shadows as the ex-soldier strolled through their glare. Where the depot by day had a languid sense of lazy slumber, by night it looked more like a closely guarded Colditz. Rivera felt the hairs on the back of his neck start to rise.

His approach had been a gamble. As the place was such a hive of activity, he reasoned his earlier method of sprinting would have aroused suspicion. With all the people moving around, he had a sense that the presence of one more wouldn't raise any eyebrows. So, he walked nonchalantly across the grass, pretending to zip up his fly. Emerging around the side of a truck, he merely looked as if he'd returned from relieving himself. A man with a clipboard gave him a disinterested nod and then, collar up and baseball cap pulled down low over his brow, the ex-soldier thrust his hands into his pockets. He walked straight across the floor of the warehouse and through the door that had aroused his suspicions earlier. All the while, he expected a shout or a challenge. None came.

Once he passed through the door, the ex-soldier looked around. Rivera didn't quite know what he was expecting, but he knew he hadn't found it. Dingy breeze-blocks lined a corridor that led to a fire exit. A horizontal steel bar sat across it with a bright yellow fixture indicating it was alarmed. The visitor frowned at it and walked on quietly, his leather boots thudding solidly on the concrete surface.

Walking along the corridor, he paused outside a staffroom. From inside came the din of voices and a fug of cigarette smoke. He glanced through the slightly ajar door and saw a football match was being shown on a television balanced on the top of a filing cabinet.

A game of darts was also being contested; a board hung on the wall. There was nothing untoward there – the indoor smoking felt quite 1970s, but he doubted the depot was the kind of place which would frequently be inspected for such things.

Rivera continued past a broom cupboard that had its door propped open, but saw nothing else suspicious. Something still didn't sit right with him, though. The transportation of drugs - if that's what it was - explained the trucks and the personnel. But the wire facing the wrong way still nagged at him.

And why have a fire door that was alarmed if the only access point near it was a staffroom?

Rivera shrugged. He'd drawn a blank so far: something was happening, but what it was remained a mystery. It just happened to be a far busier mystery by night. Looking around, he took in the piles of goods on pallets. He knew that searching for narcotics in the midst of legitimate cargo would be tricky. And he had no idea if that's what he was really looking for, anyway.

So, he approached the door and thrust his hand against the bar. He expected one of two things to happen. Option one: the door would open in silence, with whichever security system it was supposedly linked to having been deactivated years ago. After all, why alarm such an exit? Option two: the door would be a dummy entrance and would lead to something more interesting.

Option three was something Rivera hadn't really considered: that the warning sign was genuine.

He pressed the bar. The door swung open onto a floodlit gravel path; a ghostly glow of grassy expanse lay beyond it. A second later, a siren began to howl. It was like a cross between a beefed-up car alarm and an air raid warning.

And then all hell broke loose.

* * * * *

Rivera paused on the gravel path, noted the complete absence of cover, and swiftly re-entered the building. To walk across the brightly lit surface would have been as exposed as trying to move from East to West Berlin and then hopping over the wall. He decided against it, and slipped inside the broom cupboard, pulling the door closed.

Outside, he heard the footfall of boots along the corridor and the agitated shouts of what sounded like a foreman.

'Breach! Check the perimeter!' a panicked voice ordered.

'Go! Go! Go!'

In the darkness of the cupboard, surrounded by the smells of cleaning products, Rivera couldn't help but wryly smile. Real soldiers knew that remaining calm and being unfazed made for far better organisation. The almost gleefully excited tones beyond the closed door suggested those involved in marshalling people were playing parts – they were revelling in the authority the situation afforded them. Whoever they were, they'd clearly watched too many war movies.

And fought too few wars.

* * * * *

Two minutes later, the sirens stopped.

Further shouts sounded out. 'Clear!' and 'Secure!'

The ex-soldier waited until the sound of boots on the gravel pathway receded before he emerged. Moving swiftly along the corridor, he peered into the staffroom, and saw it was now empty. Peeking out through the door to the warehouse, he realised the yard beyond it was serving as a muster point. Employees and drivers were lined up, grumbling as a fire marshal bellowed instructions.

Rivera turned and headed up a stairwell. His boots rang out lightly on each of the steps. He held himself in a fighting stance, but encountered no traffic from the other direction. Emerging onto an upper corridor, he reached what appeared to be an administrative level. A bank of what looked like glass-fronted offices sat before him. At the far end was another door which would - he realised - be visible from below. It was marked with a large, red-lined sign: *SAFETY EQUIPMENT MUST BE WORN BEYOND THIS POINT.*

He ducked down behind the barrier of the balcony which overlooked the yard and crawled along it. As he did, his ear caught the voice of an overseer barking through a loudhailer. Rivera remained confused. The reaction to the alarmed door being opened was akin to one which might meet a prison break. Why bother with people breaking *out*? If the cargo was inside, then surely Denton Laine should have been more concerned with people breaking *in*.

Rivera crawled on.

* * * * *

The boss' office was located exactly where one would expect. It was in the centre of a bank of windows, but was double-fronted where the other offices had single casements. Helpfully, unlike the others, which were all labelled with generic bronze plaques, this one was marked by an enormous sign bearing the legend: *IF THE HOUSE IS ROCKIN' DON'T BOTHER KNOCKIN' - JUST COME ON IN!* Rivera shook his head, frowning a little. The sign looked like a cheap furnishing from an outlet of *The Hard Rock Café*, and he again found himself doubting the professional status of any of the men on the site.

Rivera reached up, turned the door handle, and found that it opened. Swiftly, he crawled over the threshold, closing the door behind him. He twisted the bolt, locking it from the inside. Moving over, he checked the door leading through to what looked like a secretary's office was unlocked, and was satisfied he had an escape route in place if needed. Then, slowly, as the fire marshal's voice grated metallically through the megaphone below, Rivera wound the handles that hung down from above the window frames, angling the blinds so he'd be rendered invisible from the outside.

The ex-soldier reckoned there would be some kind of siren which would serve as an 'all-clear' and would tell employees they could get back to work. Given the seriousness of the procedure, he reckoned he'd have around five minutes.

He got seven.

Sure enough, a loud, intermittent high-pitched wail sounded as a second signal. Peering through the blinds, the intruder saw the crowd outside dispersing. Their movements weren't much more enthusiastic than they'd been when they assembled. He unlocked the office door and exited through the secretary's room, quickly descending the stairs and secreting himself back into the broom cupboard at the end of the corridor. Outside, the shuffling noise of footsteps sounded out and then faded.

Standing in the darkness, he reflected on what he'd learned. His search had revealed little. He'd quickly rifled through a sheaf of documents he'd removed from the top drawer of a filing cabinet. While the numbers looked eye-wateringly high, most of the shipping manifests and documents of transport looked genuine. Rivera found the desk drawer to be open, but there was little of interest inside it. In fact, the only thing that didn't really seem to fit with the setting of a provincial haulage company were the opulent furnishings within the office. Yes, so the business was profitable, but the place seemed stuffed full of gaudy golden artefacts and glittering ornaments that were completely out of place - it looked more Las Vegas than Lyme Regis. It was this which was puzzling. He'd expected to be face-to-face with calendars of naked page three girls and overflowing ashtrays. But the possessions looked like the kind of things people who were cash-rich would buy purely because they could. It looked - he reflected – dodgy; the office displayed a Trumpian lack of taste. There was clearly something illicit going on. But what it was, he was still none the wiser. The only thing he knew for sure was that the strength of reaction he'd witnessed in response to him setting off the alarm on the fire door was massively disproportionate.

There was clearly something significant being hidden. And whatever it was, the people in charge of the depot wanted to protect it. He sighed, breathing deeply. The fumes of the various cleaning fluids made him feel a little light-headed.

* * * * *

After twenty minutes of distant noises, Rivera exited the broom cupboard. He turned right and walked slowly across the loading bay, willing himself to act calmly. He was holding a clipboard he'd found tucked behind a heating pipe, and he gazed down at it before looking up at the vehicles in the distance.

On reaching two stationary trucks, he nodded at a couple of drivers who were smoking while forklifts filled their trailers with boxes. He then made to look at his clipboard again, frowned and walked around to the other side of the trailers, and onto the grass. Once again, he moved slowly, looking down and pretending to study a non-existent form before appearing to frown. To anyone watching, he would have appeared deep in thought, carrying out official business. In this fashion, he approached the fence.

As the floodlights were angled towards the warehouse, he was almost entirely in shadow by the time he reached the chain link barrier. Risking a glance back, he saw nothing to make him suspect he was being observed, and so he swung himself over the razor wire, leaving the same way he'd arrived.

He left the clipboard in the brambles close to the fence, not knowing when it might serve a useful prop once more.

Chapter 31.

Hakeem watched.

He sat in the large, black, rented Mercedes with its smoked-glass windows. The interior smelled strongly of plush leather. New. It wasn't the most ostentatious car he'd driven; this wasn't the most moneyed locale. A car to him was a mundane, functional item – a tool. He was in town to look for leads.

Finding one hadn't taken long.

He'd been looking for Harley Davidsons - there weren't many of them. But, fortunately for him, he'd simply driven around for a while and then sighted a pair of them on the forecourt of a garage. His search had been systematic – he just hadn't expected to find such obvious indicators so quickly. He would have preferred to locate their riders, but he reckoned that having the bikes was a decent start.

Knowing the place the riders would eventually have to return to was enough.

And so, for the past few hours, he'd simply sat. Observing. He was calm. He was always calm. He was patient. But he was always patient. Sitting there, across the road from the garage, he simply stared and remembered everything he saw. That was why he was so good at his job. Time - to him - meant nothing. Some people are incorruptible. Others consider themselves crooks. But even they might – at times – show cracks of conscience. Some, though, are utterly without morals. Like Hakeem. Sociopaths. His patience was borne of a one-track mind, and an inability to empathise with anyone who wasn't him. Or someone paying him. He would simply wait. And watch. Until he got what he wanted.

It was still early in the day.

* * * * *

When he'd received the call, it had come through an encrypted route like it always did. A short exchange.

Someone along the chain would have uttered the words they always uttered when something was wrong: 'Call Hakeem.' He didn't need to know the circumstances. He didn't care. He would simply receive his instructions and send over the details of whichever bank he wanted the money wired to this time. It was always the same.

Zurich.

Half in advance.

Half on completion.

Talk was cheap. Life was cheaper. It was death where all the profit lay. He wasn't like the braggarts who hang around snooker clubs and card games boasting of contract killings. He simply made people disappear without trace. And that's why he commanded such fees.

He'd been in Berlin when the call had come through. Men like Hakeem didn't operate on normal terms. They didn't work nine to five or have mortgages and pension plans. They simply made a lot of money by doing bad things.

And then, when the bad things were done, they moved on. Fancy hotels. Fast women. Slow horses. It was a well-worn path to him; at least these days. He'd gamble until the money ran out, enjoying all the accoutrements that came with it.

It took a very definite skill-set to do what he did. Most people couldn't do it. Fewer still could do it well. And hardly any fell into Hakeem's category: they actually enjoyed the work when it was given to them. He'd always been the same – ever since he first set a scorpion in the midst of a ring of flaming petrol. Watching it sting itself to death in a panicking *paso doble*, he'd learned a love for wielding the power of life and death over something weaker than him.

But having a life like the one he led meant that when he worked, he had to work hard. He had to be better than anyone else out there. Otherwise, the work wouldn't come.

No morals.

No scruples.

Nothing other than getting the job done. And when a job came, it was all-consuming. No sleep. No distractions. He was just a body of energy until the conclusion was reached. Once he had a target, he was like a pit bull. He'd bite and hold on until the target was down. And then he'd put them down permanently.

No witnesses.

No trail.

He'd been in an upmarket hotel close to Potsdamer Platz with two prostitutes asleep beside him. He had no use for personal attachments, but the intensity of sex was something he relished. An hour later, he was at Tempelhof awaiting a plane, the dawn sky just beginning to turn a lighter hue of grey.

When the call came, the clock started ticking. Hakeem didn't hesitate. Of course, he travelled under fake documents. Hakeem was the name they asked for, but that wasn't the name he would be known by in the place he was heading.

It never was.

* * * * *

The call on this occasion came from Lisbon. They were always routed through a variety of connections. As the information bounced from the underside of satellites, it edged its way around the globe at lightning pace; an electronic encryption. Par for the course in his line of work.

Untraceable.

Hakeem didn't know the details. He didn't need to know. He wouldn't have cared anyway – he paid someone else to reroute his calls. If he was contacted, it meant things needed to happen fast, and that someone was willing to pay.

And pay big.

Someone, somewhere, would have given the order that was always uttered at such times.

'Call Hakeem.'

* * * * *

It was because of this that Hakeem found himself in Saltmarsh Cove with a driver's licence in someone else's name. In the glove compartment of the rental car, he had three other licences - all in different names; three passports; a smorgasbord of cloned credit cards, and a variety of weapons. His Star 30M, though, was in a shoulder holster, close to his heart.

It always was.

He cared little for his surroundings. Things like that didn't matter to him. At least not when he was working. He'd only been twelve when the Mullah had sat him down on the blanket in his hut. Over sweet tea, he'd told him of the men who would collect him; the warriors whose faces were covered with scarves. And so he'd waited for them as instructed. He'd joined them by climbing into the rear of the pickup truck at the edge of a dust-scarred highway.

By fifteen, he knew more about power than most men learn in a lifetime. He'd lost count of the number of kills he'd made. Of the number of times others had attempted to kill him. But he'd grown bored – his idealism had waned. His faith had faltered. Hakeem had found a new religion: money. Once upon a time, he'd have called the daytime drinkers and scantily clad female holiday makers infidels. He'd have wanted them dead because of what they stood for. Now, though, he turned a blind eye. Times had changed.

Once upon a time was a long time ago. A *very* long time ago.

A different lifetime.

Since then, he'd learned to embrace some of the excesses of the West. Ever since he'd discovered how much his work was worth, he'd found his attitudes had shifted. After all, why should he take such risks if he couldn't enjoy the fruits of his labours? He was doing little more than he'd done years ago. Only now, he ate caviar and not flatbread. And he was cashing in the rewards promised in heaven in advance; he took them on earth – made into flesh.

The job was easy. At least it appeared easy. But somewhere along the chain, a link had become problematic. His job was to get rid of the link. It was - Safia had assured him - straightforward. The link had bragged about having his own army of security guards who ruled the town on Harley Davidsons. That had been a mistake - it would make him easy to find.

Follow the bikes - Safia had told him - and you'll find the problem. And when you find the problem, get rid of it.

Easy.

The only issue was that this was such a mono-ethnic town; Hakeem was conscious of standing out as a foreigner. It was a tourist place during the season, so he wasn't the only person of colour, but he wanted to keep a low profile, nonetheless. It didn't do for him to be recognisable or memorable in his line of work. He was no stranger to Britain, but he knew the country saw him as an outsider. People rarely voiced such opinions; they hid their hostility behind veneers of civility. But it was there nonetheless. Always.

It wasn't as if he was scared of anyone - he never had been. Not since he'd seen how easy it was to lose everything you once loved. Sometimes he recalled the burning embers of his childhood in dreams. But it was a different motive that drove his actions now – he'd avenged his family many times over. Even so, fear or no fear, his work was always easier when he could remain undercover. Even though he was armed and dangerous, the element of surprise remained his most potent weapon.

Hence the tinted windows.

He peered at the forecourt again.

There was movement from behind the bikes.

The garage was opening up.

Chapter 32.

Rivera woke with a start. The sun streamed through the blind he'd closed on Iris' side. He'd been meaning to replace it - it still held the burnt tobacco smell of myriad cigarettes from back when the idea of stepping outside for a nicotine fix was tantamount to a violation of one's Civil Rights. Whenever the sun hit, it seemed to unlock the aroma anew. Rivera was a light smoker himself, but stuck religiously to his rule of no smoking in the van. It was his home, after all. He didn't know if cats suffered from asthma, but he felt a moral obligation not to use Rosie as a guinea pig in this regard.

Rolling over, he looked at his watch. It was early. The cat slept on, purring her way peacefully through whichever feline dreams she was chasing mice in.

Rivera yawned and sat up. His back and his neck felt stiff; he'd noticed how such aches and pains were more frequent these days. The ex-soldier didn't welcome the idea of growing old. He consoled himself with the fact he hadn't woken up next to Janine at least.

The night before had been a disappointment. He'd hoped to find answers on returning to the depot when it was busy, but he'd ended up with just as many questions as he'd had previously. If not more. He raised himself up and padded towards the stove to brew coffee.

As he did, he pondered the fact that the key to the Lomas mystery clearly had something to do with the depot. He just hadn't found what it was yet. But he knew there were areas of the warehouse he still wanted to take a look at - the sealed off section at the end of the administrative corridor in particular. And he was sure that if he spent longer in the office he'd find something.

Lighting the stove, he lay back on the bed and closed his eyes, his thoughts whirling.

* * * * *

The moment he knew he had to leave the forces was a point he'd revisited a million times. He'd been up-country in Helmand, working with a specialist unit. At first, he'd gone in as a sniper - plucked out of his cushy office role, removed from days spent balancing books and scrutinising spreadsheets. He'd found everything about the country both brutal and beautiful: the mountains that stretched up to the sky; the harsh terrain not troubled by crops; the people - warm and welcoming and then terrifying in the same breath. After a short stint with a group trying to flush out Taliban fighters, he'd been seconded to another unit.

This time, instead of trying to win a war with bullets, he was employed in trying to do so with charm.

The military enrolled him on an intensive course to learn Pashto and Dari. He wasn't fluent - not by a long way - but he was able to hold conversations in each tongue. That's why he'd ended up shadowing Mitchell Tyler. Tyler was a languages specialist. He would have been mentally certifiable under normal circumstances, but in Afghanistan, that classed him as being relatively sane - if not perfect for the job at hand. He was something of a legendary figure; on his language course, he'd been put on a charge for painting the entire interior of his room in the barracks black; on one of his first missions in the country, he'd won the hearts and minds of local warlords by serenading them over a makeshift PA system with popular Pashto songs. Where other students had spent their time listening to political addresses to sharpen their vocabularies, Tyler had tuned into the radio. It was a tactic which had worked extremely well.

The linguist was a wild card, but a good man to have on side. He knew Afghanistan as well as anyone else Rivera had ever met; any time he was set to be shipped home, he seemed to have the knack of finding himself placed on a charge. The easiest way to have it waived was to sign up for another tour of duty. And so that's what he'd done - repeatedly. It meant he was a mine of information for younger colleagues. But it also meant he was unhinged from all the years he'd spent in-country.

Translators - Tyler explained to Rivera - had a huge number of challenges. The problem, as he outlined it, was that British people always think of languages in the same way. When you're on an island, the language stops when you hit the sea. The rest of the world - Tyler had shrugged - doesn't work like that. Most countries' languages bleed over borders. They borrow bits and pieces from other dialects, and what you end up with is millions of people speaking distorted, confused versions of their own mother tongues. He'd sat Rivera down and attempted to draw him a map in the sand.

What you had in Afghanistan - he'd explained - was even more confusing. The lines on the map which made up the country had been drawn by westerners years ago in an attempt to pigeonhole the place into a convenient box. People on the ground, though, didn't think in the same way. The idea of a country didn't make sense to most of them. Many of them had never even seen a map. This was a land of tribes and family clans - the kind of place where each valley had its own dialect and, sometimes, even each village. It had been like that for centuries and wouldn't change just because there were troops on the ground.

It had been a steep learning curve for the new arrival, but he'd swiftly figured out how to approach communication. What he'd found more difficult to accept, though, was the continual need for compromise.

'Sucks, no?' Tyler grumbled one morning.

'What?' Rivera enquired.

'Well,' his friend had shrugged, 'we're over here trying to do good, but all we've done is let the people switch one bunch of corrupt leaders for another.'

'How so?'

'You remember that clansman?' the translator asked. 'The one who was wearing the Mazari cap and the eye patch?'

Rivera nodded. The memory was still raw.

'Well - you think he's as pure as driven snow? He's got blood on his hands, just like the rest of them. I'm sure I remember him from photographs taken years ago – he's a dead ringer for someone who was executing a Soviet soldier; he cut his throat like he was slaughtering a goat.' The translator laughed, shaking his head. 'But, by getting into bed with us and the Americans, he knows that we'll protect him - for now, at least.' Tyler paused. 'And you know those trucks of his - they're full of the fruits of the opium harvest.'

Rivera had pursed his lips and nodded. It was an unwinnable war. No matter how it was approached, they would be on the losing side; the military held no sway. All the millions of dollars being pumped in just felt like they were there to paper over the cracks. A façade of control. A flimsy construct that could be shattered at any moment.

* * * * *

It was later that day when Rivera's world changed.

The village was much like any of the others they visited - a batch of ravaged outhouses and broken down huts. They'd been given sweet tea, just like always. Tyler had led the conversation, and Rivera had done his best to tune in. The usual promises had been made: there were no fighters in the village or in the area nearby; any fighters that were seen would be reported. It was almost like a script. Tyler handed over two cartons of American cigarettes and several bricks of banknotes, and the men made ready to leave.

As they awaited their transport helicopter, the pair leaned on a fence post, smoking. The other soldiers present were in strategic positions, serving as guards. The translators' skill-set, Rivera had been told, made them an asset worth protecting. They didn't pull sentry duty – not often, at least. And they remained in the inner circle during such situations. It didn't make them any less vulnerable to mortars, though, as Tyler was fond of pointing out. The other man knew a Dari specialist who'd lost a leg in such circumstances. But Tyler always knew someone with a story behind them.

At first, a ragged group of emaciated children had approached them, but then a harsh bark from one of the elders sent them scurrying away.

'Lot of children,' Rivera had commented idly. 'I wonder where their mothers are?'

'Well,' Tyler sighed. 'The mothers will be kept out of sight from you and me - standard practice. But they're not all from here. Poor little bastards.'

'What do you mean?' Rivera had frowned.

The translator had looked hard at his colleague for a moment. 'Wise up, soldier! Remember what our brief is here? We win the hearts and we win the minds.'

Rivera nodded.

'We grease the fucking wheels of diplomacy,' Tyler continued. 'Meaning we don't do anything to fuck things up. That's why we have to turn a blind eye sometimes - for the greater good. At least that's what they sell it as. But try telling that to those ragged little fuckers who can't get a decent feed from anyone.'

'What are you on about?'

'Those kids,' Tyler had gestured. 'They're orphans, most of them. It's not like anyone's going to come and look for them. And so the elders in there...' he paused. 'They sell them.'

'You're shitting me!' Rivera's tone was incredulous.

'Straight up,' Tyler nodded earnestly. 'They'll sell them over the border. And from there... God knows. All I know is that there are some very fucked up people in the world. And if those kids end up with them... they'll make slaves of them. Or catamites or some shit. Or worse.'

Rivera shook his head in disbelief.

'And there's not a damn thing we can do about it.' Tyler flicked his cigarette away in disgust. 'Because we can't rock the boat. We can't fuck up the mission... we can't rescue any of those kids.'

It was that moment which Rivera came back to time and again. Seconds later, he'd hit the floor as an incoming round struck a nearby rock. Fire was returned towards a group of hostiles up on the ridge. It wasn't until he was out of bandit country and Tyler had been moved to Kabul that Rivera had time to think about the other man's revelation. It hadn't seemed like much at the time, but it had grown in his memory, like the banking clouds of a gathering storm, until it was almost all-consuming.

The vision of poverty-stricken children in their rags looking pleadingly at them through big eyes before being called away endured. He couldn't shake that from his mind, and he knew deep down it was that which had caused him to crack up. The guilt. The shame. The powerlessness. It was their imploring gazes that he saw in his dreams; their desperation.

The kettle on the campervan stove bubbled, gurgling noisily. Somewhere inside his head, a cog turned, and gears clicked into place.

A thought arose.

Chapter 33.

The kettle began whistling at exactly the same moment Lomas knocked on the door. His hair looked greasy; there were bags beneath his eyes.

'Good timing,' Rivera nodded. 'Coffee?'

Lomas nodded. 'Do I ask?' he began uncomfortably, before continuing with an increased urgency. 'Did you find anything?'

Rivera sighed. 'Well, I know that they're hiding something up there that really matters to them.'

'But you don't know what it is?'

'Correct.' He stirred at the instant coffee. 'Investigating's a bitch, huh?'

'So...?'

'So, I ended up opening a fire door, and an alarm went off, but it felt like a jailbreak from Alcatraz or something. The shit really hit the fan – you had people running around like it was Doomsday or something. The powers that be are very, very worried about something over there. If I was a gambling man, I'd say that your sister discovered what it is.' He paused. 'No proof, of course. I still haven't cracked it. But I've got an idea.'

Lomas looked expectantly at him as Rivera handed over a cup of coffee. The two men headed outside into the bright sun of the early morning. An oil tanker sat on the horizon – a huge, grey hulk against the azure, Mediterranean blue.

As they sat down on two folding chairs, Rivera turned to the visitor. He frowned. 'You know how we've been thinking this is all about drugs?' he began.

Lomas nodded.

'Well... I'm not so sure,' the ex-soldier continued. 'And then I started thinking about guns, but neither of those things makes sense.

Why would you need somewhere as out of the way as this to bring things like that to shore?'

'So, what do you think now?'

'Honestly?'

'Yes, fucking honestly!' Lomas rarely swore. Curses sounded almost comical coming through in his perfect diction. But there was no doubting his sincerity; his eyes burned. 'Tell me.'

Silence.

Rivera sighed. 'People.'

'People?'

'Yeah, like trafficking, you know? Think about it. It's perfect. You load up a bunch of migrants on the French coast and ship them over on a night when the sea's calm. Then, a few miles offshore, you switch them onto a local boat. They come back here under cover of darkness and they're whisked away. After all, if you've got a reputable haulage company, then you can use it to transport things anywhere. No questions asked.'

Lomas frowned for a moment and then sipped at his coffee. 'OK,' he began doubtfully. 'But where's the money? Those migrants are dirt poor. None of them are going to have enough cash to make people act like they're acting here – they're fighting tooth and nail; throwing up roadblocks. I don't get it. And anyway, they come over on death-traps and floating bathtubs. They go from Calais to Dover - they're not going to reach here. Surely?'

Rivera nodded. 'We're not talking floating bathtubs here. Not to land on local beaches. I reckon they're legitimate boats - big ones that people won't ask questions about. You know how we've said that this is just part of a chain? Well, my guess is that they pick out the migrants who are young; good-looking. The ones they can sell for a high price - like cattle.'

'What, for...?' Lomas' question hung in the air.

'There are bad people out there,' Rivera nodded grimly. 'People with money and perversions and too much time on their hands.' He chewed his lip, thinking of Tyler. 'Really fucking bad people.'

'That's quite a leap,' Lomas began. 'From drugs, I mean.'

'Yeah, well – you have any better ideas?' the ex-soldier shrugged. Silence.

'So slavery is alive and well?' Lomas said eventually, raising his eyebrows. 'Well, that would certainly fit with the way Katie saw the world. But we need proof, right?'

'We do. So I'm going to go back there this afternoon.'

'The depot? Again?'

'Yeah. There's a part of the warehouse I haven't looked at yet. There's got to be something I've missed. I can't believe they're smart enough to cover all their tracks.' He shook his head. 'These guys are pretty much just a bunch of yee-hahs – they're bloody useless for the most part.'

'Can I help?' Lomas pressed. 'I mean - I feel a bit useless here otherwise.'

'Do you know anywhere I can hire a suit?' Rivera asked bluntly.

'I do,' the other man replied, frowning. He cast his eyes up and down the ex-soldier. 'But I've got one with me - it should fit you, just about, if you breathe in. Why?'

'Well - I've been up to the depot through the back door twice now. I don't want to push my luck too much. This time I'm going in through the front. I'll do a bit more research on the company, but I was thinking I could pose as a tax official. That should get me in at least.'

'Isn't it a bit risky, though?' Lomas frowned. 'After what might have happened to Katie, I mean.'

Rivera swilled his cup, pouring the remaining liquid onto the grass. 'Maybe. But I think they'll swallow the idea of me working for the government. I know how people like that talk.' He looked at the other man. 'I've got a few errands to run, and then I'll meet you at your hotel. You can pose as my driver. If that's OK?' He scratched at his stubble. 'I'll clean myself up - can you help me with a pass or something that looks like an identity card?'

The other man nodded, slowly. 'I still say it's quite a risk.' He narrowed his eyes, unconvinced.

'Look,' Rivera sighed. 'Once I'm inside, start the countdown. If you don't hear from me by five, then call Christie. Explain everything to her. Got it? Then she can bring in the force – or any of them she trusts at least.'

Lomas nodded. Then he frowned. 'Hang on,' he began. 'They saw you in the pub – remember? When you were reading.'

The ex-soldier pursed his lips. 'It was only for a split-second.'

'But what if they recognise you?'

Rivera shrugged. 'It's a chance we'll have to take.'

Chapter 34.

Entering the library, Rivera was greeted once again by Belinda. She seemed flustered. Her cheeks were blushing, and she was holding a tissue to her nose. When he asked her if she was alright, she told him she was fed up with the derelict outside who saw fit to come and go as he pleased. It transpired she'd had to clean up one of the bathroom stalls after he'd visited that morning. She opened her mouth to provide more detail and then recoiled – as if in horror.

'I'll have a word with him,' the visitor promised, raising a hand as if in appeasement. 'I think I can get through to him.'

'Do,' the librarian replied, looking at him gratefully. 'Please.'

After he'd explained that he needed access to the same documents he'd looked at previously, she ushered him through to the reading room and left him to his own devices. There were only a couple of other people browsing that morning, so he had little concern about being disturbed. The tables were polished and had several layers of cracked varnish on them. Shelves lined the room with local interest books: *Saltmarsh Cove in Wartime*; *Saltmarsh Cove – Literary Heroes*; *Saltmarsh Cove of Yesteryear* - they were huge tomes. On the grey carpet, journals and periodicals were piled high. Rivera liked libraries – he'd spent hours on base hiding away from other people in them. These days, he rued all the time he hadn't properly spent perusing the shelves, though. He vowed he would make amends.

The ex-soldier eventually found what he was looking for. The various changes in titles and the constant shuffling of directors meant that the whole operation at Denton Laine was shrouded in a smokescreen. But he eventually located the name that mattered. It meant cross-referencing paper files and going online to search a database at Companies House. But there was a brief record of the haulage company passing into new ownership.

Garry Naylor.

That was all Rivera needed. Replacing the various books he'd pulled from the shelves onto the trolley, he prepared to leave. He'd left Lomas instructions to meet him by the service entrance of The Cliffside Hotel. The plan was loose. The be-suited Rivera would act as an administrator who'd been tipped off about a shortfall, while Lomas pretended to be his chauffeur. Katie's brother had assured him he'd be able to print official-looking accreditation that would pass the scrutiny of any guards and, indeed, the boss himself. Once inside, he'd improvise.

Exiting the library, Rivera spotted Fraser. The homeless man had been absent earlier, but now he'd reappeared. As he nodded at Rivera, he looked at him through his one good eye. The other was surrounded by a welt of purple and black bruising. He was smiling, though it might well have been more of a wince; holding himself straight seemed to be an effort.

'How are you then, chief?' he enquired, grimacing a little as he spoke.

Rivera frowned. 'I feel like that's a question I should be asking you instead.'

Chapter 35.

'You need a doctor,' Rivera announced seriously. He stood back a little from the homeless man, aware of how his aroma was exaggerated by the occasion.

'Ah, it's nothing,' Fraser replied. 'Besides, I cleaned myself up in the library bathroom.' He looked at the other man sheepishly. 'I'm not sure the old Doris behind the desk was too impressed, though. Lots of claret.'

Rivera paused, handing him a cigarette. 'So...' he began. 'What happened?'

'It's a long story,' he shrugged. 'But I've got a little information for you. You know – you were asking.'

'Yeah?' The ex-soldier looked expectantly at him. Then he paused. 'You ever heard of someone called Garry Naylor?'

The homeless man sighed and drew heavily on the cigarette. As he spoke, smoke poured from his mouth. 'Nobody around here calls him that - Garry, I mean. They all call him Grizzly, on account of the fact that he's built like a bear. He's the owner up at the depot. I told you that before, right?'

Rivera nodded.

'Anyway,' Fraser went on, 'I didn't think Grizzly would be news worth telling before, but he's the bastard who did this to me. Who told you his real name, anyway?'

'I was doing a bit of research.'

Fraser nodded. 'I was having a chat with a bloke called Roy.'

'Oh yeah?'

'Yeah - mechanic. Nice fellow. Anyway, he had a couple of Harleys bought into his workshop. And he started telling me about how their owners had been given a kicking by someone.' At this, he turned and looked at Rivera in admiration. 'And I think it was you that did it. So cheers.' He spat a globule onto the pavement. 'Shame you weren't around when Grizzly stopped by last night.'

The ex-soldier raised his eyebrows. He wasn't sure how early Fraser had started self-medicating with booze. He wondered how lucid he was. 'Why would he give you information?' he pressed. 'I mean you're...'

'...a tramp?' Fraser shrugged. 'Yeah, well – he's one of those blokes that's a bit of a do-gooder. He comes and sits with homeless people from time to time. You know the sort. Makes them feel more worthy or something. But once he started talking, I couldn't shut the fucker up.' He opened a can of cider. 'So, I got to thinking I'd tell you. I wondered if knowing about the bikes might be useful. You know – being as you're looking for the lass that's gone missing and all.'

Rivera nodded.

'There's two brothers, you see. One's Garry - Grizzly - the big one, and the other one is Spice.'

'Yeah - I've seen them around. At The Royal George.'

'Yes - that's their stomping ground. You don't need to be Columbo to hear about them – their names crop up all the time around here. Anyway, this bloke said the three bikers who usually tag along with them are Grizzly's mates from the Navy. Pugwash, Pluto and... can't remember the other one. Stupid dumbass names, they are. They're the security men. Or at least they were until you put them out of action.' He half-grinned, half-grimaced.

'Grizzly's the head honcho,' Fraser went on. 'But he's the one who was out doing the legwork. At least that's what Roy said. And he must be really pissed off, I reckon, because when he thumped me last night, it was completely unprovoked.'

Rivera nodded. 'What's the other brother up to, then?'

'Spice,' Fraser replied. 'He's mean - I mean, proper mean. But then, a lot of small guys are. I don't know much about what they do. I only know how shit-scared of them everyone is.' He paused. 'Who knows what he's up to? What either of them are. I don't give a shit – I just want them to leave me alone. But you find Grizzly, you'll find Spice too,' Fraser answered. 'And feel free to dish out a kicking to either one of the bastards. Or both.' His tone was understandably bitter.

* * * * *

Rivera reached the garage where Roy worked five minutes after leaving the library. Fraser had pointed him in its direction.

The forecourt was still. A chain was drawn up between the posts of the entrance to indicate it was closed; the rolling doors to the workshop had been lowered down to the ground. A pair of Harleys stood in front of the office door.

Rivera glanced at his watch then looked back at the sign on the wall advertising the fact the garage was open each weekday from 9 until 5. He considered waiting around, assuming the proprietor had skipped out for an early lunch, but thought better of it. If Roy was anything like Fraser, he could be waiting a long time.

He headed off to rendezvous with Lomas instead.

Chapter 36.

'Mr Lomas,' Christie announced upon answering the call. She was in her office. Her desk was a mass of post-it notes. They clung to the edges of her computer monitor. Other surfaces were littered with half-drunk mugs of tea; Christie was known by her colleagues as never getting around to finishing her drinks. Sometimes the dregs remained for weeks, growing strange, alien-like cultures of furry mould. 'What news?' Her tone was business-like. Blunt. Organised – in complete contrast to her clutter.

'It's about Rivera,' the caller began.

'And?' The Detective Inspector leaned back in her chair, chewing at the end of a pen. She scrolled her mouse cursor idly across an item on the computer screen with her other hand. 'What about him?'

'He's... We're going up to the depot together this afternoon. And...'

'...I strongly suggest that you do *not* do that,' Christie interrupted. 'Why are you going with him, anyway?'

'Rivera has a hunch,' Lomas explained. 'He's going to pose as a government official. And I'm going to act as his chauffeur,' he added. 'He thinks it'll work. I'm lending him a suit for it.'

'Right...' The police officer's voice was laced with doubt. She lifted the pen from her mouth and began doodling.

Silence.

'He said to tell you that if you haven't heard from him by five, something's gone wrong.' Lomas paused, uncomfortable. 'And because I'll be there too, I thought I'd let you know. Just in case. You know?'

Christie paused. She worried a strand of her hair, twisting it around by her ear. Her open notebook page was filled from where she'd been etching repeated pictures of a flower. In the silence, she went over the lines she'd drawn, pressing the nib of the pen harder into the paper.

'Mr Lomas,' she began. 'I'm of the mind that Mr Rivera can look after himself. He knows how to fight. Knows how to survive. You... don't.'

'None taken,' Lomas retorted.

'These are not good people. Understand?' she protested. 'Me getting a warrant is impossible – there are people who'll block me every step of the way.' She ground her teeth for an instant. 'I can't come with you and I won't be able to get there unless you call me claiming that one or both of your lives are in danger.'

'I'll keep you posted then,' the caller announced, a little admonished.

She nodded. 'Do.' Hanging the phone up, she gazed at the sun as it streamed through her blind-slatted window. Christie knew there was no way she'd be permitted to go to the depot.

She wondered whether she should head there all the same.

Chapter 37.

Roy, the mechanic, whimpered a little as he came to and realised the predicament he was in.

One moment he'd been stooped over, his head beneath the bonnet of a car, and the next he'd heard footsteps and a voice saying, 'excuse me.' But as he'd straightened himself up, a wrench had flashed towards him. In the split-second for which he saw it, he realised he was powerless to dodge out of the way. His knees had buckled on impact and he'd crashed onto the floor, descending into a dark fog.

Now, though, he was awake and in pain. 'Who are you?' he asked groggily. Every word stabbed; every syllable was an effort.

A well-dressed man with a swarthy complexion stood before him. His dark hair was parted immaculately and, as he looked at Roy, he began rolling up the sleeves of his shirt, holding two silver cufflinks between his teeth. His dark irises were small; they were entirely afloat in the milky whites of his unblinking eyes. It gave him the appearance of being sculpted. Unnatural.

'My name is Hakeem,' he announced, sniffing, after placing the cufflinks into his breast pocket. 'So?' he asked, raising his eyebrows.

'So fucking what?'

Silence.

'Those bikes.' The man in the suit began. 'Belong to who?'

The mechanic's head pounded. He tasted blood and wondered if he might vomit. 'Why?' he asked.

The man frowned. 'Look at yourself,' he ordered. 'Your – er – situation.'

Roy's hands were tied behind his back with an electrical cord. A further length of cord was tied around his neck. The other end of it was looped over one of the ceiling struts above. As Roy's eyes followed the taut line to the skylight above, he swayed slightly. His feet scrabbled for purchase and, he realised - to his horror - he was positioned right at the edge of the vehicle inspection pit.

'Your choice,' the man said quietly. 'But if you slip, then all will be over.'

Roy's eyes widened. His pulse quickened, and his gasping breath sounded ragged in his throat.

'The bikes' he pressed, 'belong to who?' As he spoke, he produced a toothpick, and began working it along the bottom row of his teeth. Roy was unable to gauge him. The confidence the man exuded was unbelievable to him. It was as if he knew Roy was bound to talk – his demeanour was relaxed; leisurely.

The mechanic began talking. 'Pugwash. Pluto. Popeye.'

The other man frowned. 'You are serious?'

'Yes,' gasped Roy. 'I don't know their real names. They...'

'... these men work for who?' The visitor interrupted, looking up as he finished picking at his teeth.

'Grizzly. And... Spice.'

'Where?' Hakeem rolled the toothpick back and forth between his fingers.

'Up on the hill. Denton Laine. The haulage place.'

The man nodded at this, thoughtful for a moment. 'Denton Laine,' he repeated to himself. 'And the soldier?'

'What soldier?'

Hakeem paused for a moment – he'd wait for confirmation on the third target. His understanding was that it was someone who'd been causing problems. An irritation.

'So you can let me go now, right?' Roy's words were panicked as he pirouetted on the spot, desperate to keep his footing. The sole of his foot slipped for a moment, then he regained his balance.

The man held his phone in one hand, scrolling across a map on the screen. Having typed the haulage company's name, he zoomed in on its footprint, looking closely at a detailed satellite view. As he did, he absent-mindedly shoved Roy with his other hand.

The mechanic's scream was stifled as the cord cut off his airway. In the next instant, it drew taut with a twanging sound; the bulk of Roy's body reached the low point of the curve. The metal ceiling strut creaked a little as his legs kicked out in a futile, twitching attempt to cling to life.

Placing his phone on a stool, the visitor calmly rolled his sleeves back down, taking his time as he replaced his cufflinks. The toothpick was now gripped in his mouth. He whistled tunelessly and checked his reflection in an unscrewed wing mirror. Then he picked up his phone.

As he left, he didn't look back at the lifeless body that now hung still, suspended above the pit. Hakeem had what he needed. The dead man would hardly imprint himself on his memory. He wasn't one to look back – he saw no value in it.

Chapter 38.

Serge Valais raised his eyebrows as Safia walked towards him. The meeting point on this occasion was just off the D35, close to Mayenne. The arrangement was always the same. He would be handed a large envelope stuffed full of cash. Then he would provide an escort. After that, he'd head to his favourite brothel and spend a sizeable chunk of the cash. Later, he'd buy a gift for his girlfriend to assuage his guilt. And then he'd fritter away the rest of the money online, gambling.

So far, it had been a foolproof system. If any of his colleagues ever grew suspicious about one of the vans carrying the cargo, he'd warn them off. It had never happened before, though – they travelled mainly in the daylight, and the vans were new enough not to raise suspicion. The only difference this time was that there were three vehicles instead of one. It wasn't enough to make them conspicuous, but Valais licked his lips: more vans meant more money.

Valais walked towards the figure who stepped out of the van.

It was a woman.

* * * * *

The rendezvous this time was the forecourt of an abandoned garage. It had been used until recently as a drive-through car wash, where illegal migrants would polish up vehicles for passers-by. The policeman had been responsible for closing it down. He'd also denied a permit to a would-be buyer. The place, he'd realised, would prove useful for exactly the kind of exchange he was engaged in now. Valais had made a gap in the high fence panels, and the vans had parked behind the former petrol station building, where they were all but invisible from the road.

'Monsieur Valais?' The woman asked.

'Yes,' the policeman nodded, looking the woman up and down. For an instant, he wondered if he might try his charms. But once he saw her properly, he abandoned the idea. He would be punching well above his weight. 'Why so many vans?'

The woman, who had been about to hand over the envelope, moved it back towards her. When she addressed the man, she did so in her second language – French. 'I am your contact, Monsieur Valais,' she announced. 'I pay your bills. I get to decide how many vans there are. One van. Three vans. Ten vans. It's all the same – your job is to do what you're fucking told. Understand?'

'I... but...' Valais stuttered.

'This conversation is being filmed and recorded,' Safia announced. 'The same is true of all your previous interactions with my organisation. So, if you value your employment as a law enforcement officer, then you'll cease your questions and do as you're told.' She paused and nodded at his badge. 'That Gendarmerie Nationale badge might mean something to your boyfriends back at base, but it doesn't mean shit to me. Not out here.'

Valais grimaced, and then nodded.

'So, your payment has been adjusted accordingly to better fit with the level of - er – risk.' She eyed him coldly. 'You will provide us with an escort. How many vans arrive at our meeting point is up to me. Always.' She paused, as a car on the D35 swept by. 'If you don't like our arrangement, then I will find another – shall we say *flexible* officer - who will be only too glad to accept my terms.' She eyed him coldly, then paused again. The policeman opened his mouth to begin speaking, but she cut him off once more.

'I will be accompanying the cargo today. All the way. We will be ready to depart in three minutes. Do we have an understanding?'

'Yes.' Valais paused, now sharply aware of the power dynamics at play. 'Ma'am.'

At this, she passed him the cash-filled envelope, turned and walked back to the lead van, her heels echoing from the roof covering the forecourt.

The shadows were beginning to lengthen.

Chapter 39.

Hakeem's car followed a similar vehicle up the hill. He hung back slightly, watching carefully; gaps in hedgerows revealed a patchwork quilt of summer fields in yellows and greens. The man had no interest in the scenery, though. His mind was solely focused on the mission. His eyes were glued to the other vehicle. The car handled well. It drove smoothly and made little noise, barely straining as it negotiated the steep gradient. Its air conditioning was almost Arctic, and a large interactive map beamed out from the dashboard, displaying the vehicle's progress as a moving dot.

As the two cars meandered up the steep road, Hakeem lost sight of the leading vehicle round a bend. He then spotted it again as it reappeared in the open. Given the lack of other traffic on the road, he suspected they might be heading to the same place. The Sat Nav map showed little of interest beyond the point he'd reached – indeed, the roads seemed to peter out into what looked like pencil-sketched cart tracks.

His suspicions were confirmed when he saw the vehicle indicating right as the road levelled out. The car ahead - like his - had tinted windows, so he was unable to see how many passengers it carried.

Or if it carried any at all.

Hakeem's initial plan had been to drive straight into the depot and act as an international trader. He had all the necessary accreditations - he could pose as pretty much anything if required. Looking as he did, and attired as he was, he was confident people would accept his alias. Of course, he might not get to meet the establishment's head immediately, but it would get him onsite.

In the end, though, he opted to wait.

The visitor drove past the site entrance, glancing back as the other car turned in. Heading along the road for a further half mile, it rose once more. He pulled over, driving a short way up a track made of compacted mud. Once the car was obscured behind a hedge, he cut the engine and climbed out. The foliage was not so thick that he couldn't see through it.

The depot was clearly visible. A butterfly landed on his lapel. He flicked it away onto the stony dust of the track. For a moment, he gazed at the impossible brilliance of its colours as it tried to right itself.

Then, he killed it.

* * * * *

The security guard approached the stationary black car and motioned for the driver to lower the window. Doffing his peaked hat in mock salute, the chauffeur gestured towards the back seat. Wheezing, the guard approached the passenger.

'Do you have an appointment, sir?' he enquired politely, peering inside.

'No.' The reply was forceful.

'No?' Frowning, the security guard stood upright, uncertain.

'No,' the passenger repeated. 'Nor do I require one - I am a representative of the tax office. This is a spot check and the precursor to a full audit.' The security guard leaned in as Rivera continued. 'I need to see a senior employee from the finance department, and I am authorised to make contact at any time.' The guard nodded; the man before him was well-dressed and clean shaven. His suit spoke of money, while the embossed identity card he waved looked irrefutable.

The guard gestured to his colleague, who raised the red and white barrier arm.

The car passed through.

* * * * *

Hakeem prided himself on his ability to read people and situations. He watched the delayed entry of the car through the barrier with interest. His military-grade binoculars rendered the scene in crystal clarity. There was nothing remarkable about the security guard - the way he carried himself suggested his bulk came from fat, not muscle. But when the passenger exited the rear of the car, something seemed wrong. Hakeem had not survived for as long as he had without noticing such things.

From his vantage point behind the hedge, Hakeem pondered the scene. Maybe it was the cut of the suit? It was expensive, but a suit of that quality would be tailored, and it didn't quite hang right. The man looked the part; he had a briefcase and some kind of accreditation looped around his neck, but those things meant nothing to the viewer. It was the brief pause that made him wonder. As the man left the car, he hesitated, as if considering whether to enter through the large, open warehouse door, or go to the hut marked *RECEPTION*.

Men who dressed like that, Hakeem reasoned, didn't hesitate. Ever. They simply marched into establishments as if they owned them. He'd made a living from reading people. It was that skill as much as anything else, which meant he'd stayed alive as long as he had. Sometimes, he mused, his eyes told him one thing while his gut told him another. And Hakeem trusted his gut. Always.

Also, while the movements of the security guard had meant he could be dismissed as a threat, there was a manner to the way the visitor carried himself, which suggested a rather more capable physique would be found under the expensively cut suit.

* * * * *

The journey from reception to the administrative level was swift. Rivera was ushered into a waiting room by a functionary and, a short time later, was escorted up the steps at the side of the warehouse, and onto the balcony housing the offices. He was careful not to appear familiar with the layout of the place.

Lomas had told him that all he would need to do was ask for the accounts and that the company was obliged to hand them over. And so far, things had played out exactly as predicted. An enthusiastic secretary gave him a warm welcome and showed him into a conference room at the far end of the corridor. The door bearing the sign *SAFETY EQUIPMENT MUST BE WORN BEYOND THIS POINT* was right next to him.

Rivera saw through the secretary's fawning; he knew she was playing for time on the orders of a higher power, but he smiled sweetly and went along with the charade. 'Are you sure it's safe to be here?' he'd joked, nodding at the sign on the door.

'Oh yes, sir. The chemicals have been decommissioned,' the secretary smiled. 'There's nothing through there now - we should be taking the warning sign down any day soon.' It was clearly a well-worn script she'd been briefed to follow.

Rivera nodded, playing the part of the concerned government employee. 'Have you ever seen what's on the other side?'

The secretary shook her head. 'I've never been authorised, sir.' She smiled again, changing the subject. 'Can I get you anything? Tea, coffee, water?'

The visitor shook his head. 'No - you'll just need to leave me in here for an hour or so, please.'

She nodded in reply, standing by the open door.

'Undisturbed,' he added, a serious note creeping into his voice.

'Of course.'

Rivera then made a play of squinting at the window. 'If you don't mind,' he began, 'I'd like those blinds closed, too. There's a glint coming off the table. It will disturb my work.'

As the secretary lowered the blinds, she spoke calmly. 'I'm sure you'll find everything above board, sir. Our record-keeping here is meticulous. We can give you access to our cloud storage too, but you will need to give us 24 hours' notice in writing for that to happen. I'm sure you're aware of this already?'

He nodded, and then his eye caught sight of the security camera on the wall. 'That will need to be disconnected too,' he announced, pointing at it.

'But...'

'Government regulations, I'm afraid.' He raised the fake accreditation that was looped around his neck on a lanyard. 'I'm just doing my job.'

As he strode over and yanked the plug out of the socket, the secretary protested lightly. Rivera didn't care. He knew the office staff would comply with him. But he had no interest in that. The box of files that had been moved onto the table in the conference room had doubtless been doctored for the purposes of any unwanted inspections like this. They were irrelevant anyway - there would be no clues within. He was sure of that. The main reason for disconnecting the camera wasn't because it would portray what he was doing; it was because it would show who he was. As far as possible, he wanted to keep people guessing – for now.

All he wanted was the opportunity to get through the door.

Having drawn a blank everywhere else, he had to know what lay beyond it.

* * * * *

Shortly after Hakeem had taken up his position behind the hedge, things began to happen.

He kept watch through his binoculars as three men approached the parked black car. They were dressed in dark clothes and walked with an officious air.

This was unremarkable.

What was more remarkable was that each of them carried a gun. They didn't do so with the calm assurance of those familiar with firearms. But, a gun was a gun.

Hakeem watched with interest as the three men removed the driver from the car. They were unhurried as they made him place his hands on the bonnet of the vehicle. Going through his pockets, the first man removed various items and handed them to his colleague.

After that, they cuffed the man's wrists behind him and conveyed him towards the building. One of them gripped his arm to prevent him from falling.

Hakeem raised his eyebrows. He knew from long experience that plans didn't last long once the target was encountered. The job of the soldier on the ground was to be flexible.

To watch. To wait. To adapt.

His orders were simple: kill the two brothers.

Nobody ever told him why. Or how.

He wouldn't have cared, anyway.

* * * * *

Ten minutes into the façade of his accounts audit, Rivera moved over to the door of the conference room. In the centre of the table, documents were piled. They were clearly set aside for such purposes – little better than stage props. He listened for a moment. Then, he slowly moved the blinds apart, just enough for him to peer through.

There was nobody outside.

He opened the door a crack, placing a miniature mirror just beyond the frame. The view it gave him was hazy, but it was clear enough to show that the balcony was empty. Rivera knew the boss' secretary would have her door open and would be watching the corridor beyond it to see if he passed. However, the company would want to appear nonchalant - as if it had nothing to hide. Therefore, they were never going to post a sentry directly outside the conference room.

It was all the chance Rivera needed.

He risked a glance over his shoulder, and then hurried out into the corridor and tried the handle of the door.

It opened.

* * * * *

Hakeem was tempted to go straight to the depot. Now that he'd seen the guns, he realised he would have to modify his approach. He would always back himself in a gunfight, but he also knew he might risk heading into a bloodbath. And bloodbaths created headlines.

The reason he made the money he did was because he was subtle. Discreet even.

He didn't leave clues.

He didn't do things that would make the authorities become interested. Bloodbaths were all well and good, but if they could be avoided, he avoided them. It wasn't a moral consideration - he had no issue with death. He simply wanted to make things as easy for himself as possible.

He opted to stay where he was.

If in doubt, wait.

Watch.

Once he had spotted the armed men, Hakeem understood that he might not be starting a war anyway. He realised it might be that the war had already begun. If he was clever about it, he reasoned, there was a chance he might be able to turn the sides against one another. And if he was fortunate, he might even be able to get them to do his job for him. He knew what civil war was like. He was well aware of the chaos it created. If – he reasoned – he could stay on the periphery, he might be able to strike at exactly the right time. If he was lucky.

Hakeem didn't believe in luck.
But he wouldn't turn his back on it if it happened to come his way.

* * * * *

Beyond the door, Rivera found another door. And beyond that, another one. Then, he found himself in a dormitory. The door opening on to this was thick and heavy. Looking at the other side of it, Rivera saw that it had no keyhole - it was designed to keep people from passing through. He reached down and grabbed a fire extinguisher, propping it open.

Inside, the room was lined with beds. Each was set a small distance apart from the next one. The beds all had low tables beside them and tall, narrow cupboards that stood behind, positioned against the wall. A mirror was tacked to the door of each. He frowned. It resembled a hostel of some sort, but it clearly wasn't for workers at the depot.

The far end of the room had another door which couldn't be opened from the inside either. Towards the rear, on the far side, was a bank of sinks. And beyond that were showers and toilets.

It was a prison.

But it was light, and it was airy. The sheets on the beds looked clean and freshly laundered. As Rivera explored further, he saw there was a long table and what looked like a service hatch built into the wall. He rattled at it, but - like the doors – it couldn't be opened from the inside.

At the very back of the room was a long rail. Attached to it were hundreds of coat hangers. The coat hangers held clothes.

Women's clothes.

This was, Rivera reasoned, not a sweatshop. It wasn't a brothel, either. It looked, instead, to be some kind of holding pen. Somewhere comfortable enough to keep people for short periods of time. For processing, perhaps? Or, possibly, for other, darker uses.

He absentmindedly placed a hand on the rail. Then he turned. Footsteps were approaching.

* * * * *

'Surprise!' A small man walked through the door holding a pistol aimed squarely at Rivera's face. He strode in with the self-assurance of one who knew his position was all but unassailable.

Behind him came a distraught Lomas, pushed along by two other men, his hands cuffed.

Rivera looked around for something to serve as a weapon, but drew a blank.

'They call me Spice,' the man announced, his voice echoing through the empty room. 'But I think you knew that already. You see, you've been asking lots of silly fucking questions.' He was smug and self-confident, entirely at ease with where he was.

'So?' Rivera shrugged.

'So this is a Heckler and Koch 45 Compact.' He held up the weapon. 'I've found out a bit about you too, you see? You're ex-military. So you know how good these guns are. You know what they can do.'

'So?'

'Well,' he sighed. 'I could show you if you like, but I don't think there's any need. It'll fucking cut you in half. So, walk here slowly and then lie yourself down on the floor over here, with your fingers laced together behind your head. Do it, and you live – for now. Don't, and I'll shoot you.' He shrugged.

Rivera, not having any other option, did as he was ordered. He made a show of limping and wincing as he moved to make it appear as though he were injured. As he approached Lomas, the other man looked ashen-faced.

'I told Christie,' he said. 'I know you said to wait, but...'

'Good lad,' the ex-soldier nodded, smiling warmly at his acquaintance. 'You did the right thing.'

Spice looked on, laughing. 'And you think that woman will save you, boys? You forget who owns all the coppers in this town! You're either dumb or fucking stupid. Or both.' He paused. 'No one's going to save you now. Not unless I change my mind... and I won't.'

Chapter 40.

Mustafa flicked the butt of his cigarette into the water. He was standing at the helm of a high-powered boat which was anchored in the shallows. That there were more vans than usual was something of a surprise. What was more surprising was that Safia had climbed out of one of them. Previously, the French coastline had been far beyond her limits. She'd always employed a go-between to deal with Valais and the rest of the transport. Her turning up on the shore was not a normal occurrence.

Mustafa raised his eyebrows as she climbed aboard the boat. It had been a long time since he'd seen her, but he said nothing.

She paid him not to ask questions. Ever. He simply lit another cigarette and counted how many girls climbed out of the van.

The boat's mooring was down the coast from Dinard. It was far enough away from any tourist beaches that people wouldn't pay attention, but close enough to the road that shifting goods was easy. It was the place they'd always used – so far, so good.

Safia's drivers unloaded the cargo from the three vans. The young women, uncertain, made their way over the rough ground. They'd been promised new lives and riches. They still thought of Britain as being some kind of promised land. There was just enough of the façade of those promises remaining that they didn't run, but even the most optimistic of them were beginning to wonder how far the promises and dreams they'd been sold back on Lampedusa were from the truth.

'Quickly,' Mustafa hissed between his teeth, turning his attention away from the drivers and towards those disembarking from the vehicles. His tone was urgent, but not angry. The road was quiet. It was the dead of night, but he'd scouted the inlet as he always did. There were no late night fishing parties; no wild swimmers; no drunken teenagers enjoying barbecues. It was deserted. Just the slow lapping of waves and the moonlight glinting on the water.

The boat was fast. It was an offshore cruiser. The kind of toys that rich men moor at marinas in expensive locales to show off their wealth. This boat, though, was a working vessel. It might have looked pretty on the outside, but the interior was fitted for fast travel across oceans. Built for speed, not comfort. Decked out to maximise profits.

As the young women climbed the gangplank, they were ushered onto bench seats that lined the edges of the hull. He held a finger to his lips as they clambered aboard.

'Any more?' Mustafa asked, speaking in the dialect Safia and he had grown up with.

'Don't get sarcastic with me!' she hissed, narrowing her eyes.

'What? I...'

'...I know what you meant, you fucking idiot,' she replied sharply.

'What?' he enquired defensively. 'If I'd known you were bringing this many, I'd have done two trips. I've only just got enough life jackets.'

Safia laughed. 'Lifejackets? If this boat goes down, then none of them are going to get saved. You know that much – they might talk.'

Mustafa shrugged.

'Shut up and drive,' she ordered. The merest hint of a smile played across her face. She thrust a handful of banknotes into his outstretched hand.

'The usual?' he asked.

She nodded.

'Er...' he hesitated. 'Are you staying on board?'

'You're wondering why, aren't you?' She looked hard at him.

'Well... it's not like this is a pleasure cruise,' he shrugged. 'I mean – if you're going all the way, then what are you going to do at the other end?'

She paused. 'Remember what we used to say when we were kids?'

Mustafa paused and looked out over the water as a fish broke the surface. He spoke quietly. 'I against my brother. I and my brother against my cousin. I, my brother, and my cousin against the world.' His voice intoned, almost like a mantra. It was an utterance that spoke of long ago. Far away.

'That's right,' she nodded sagely. 'Just like always.'

'Has somebody wronged you, cousin?' he enquired.

'You could say that.' She nodded, grimacing. As she did, thin lines grew visible around the corners of her eyes. 'Anyway, enough fucking chatter. Are we ready?'

He nodded, making his way back to the helm. She walked in the other direction until she reached the prow.

Moments later, the large engines lumbered into life and he eased the vessel away from the shore. The whole operation, from arrival to departure, had taken a little over seven minutes. Once they were rounding the headland, the pilot looked back and saw the headlights of the vans switch on as they turned, making their way back onto the coastal road to travel the return leg towards Paris.

He turned his face north. On a night like this, with little swell, the journey would be fast. If things went according to plan, they would intercept the other vessel around four in the morning. Stuffing a plug of tobacco into his cheek, he thought about his cousin. What she'd told him was far too enigmatic for his liking. Mustafa was a man of simple pleasures; he disliked things growing complicated. The pair of them took enough risks as it was. And, with her aboard alongside him, the risks seemed so much worse. She may well have been his cousin, but it didn't make her any less terrifying.

She was - he reminded himself – always unpredictable. He didn't much like to think about what she was capable of if pushed. He remembered how they'd strung a boy up from a neighbouring village when they were children. It was a joke – at least that's what Mustafa had thought until Safia kicked away the stool on which he stood. He vividly recalled the boy's worried smile – a grin borne of thinking his tormentors would see sense at any moment – vanishing. His horrified expression was then accompanied by a choking noise as he grabbed at the frayed rope. It had been Safia who'd dragged at his feet, cackling delightedly as the life was throttled from him.

He knew that, whatever it was she had planned, it would not end well for someone. Deep down, he just hoped he would emerge unscathed. He had an appointment near La Rochelle in a week's time. A chance to leave behind this business once and for all.

When he'd first started working with Safia, he'd been penniless. He'd had no choice. Now, he had more money than he'd ever dreamed of having. It was enough for him. But it wasn't enough for her. He knew that now.

Nothing would ever be enough for her.

And when she had a look in her eye like she did tonight, she reminded him of a cornered animal. If she felt like she was under threat, then she'd fight to the death. The way she'd spoken, she sounded like she was on high alert. He spat over the side, remembering how small and innocent the boy they'd left hanging from the lamppost had looked.

Someone must have crossed her, he mused.

Pity the fool.

* * * * *

Two hours later, the vessel powered past the Channel Islands. The twinkling lights of Jersey and Guernsey appeared on the starboard side of the *Arabia* as she scythed her way through the gentle waves. Mustafa stuffed a fresh plug of chewing tobacco into his mouth, wedging it between his teeth and his cheek. It was too breezy to enjoy a cigarette, but the tobacco would give his system the surge of stimulants he craved. As he spat across the side of the boat, he caught sight of his cousin at the prow. She was standing, statuesque, staring out at a distant green light across the water.

She hadn't moved for nearly an hour except on a single occasion when she reached for her phone. She tapped at the screen for a moment and then tucked it back into a pocket.

It happened only once.

That made him nervous.

Whatever thoughts were spiralling through her mind, they were not being lightened by the luminescent moon. The night was calm, but within her, a storm was clearly brewing. Standing there, she looked like a hunter. What worried him was wondering who her prey might be.

The radio crackled for the first time since they'd set out.

It was the other boat. Echoes from the distant shore ahead. Contact had been established.

Chapter 41.

Lomas was worried. But nobody gets imprisoned in a shipping container without getting worried. A weak light shone into his cell through an exterior grille. He'd listened intently to the strange noises from outside, and had risen into an approximation of a fighting stance whenever he heard footsteps. By this stage in proceedings, though, he was no longer attempting a brave face; he'd graduated to feeling scared.

All afternoon, the container had been in the direct sun. The two inhabitants only had a bottle of water between them. That had been bad enough, but Lomas felt - somehow - that if he was with Rivera, he might have a chance. The man had seemed superhuman when he'd watched him in action against the bikers before. It had been that which had initially given him a sense of hope.

But those had been fistfights. When the pistol was levelled at him, he'd shrugged and submitted.

'Wise choice,' the man known as Spice had nodded. 'Maybe you're not so fucking stupid after all?'

Instead of cuffing him as he might have expected, the man had jabbed the ex-soldier in the neck with a syringe while his two accomplices took an arm each. Whatever the liquid was that had coursed through the man's body, it took only seconds to knock him unconscious. As Rivera's legs crumpled, Lomas tensed. Ready for his dose.

'No, no, sweet cheeks!' Spice had chuckled. 'We don't need to knock you out. You look like a fucking fairy. We only need to incapacitate the ones who pose a threat. As long as you keep your mouth shut, then we'll have no worries about you. You don't look like you could fight your way out of a wet paper bag!'

Lomas' face burned. He didn't know what was worse - the fact he was considered so impotent a fighter, or the fact that - secretly - he was relieved they didn't want to inject him. He was scared of needles, after all. Moments later, they'd bundled him into the container with the snoring Rivera, and slid a bottle of mineral water across the steel floor. Then they'd cranked the handle shut.

Quietly sweating, the journalist's brother felt bile rising. It was partly due to the hopeless situation he was now in, and partly due to the dawning realisation that this was similar to the fate his sibling must have suffered.

His demise would doubtless mirror hers.

* * * * *

It wasn't until later in the day, though, that Lomas truly gave up hope.

As the daylight dimmed, footsteps approached the container from the tarmac outside. Its handle was wrenched open once more. The door swung wide, and the shrill voice of a woman became audible. She protested at the handling she was receiving.

When the door shut behind her, she trapped her foot in it, preventing it from closing.

'Move it!' Spice growled. 'Or you'll fucking lose it.'

'You don't fucking scare me!' Lois Christie's voice was laced with venom as she stood silhouetted in the doorway, her back to Lomas.

'Yeah, right,' Spice scoffed. 'Big fucking words.'

'You won't get away with this, you know?' the Detective Inspector protested. 'I've informed my superiors. They'll have a squad up here in no time.'

Spice paused for a moment. 'But your superiors are going to be chasing their tails for months, darling. Beatty has buried all the paperwork. By the time they catch up, you'll be long gone. I mean... forever kind of gone. So make the most of your last few fucking hours here. Bitch.'

With this, he shoved her through the door, where she landed awkwardly on the floor. It was only as her eyes grew accustomed to the light that she perceived her fellow inmates.

'You?' she began. 'And him?' She nodded, indicating the slumbering figure who lay propped up against the side of the container. 'But...'

'I thought you were going to get us out of here?' Lomas frowned.

'So did I,' she replied through gritted teeth. 'But they got me at the station. It was that bastard Beatty – he's in their pocket, clearly. I should have guessed it was him. He told me I had a visitor. Said it was a young woman who'd been violated and would only talk to a female officer.'

'And you believed him?'

'Well,' she sighed. 'I never trusted him exactly, but I charged in there without a second thought. Of course I did. And when I opened the door...'

'... let me guess. A welcoming committee?'

'Yeah. Spice and one of his fucking hard men.' She shook her head ruefully. 'They bundled me out of the back door and the next thing I know - I'm here.' She kicked against the wall of the container, hissing.

Lomas stared at her. 'You know... I really think this might have been what happened to my sister. And now we have no way out. Nobody knows we're here. We...'

'Never mind about that!' She cut him off. 'We need to find a way out of all this, so stop bloody moping. That won't do us any good.'

The contrast between his inertia and her energy was pronounced.

Silence.

'Who knows we're here?' she asked.

Lomas thought for a moment. 'Just us three,' he replied morosely. 'As far as I know, that is.'

'Dammit!' Christie stamped on the floor in frustration. As she did, a sliver of rusted steel became slightly dislodged. She kicked it a few more times. Then she began to wrench at it.

'What are you doing?' he enquired.

'Well, we can't just do nothing,' she exclaimed. 'If I'm going to die, then at least I want to go down fighting.' She straightened, holding the shard of metal aloft in triumph before gesturing towards the inert Rivera. 'What about Sleeping bloody Beauty down there?' she enquired. 'How long has he been out of it?'

Lomas shrugged. 'Maybe three hours.'

She nodded, and walked over to the unconscious man, placing her fingers on his neck to take his pulse. 'Well,' she reported. 'His heart's still beating like a sledgehammer. But whatever it is - if it's been strong enough to put him under for three hours - then it'll probably be strong enough to keep him under for another couple at least.'

Sitting down, Christie reached over and sipped from the bottle of water. 'We'd better ration this,' she advised. She looked hard at him. 'Do you have any bright ideas?'

Lomas shook his head. 'I was rather hoping that telling *you* was my bright idea.'

She held the lukewarm bottle against her forehead and sighed. 'Well... whatever they're planning on doing to us, I'd say they've done it before.' She paused. 'I reckon they're pretty confident about not getting caught. These are bad men; they've abducted a police officer in broad daylight.' She paused. 'I think we can assume this is pretty much life or death – so we need to bloody do something.'

'You're not making me feel much better,' Lomas said glumly.

'No - but when people do the same thing time and again, they get lazy. They get complacent. They make mistakes. It's human nature. Human error. It might only be for a split-second - but that might be all the chance we get. So keep your eyes open and be ready.'

'To do what?'

She handed the makeshift knife to him. 'Take this,' she ordered. 'They'll know I've had weapons training. But you...' she regarded him and shook her head.

'Fuck's sake! People are full of compliments today,' Lomas grumbled. 'Even locked up in here.'

'Just shut up and stuff it inside your shirt. Try and wedge it under your arm. That way you might still be able to reach it even if they cuff your hands behind your back again.'

Lomas nodded. 'What do we do now?'

Christie shrugged. 'We wait. And when the time comes, we fight like crazy. That's all we can do.'

Chapter 42.

With sunset, the container darkened completely. Lomas and Christie kept up a whispered conversation at first, but they soon settled on bouts of silence. Periodically, she would stand up and slam her boot against the container's sides. But then she'd sit once more, brooding.

'You said they'll make a mistake?' Lomas repeated, his voice hoarse.

'Guaranteed,' she replied. In the darkness, he couldn't read her expression to gauge how much she meant what she said. 'It's whether or not we get to capitalise on it. That's the question.'

In the dark, Lomas nodded. A thin finger of moonlight played between the bars of the grille. He peered up at it. As he did, his mind wandered; it seemed strange that the moon could look down with such indifference. He pondered how many deaths it might be staring at during that exact moment. With each passing minute, his heartbeat raised. His senses felt alert.

Rivera, meanwhile, continued to snore.

* * * * *

It was an hour later that footsteps again sounded outside. Accompanying them was the whine of an electrical engine. A grating noise sounded, and something juddered the crate's interior. Both Lomas and Christie gripped at the walls as their prison rocked like a room in an earthquake.

'What the hell's that?' hissed Lomas.

'Forklift prongs,' Christie replied.

'How do you know?'

'What else would they be?' she sniffed.

Moments later, with a whir of hydraulic gears, they felt themselves being jolted and then lifted through the air as the forklift's arms gained purchase on the container.

It was at this instant Rivera began to come round, groggily enquiring where he was.

'We're in a steel container,' Lomas explained quickly. 'They knocked you out. Christie's with us.'

'We think they're going to take us down to the shore,' Christie added. 'It doesn't look good.' She paused before continuing morosely. 'It actually looks fucking terrible.'

'Huh?' Rivera replied sleepily. 'I forgot to feed my cat.'

'Your cat?' Lomas frowned.

'Who cares about your bloody cat?' Christie spat.

'I do,' the ex-soldier said bluntly. He then continued, in a disinterested tone. 'Anyway, Detective Inspector – you know what happens in Armageddon?' The ex-soldier paused. 'How about it?'

'Fuck you!' Christie spat, laughing despite herself. 'This is like the least horny situation ever.'

'I don't know...' Rivera said pensively. 'Anyway, have you guys figured out a plan to get us out of here yet, then?'

'Lomas has a knife - of sorts,' Christie explained quietly.

'Well, that's better than nothing,' Rivera replied, laughing drily. 'Anyone got a drink?'

Christie handed him the water.

'What's going to happen to us?' Lomas wailed. He'd banked on feeling better once Rivera was awake.

He didn't.

Silence fell for a moment and then the trio felt the container being slapped down onto a surface. They were thrown bodily upwards – the jolt rattled through their bones, and Lomas tasted blood where he'd bitten his tongue. A metal clang echoed.

'Well...' Rivera began, calmly. 'I hate to break it to you, but I reckon they've put us on the back of a truck. I'd say they'll be thinking about driving us to the coast. After that, they'll put us on a boat, and after that, my guess is they'll try to drown us.' He paused. 'So make the most of taking it easy - the fun and games aren't too far away.'

'What?' hissed Lomas, his voice barely more than a whisper.

'You up for some fighting?' Christie asked.

'Should be,' Rivera answered. 'You sure I can't tempt you into anything else?'

'Let me refer you to my previous answer,' Christie shot back angrily.

Silence.

Rivera spoke once more. 'They'll tie me up. They'll tie us all up, I should think. These guys know what they're doing, don't they? They're not going to take any chances.'

'But they'll make a mistake,' Christie protested, her tone less certain than before. 'People like them always do.'

'Yeah?' Rivera laughed drily. 'If you say so.'

Chapter 43.

'Shall I rush at them?' Lomas whispered as the footsteps approached the door. The interior of the container seemed to shrink for a moment – it was as if the three inhabitants breathing in simultaneously somehow dragged the walls closer. Someone had climbed up onto the flatbed of the truck where the steel box now sat, and had started pulling at the handle of the container.

Rivera waited until the handle was being cranked before replying. 'No - don't be stupid,' he hissed. 'Bide your time. Otherwise, they'll just break your legs.'

Once the door swung open, the container's inhabitants had to shield their eyes against the glare of the flashlights. It was clearly a technique their captors had used before.

'Wakey, wakey losers!' a voice rang out.

Silence.

'Kneel down!' Spice barked. On either side of him stood a dark figure brandishing a gun. 'Lace your fingers behind your heads. Or Wozza here will blow your fucking heads off.'

The three captives did as instructed, muttering curses as they lowered themselves.

Spice remained by the door as his two men made a beeline for Rivera. One stood in front of him while the other stepped behind, raised the butt of his rifle, and clubbed the ex-soldier in the back. He fell, winded, and the pair pinned his arms behind his back, swiftly cuffing him with plastic cable ties.

Having witnessed the other man's fate, Lomas put up little resistance. Christie, though, unleashed a stream of fiery invective, grabbing at the guard's collar before he wrenched her arm behind her so hard she yelped.

From the doorway, Spice laughed. 'You're a feisty one, aren't you?' he chuckled. 'Shame...'

'What the fuck do you mean?' Christie snarled.

'Now, now,' Spice chuckled. 'Protect and serve. Uphold the law. Be nice and polite and all that bollocks.'

'Fuck you!' Christie spat.

Silence.

'I mean,' Spice announced. 'It's a shame - you're the kind of girl that I might not have minded fooling around with.' He let his comment hang in the air for a moment. 'But in a little while, you'll be at the bottom of the ocean where you fucking belong. Just like this twat's bitch sister.'

'Dead?' Lomas frowned.

'Of course she's bloody dead, dumbass. Just like you will be.' Spice shook his head disdainfully. 'Unless you've grown gills since we put you in here.' One of his henchmen laughed.

'Why, though?' Rivera asked.

'Why not?' Spice shrugged.

'Well... me,' Rivera began. 'I get it. I'm annoying. I beat up your boyfriends...'

'Shut the fuck up!' Spice growled. 'I'll fucking club you myself next time.'

'What difference would it make?' Rivera sighed. He paused. 'But these two.' He indicated Lomas and Christie with a nod of his head. 'What have they done?'

'You know...' Spice began calmly, 'I'm an organised kind of guy. Clean. Fastidious. I don't like loose ends. And they're loose ends. Him,' he indicated Lomas, 'because he's as bad as his whore of a sister.' He nodded towards Christie. 'And her, because she won't keep her fucking nose out of what doesn't concern her.' Spice looked directly at her as he spoke, a snarling expression on his face.

'Oh, and that's it, is it?' Christie's voice rose angrily. 'You can't bear to lose so...'

'... that's right.' Spice interrupted, smirking.

'This is the *law*!' she protested. 'You're thinking about killing a serving officer. You know what that means?'

Spice shrugged. 'You know, dear, I tend to believe that the letter of the law is best enforced by the person holding the gun. Don't you think?' He shook his head, tutting. 'You see – as far as I'm concerned – the moment they started having female coppers, society was shafted.'

'You're a madman!' All of Lomas' suppressed rage rose up within his venomous cry.

Spice grinned. 'Is that the best you can do, posh boy?' he sneered. 'Listen – tomorrow night I'm going to a charity auction at the golf club. I'm going to spend a shitload of money, and then everyone'll think I'm a humanitarian hero.' He laughed. 'My plan is to get good and drunk and then bang a barmaid or two – once they get dollar signs in their eyes, they're always easy meat.' He smiled again. 'I might even spare a thought for the three of you. But don't hold your breath!'

Silence fell on the container once more. Behind his back, Rivera relaxed his arms. He'd tensed them the moment he'd heard the cable ties being tightened and had kept them clenched ever since. There was a tiny amount of give between the plastic and his skin. It was, he hoped, better than nothing.

'It's time, lads,' Spice announced to his goons. 'Let's get this done, shall we?'

He looked hard at the prisoners. 'Gag them.' Christie took a breath to protest. Spice noticed. 'Make that one especially tight.' He grinned; the officer's eyes widened in pain as a rag was stuffed harshly into her mouth.

Chapter 44.

Through his binoculars, and later with a pair of night vision goggles, Hakeem had watched the scene unfolding with interest. Insects flitted around him, and the distant drone of a tractor ploughing a field came to him across the hillside. Once darkness fell, its floodlights occasionally flashed across the sky. It remained faraway, though. All the while, the watcher remained hidden in his nook. He witnessed the three captives being incarcerated in the shipping container and remained where he was.

Watching.

The sun blazed down upon his head as he'd remained there throughout the afternoon.

It didn't bother him, though. He'd been in hotter places before. And patience was a quality he possessed in bulk. That the loading of the captives had taken place in broad daylight told him how confident the captors were of avoiding detection.

As the night had drawn in further, he'd imagined he would have to advance to the depot. The brothers were not going to seek him out. They didn't know he existed. But he had a job to do, and he didn't want to waste any more time than was absolutely necessary. He had unfinished business in Berlin. And he fancied a trip to Mauritius.

It was time for him to act.

Then, though, the yard leapt into action. He watched the scene before him – illuminated by the depot's security lights: the small man emerged from inside with his henchmen and supervised the loading of the container onto the back of a truck. Hakeem had then watched how the man in command climbed onto the flatbed and addressed his captives.

At the last moment, a huge man joined them, climbing into the cab of the truck. However, he then changed his mind and retreated into the warehouse, speaking back over his shoulder.

Hakeem had seen all he needed to see. There would have been no point revealing his existence before he'd found his targets. But the two men's appearances matched the descriptions he'd been given exactly. He walked over to his parked car, ready to move.

That was the moment when the phone in his pocket buzzed. He reached for it, shielding its glare lest anyone should spot the glow.

The message was brief. There was only one number in the phone anyway:

S.

Messages from it were always blunt.

TERRA FIRMA TOMORROW. TAKE THE SOLDIER TOO.

Hakeem frowned, pocketing his phone. In the distance, the large engine of the truck spluttered into life. He watched as it slowly pulled out of the yard, and then traced its progress by the dancing of its headlights as it wound its way down the darkened hillside.

The plan had changed.

Chapter 45.

The trucking compound was quiet as Hakeem approached. He'd toyed with the idea of bringing his car, but had decided against it. It remained hidden beside the vantage point where he'd spent most of the day. If he had to shoot his way out, he'd simply take one of the vehicles that now littered the yard.

He wasn't particular about such things.

Growing up where he'd grown up and at the time he did meant Hakeem wasn't particular about anything. He knew that whatever wealth he managed to accrue might just as easily vanish tomorrow. When you've seen most of your family killed before your eyes. When you've grown up hungry. When you've grown up poor. When you've slept on the earthen floor of a stone hut and watched as warplanes swoop down through your valley like deadly eagles, then you understand how cheap life is. You realise how fleeting existence can be. You know that, just because you have something one day, it doesn't mean you'll have it the next.

People live.

People die.

Plans change.

Hakeem shrugged. The rental Mercedes was a pleasant perk of the job. But it belonged to someone else. He was simply the custodian.

He reached into his pocket. The Star 30M was his. At least it was his preferred *model* of weapon; he hadn't been able to transport his own version into the country. The substitute had been waiting for him in his hotel room when he arrived – he always requested the same make and model. Hakeem didn't know exactly how Safia secured such firearms in a weaponless country. But he knew that it came down to money.

It always did.

*****

Hakeem crossed the empty yard. There was nobody there. Even if there had been, he was sure he'd have been able to progress unnoticed. If you grow up on the margins of society, you learn to turn it into a strength. You learn to switch on a cloak of invisibility whenever you require it. Walking over to the black car he'd seen arriving earlier, he inspected it briefly, picking up a couple of discarded cable ties from where the captives had been cuffed previously.

Waste not. Want not. Usually, Hakeem found the buoyant rhythm of English idioms irritating. Here, though, the brevity was appealing.

He strolled across the floor of the depot. The place stank of engine oil. Moving out of the shadows cast by a stack of crates, he stepped into a pool of light. But there was no reaction. He wondered if he'd encounter a shout. Or a shot. But it dawned on Hakeem that there would be no reaction, and he smiled grimly as further idioms came to mind - this was a ghost town. This was Dunsinane Castle, with Macbeth awaiting his fate. The circus had left town.

Looking up, he saw a light in one of the banks of windows that stretched along a balcony above. Everything else was in darkness. In a calm, unhurried fashion, he made his way over towards the end of the giant, hangar-like space and began to climb the stairs. He still walked with caution, checking for unseen threats. But the place was deserted. Hakeem could tell. The presence of another human changes a place. Their breathing alters the atmosphere; their energy burns. It was something the assassin was finely attuned to. A sixth sense. But there was no buzzing or sparking of energy in the building. He was confident of that.

Hakeem pulled out the pistol.

*****

'I thought you'd gone already,' Grizzly grumbled. He was bent over the open drawer of a filing cabinet, rifling through papers with his back to the door as Hakeem entered.

The visitor said nothing.

'What's going on...?' Grizzly paused as he turned, taking in the situation. He cast his eyes around the room quickly.

'If you're looking for a weapon,' Hakeem announced coldly, 'forget about it.'

'Who the fuck are you?' Grizzly growled. He breathed in, puffed his chest out, and looked ready to charge at the other man. Then he eyed the Star 30M and thought better of it.

'Not important,' the visitor replied. He threw the cable ties onto the other man's desk. They landed with a gentle, skittering noise, like an escaping arachnid.

Grizzly looked at them, sniffed, and shrugged. 'What the fuck do I need them for?'

'You need to fasten one of them around your wrists,' the man explained calmly. The whites of his eyes glowed, unblinking.

'How?' Grizzly complained, sensing an opportunity. 'Aren't you going to fasten them for me?'

'What do you think I am? An amateur?' Most of the time, Hakeem's accent was almost imperceptible. But it bled through slightly with his irritation. 'Do it yourself. Now.'

Grizzly sighed, fastened the cable tie and then tightened it with his teeth.

'Tighter,' Hakeem demanded.

Grizzly muttered bitterly, but did as he was told, wary of the pistol pointing at him.

'Now,' Hakeem ordered. 'Move everything from the desk - so it's a clear surface.'

'Everything?' The big man frowned.

'Everything.'

'But that lamp cost a grand.'

'I'm not playing games, Mr...'

'Naylor.' Grizzly plonked his tied arms down on the desk and, in one broad movement, swept everything from its surface. A sheaf of paper splayed out across the floor, and the lamp clattered, its bulb shattering. The phone receiver hung on its wire, swinging back and forth, and an array of expensive pens bounced on the carpet. 'Happy now?' he enquired bitterly as silence returned to the room.

'Very,' Hakeem nodded, speaking tonelessly. 'Now... the three prisoners. Who are they?'

'I don't know what the fuck you're talking about...' the big man replied sullenly.

Hakeem sighed. 'I advise you to talk. And... if you don't feel like talking, then I have ways of making sure you change your mind.' He paused, eyeing the other man with contempt. 'That is not a threat. It is a promise.'

Grizzly stared back, his eyes boring beams of hatred across the room. Then he sighed. 'Detective Inspector Lois Christie,' he began.

'Man?'

'Woman.'

'Job?'

'Police.'

Hakeem whistled through his teeth and then chuckled a little. 'Brave man. Not clever though - this thing you are running here. You know police hunt in packs, don't you? If you get rid of one, they have an annoying habit of reappearing. And there are more of them than you.'

Grizzly shrugged.

'And who else?' Hakeem pressed.

'Why should I tell you?'

'Because I have a gun, my friend.'

The big man sighed. 'Lomas - Eddie Lomas.'

'And why is he here?'

'He's the brother of a journalist who caused us problems a while ago.'

'This is good,' Hakeem nodded. 'You are cooperating.' He smiled sweetly, his lack of regard for his counterpart clear, nonetheless. His eyes showed none of the warmth his voice seemed to hold. 'And the third?'

Grizzly paused. Hakeem waved the gun as if in encouragement. 'Rivera,' the big man began. 'He's a soldier - used to be. I don't know why he's here. Don't know who he's working for. Don't really know anything about him – I've never spoken to him face-to-face.' He sighed and carried on, almost in admiration. 'That one's a tough sonofabitch. He's caused us real problems.'

Hakeem did not react. 'Where are they taking them?'

Grizzly narrowed his eyes. 'None of your fucking business.'

Hakeem smiled thinly. 'Who's Spice – the leader?'

'Fuck you,' he announced, half laughing. 'I'm not giving you anything else.'

Silence.

'You have enemies, yes?'

'Everyone has enemies.' Grizzly paused. 'Who sent you? Safia?'

Hakeem went on, ignoring the question. 'Business is business, my friend. Everyone wants pieces of the pie.'

The big man shrugged.

Hakeem chewed his lip for a moment, pensive, scanning the room. 'Is that him?' He indicated a framed photograph hanging on the wall. It depicted the two brothers standing on either side of a local dignitary, presenting an oversize cheque. Each was smiling.

Grizzly shrugged.

'So why aren't you on the boat?'

The big man looked back in vague amusement. 'I quit.'

'There is saying where I come from,' Hakeem began.

'That so?' Grizzly's tone was one of disinterest.

'I and my brother against my cousin. I, my brother, and my cousin against the world.' Hakeem smiled.

'So?'

'So, you screwed up.' As the assassin shook his head, he pursed his lips and looked at the other man in what seemed to be genuine disappointment. 'You part ways with your brother; you become weak. You stay together; you're strong. That's what family is. But this... this is not how the world works.'

'We have a saying here too,' Grizzly rasped. 'One bad apple turns the barrel.'

Hakeem grimaced at yet another idiom. 'Meaning?'

'Meaning you get someone like Spice involved, and he'll fuck everything up.' The big man sank into his chair a little. His visage looked suddenly more tired.

Hakeem nodded, a smile playing across his face. 'You know? I like it. One bad apple. I shall remember that one, I think.' He tilted his eyes a little towards the ceiling, his glance caught by a moth that pinged from the overhead light. It was at this moment the big man began reaching across the table towards him, his bound hands gnarled sledgehammers.

Grizzly began to snarl just as Hakeem shot him for the first time.

He was dead before the second bullet entered his heart and passed through him, embedding itself in the mahogany frame of the chair. Within the confines of the office room, the shots sounded like cracks of thunder.

As the echoes died, Hakeem listened carefully for any noises elsewhere in the depot.

Silence.

Grizzly was slumped lifeless in the chair. Both eyes were open, and there was a look of slight bewilderment on his face; after so many years of dominance, it must have been utterly surprising to have been bested so easily.

Hakeem walked back to his car, looking up at the stars as they twinkled over the hillside. The night was quiet, save for his expensive shoes crunching on the ground.

One down. Two to go.

In the meantime, he had a boat to wait for, and the hope that maybe the soldier would take care of the other brother for him.

Chapter 46.

The three captives were aboard. Spice sneered at them.

When they'd been dragged out of the container and onto the deck, the sea front had been silent. Lomas, his anger gathering, took a fist to the face – he'd shouldered his full weight into one of the heavies, but it had made little impression. Rivera was strangely compliant. Spice's frown suggested that he remained suspicious of the ex-soldier, and he regarded him warily as he watched him being led to the bench on the starboard side. The captor's eyes were a little nervous, darting, cat-like as he surveyed the scene.

The gags they'd had fixed to them were rough. Oily rags were stuffed in their mouths and duct tape was applied on top. Only Christie, her fury writ large in the way her eyes bulged with rage, attempted to shout out.

Spice laughed at her, recovering his poise, enjoying the feeling of being in control. Then, he grabbed her by the hair, twisting her head to face along the seafront.

'So then. Lois... Detective Inspector Lois Christie,' he began, grinning. 'I thought you might like to know that the camera you had footage from has been destroyed. No evidence exists of our previous fandango. All the cameras along the seafront have been deactivated. And any fucking lunatics who walk their dogs at this time will just see a fishing boat heading out to collect the catch.' He chuckled. 'Beatty will shut down the investigation, so everything you've done will have been for nothing. You - young lady - will have died for nothing.'

Her eyes blazed.

'This,' he announced smugly, 'is Saltmarsh Cove. I run this town now. Everyone here is my bitch – you included. And if there's anyone who doesn't like it, I get my big old useless lug of a brother to sort them out.' As he spoke his next words, he punctuated them with staccato flicks of his fingers to her face.

'I-can-do-any-thing-I-like.'

She bridled a little, but refused to flinch. He laughed, bitterly. 'Right then,' he announced to his two accomplices. 'You know the drill. Get them set.' He pointed to Rivera and Lomas. 'You can leave them there, but keep an eye on them – they're dumb enough to do something stupid.'

'What about the chick, boss?'

Spice looked Christie up and down. 'Yeah - change of plan with her. Take her down below and tie her to the bed.'

'Yeah?'

'Yeah,' he nodded. 'Might as well get some use out of her while she's still here.' The two men laughed in response and pushed Christie towards the cabin doorway. At this, the boat's engines started, and the vessel began to move slowly away from shore.

He eyed the other two captives coldly.

'Have you figured it out yet then, Clouseau?'

Rivera simply stared back at him, gagged.

'You must be fucking dumber than you look.' He grinned. 'Not such a hard man now, hey? It's pretty easy,' he shrugged. 'Good-looking girls from desperate places get intercepted along their way to a better life. Our people on the French coast bang them into obedience, ship them over, and we sell them on.' He paused. 'You'd be amazed at how much some people are willing to pay for an obedient housemaid who has no choice but to cater to their every whim. They're kind of like blow-up dolls that cook and clean. You don't need to inflate them every few weeks, either.' He paused. 'Still have to hose them down, mind.'

Spice lit a cigar. 'You see, I've thought of fucking everything. No stone unturned. The only weak link is Pugh back there at the wheel.' He raised his eyebrows at Rivera. 'But since you put my usual pilots out of action, you left me little choice.' He drew hard, the smoke catching in his throat. He coughed slightly. 'Of course, the poor bugger's half blind and almost completely deaf.' He sighed. 'He's going to have an accident tonight, you see. I can't have any witnesses.' Spice looked hard at the two captives once again. 'And that's your fault, gentlemen. You'll have his blood on your hands... well, your souls.'

At this, Spice's two accomplices emerged.

'She's ready for you, boss,' one of them announced, smiling.

'Jolly good,' he replied. 'Now get these two fuckers sorted.' He nodded to Rivera and Lomas.

* * * * *

The boat was a couple of miles offshore by the time Spice's men were finished. Though both men had fought back, there was little they could do against such overwhelming force, especially when their arms were pinned behind them. Each of them had their feet forced into a bucket, and each was then held firmly as quick setting concrete was poured into both of the steel containers.

Lomas panicked, looking like he was going to faint. He made a strange snorting sound, as if he was hyperventilating. Kicking out violently, he made little impression – he rattled the bucket a little against the deck.

Spice simply laughed.

Rivera remained calm. He'd been in difficult binds before. Not like this, but situations tricky enough to know that panic was just wasted energy. As Spice sat watching him, he moved his feet and ankles within the setting mixture as much as he could, continually flexing and un-flexing his calves. He could feel the concrete gripping at him – he just hoped he could weaken it.

Ten minutes later, one of the heavies tapped the concrete, satisfied it had set. A shout came from behind the wheel.

'That's them,' Spice announced. 'The other boat is approaching.' He turned and looked at the two captives. 'The average depth of the water out here is a hundred and twenty metres.' He paused. 'So no diver will ever find you – no matter how fucking good they are. You'll be crab food, boys. Throw a tarp over those two,' he ordered, turning to one of his accomplices. 'I don't want them scaring the cargo away. And when we're done loading, we'll take our time.' He smiled again, his eyes narrowing at the trussed up pair. 'I'm going to enjoy your demise, gentlemen.'

'What about the girl?' one of the men asked.

'Leave her there for now,' he replied. 'I'll let you know.'

* * * * *

As the French boat drew alongside its British counterpart, its lights created a ghostly green glow beneath the tarpaulin. The two men turned to look at each other. Neither could speak, but neither needed to. They both knew this was their chance - the one moment when their captors' eyes were obviously elsewhere.

Lomas lifted his tied wrists to the base of his shirt. Then, wedging his head against his shoulder, he gyrated until, inch-by-inch, the tip of the shard of sharp, rusted metal protruded. It cut his back in several places, and he felt a searing pain along his spine, but he eventually had the makeshift weapon gripped tightly in his bound hands behind him.

Rivera, peering through the gloom, nodded in readiness. He shuffled along the bench seat with his back to the other man until he was in a position where he could rub his wrists along the blade. Anyone looking at the heaving tarpaulin would have been forgiven for thinking a couple were engaged in fits of passion beneath it. The ex-soldier only hoped their captors' eyes would remain elsewhere.

The knife worked.

By the time the plastic strand snapped, Rivera's forearms were cut and bloody. But the cable ties were broken.

He quickly ripped the tape from his mouth and spat out the cloth. Then, he reached down and sliced the ties securing Lomas, who quickly removed his gag.

'What now?' the other man whispered, breathing deeply and rubbing at his wrists.

'You stay here,' Rivera announced.

'What?' The other man's tone was incredulous. 'But...'

'I reckon I can deal with them.' He looked at Lomas in the green glow. From the front of the boat, excited voices chattered. The cargo was being unloaded.

'Don't take this the wrong way,' Rivera continued, 'but you'll be more of a hindrance than a help, I'm afraid. Besides, I need you to stay here as a shock tactic. It'll buy me enough time for what I need to do.' He looked hard at the other man. 'Whatever you do, don't move from this spot.'

'What are you going to do?'

'You'll see.'

Begrudgingly, Lomas acquiesced.

* * * * *

Spice and his helpers stowed the forty girls unloaded from the French boat in the hold. 'Don't worry ladies,' he announced cheerily above the sound of the surf. 'You'll be living in the lap of luxury soon.' Whether he was understood or not made no difference to him. His tone seemed almost soothing. The glint in his eye was deranged. He swaggered around the deck, occasionally grabbing a girl and conveying her towards the hold as if in benevolence.

Forty girls - just as agreed. So, it came as something of a surprise when a forty-first stepped onto the deck. This girl, though, clearly did not belong to the same party. She was well-dressed and, even in the light of the torches, had the glowing, healthy sheen of money. Of living well.

'Spice, I presume?' she announced confidently. She stepped purposefully over to where he was standing next to a door that led into the cabin.

'Safia?'

She nodded.

'At your service, ma'am,' he replied theatrically, tilting his head slightly. His poker face was betrayed by the crows' feet at the edge of his eyes, puckering slightly. Safia noticed immediately. Spice extended his arm and leaned nonchalantly against the door frame, looking at the woman's chest.

'Change of plan,' she continued. 'I accompany the cargo now. I have plans. Bigger plans for the future. If I'm happy, then we increase the - ah - operations.'

'That's music to my ears,' Spice nodded. The glimmer of greed glowed in the features of his half-lit face.

'Cigarette?' She offered a pack to him and held out a flaming Zippo lighter.

'Good - er - trip?' he enquired uncomfortably.

'That is - how you say - small talk, no?' she grinned. 'Never mind. These girls – they're some of the best I have ever traded. I think you and I do good business together already, no? But we can sell for even higher prices in future. Don't you think?'

Spice laughed and drew on his cigarette, exhaling contentedly. 'I think so, Safia. Absolutely.'

* * * * *

Rivera had half-dragged, half-jumped his way across the deck from the tarpaulin, then hauled himself up onto the roof and waited. Launching and then heaving himself upwards had taken all his strength and three attempts. He wondered if the noise would attract anyone, but it seemed their attention was elsewhere. His plan was simple. He would wait for an opportune moment and then jump down. Whoever he landed on first wouldn't stand a chance. His hope was that moving his ankles and calves would have weakened the concrete. If it shattered, then he might be able to move quickly against whoever he faced second. It wasn't a great plan, but it was the best he could do under the circumstances.

Most people would have cursed when the two traffickers came to stand beneath them talking. Rivera, though, held his breath; he heard the name Safia and then watched as Spice moved directly beneath him. The ex-soldier didn't hesitate. This was his chance.

His one shot.

And so he launched himself and simply dropped. One moment the pair were talking and the next, Rivera's feet, encased in a bucket filled with concrete, smashed into Spice's shoulder. As his feet hit the deck, the concrete split and the ex-soldier - in a fluid motion - brought his elbow crashing into Safia's face, sending her flying back against the closed door.

Rivera pulled his feet out of the bucket, kicking shards of concrete away from him as he did. Spice sat, groaning, clutching his shattered collarbone. The ex-soldier removed the 45 Compact from the waistband of the other man's jeans. He then whipped it across his adversary's temple – the man's face smashed into the deck. Then he grabbed Safia, dragging her along by her hair.

Sweeping aside the tarpaulin, he grinned at Lomas. 'Here,' he hissed. 'Can you raise your legs?'

It took the other man considerable effort, but he managed to raise them. Rivera helped him the rest of the way, and slid Safia beneath him, blood pouring from her nose. He then positioned Lomas' concreted feet above her shoulder. The trafficker moaned groggily.

'Two possible outcomes here,' Rivera announced. 'If Safia heard, she gave no indication. The ex-soldier continued. 'The concrete cracks. Or your collar bone cracks.'

As it was, Safia's collarbone shattered. The bucket bounced off her, hitting the deck and making a loud crashing noise. Rivera wasted no time in dragging Spice's inert form over to the same place.

Despite the obvious pain she experienced, Safia gave out no sound, although her breathing came in ragged gasps. The ex-soldier bit his lip. 'That might well bring someone out of hiding,' he explained to Lomas. 'I'll get you out of the concrete in a bit. For now, though, I'm going to leave these two in your capable hands.'

He picked up the discarded rags from the deck and stuffed one into each of the injured people's mouths. Then, he picked up the unpeeled duct tape that he and Lomas had suffered previously, and secured it across the traffickers' mouths. Grabbing each of them by a section of broken shoulder bone, he dragged them up onto the bench so they were seated beside the journalist's brother.

The ex-soldier then retrieved the bucket which had housed his feet. He positioned it beneath the insensible Spice and shoved the man's feet into it.

Lomas raised his eyebrows. 'We're not...?'

'They wouldn't have thought twice about ditching you over the side, mate,' Rivera said bluntly. 'Don't go getting all humanitarian on me now. Not for him, at least.' He nodded at Safia. 'She's a bigger fish - the police will want her, and they'll hopefully be able to stop her whole operation.' He paused. 'Him though - he's a worthless man. A useless sack of shit. Hold him still if he struggles, will you?'

Lomas did as he was asked. Rivera dragged the weighty sack of powder back across the deck and then filled the bucket in front of Spice with the mixture; he grabbed the same hose that had been used on him a short time before, twisting the nozzle to open the water flow. The barely conscious man rocked his head groggily from side-to-side as the cold water contacted his skin, but then he fell back into a stupor.

When he was satisfied with the consistency, Rivera twisted the hose's nozzle, turning it off. 'I need you to keep an eye on them now,' he announced to Lomas.

'Really?' The other man's eyes widened.

'Yeah,' Rivera nodded. 'I'm going to put you all under the tarp for now while I take care of Tweedle Dum and Tweedle Dee.'

Lomas shrugged. 'And?'

'Have you still got the blade?'

'Yeah,' the tall man replied, picking it up from the bench.

'Good. Either of them tries to move. Kill them.' He paused. 'I mean it – don't fuck about. Stab them right in the throat.' He thrust his hands upwards in a savage gesture. 'Don't even think twice.'

Lomas looked hard at Rivera. He nodded slowly.

Chapter 47.

For someone pretending to be a soldier, a gun is a prop. It's there to scare people. They haven't slept with it in trenches; haven't kept it with them through endless training exercises; haven't lovingly cradled it on the firing range.

For a *real* soldier, a gun is something they're so familiar with that it almost becomes part of them. An extension of themselves. The essence of their survival. Spice's biker friends knew that feeling.

The younger sibling's new helpers, though, had never lived such a life. They'd been drafted in as dogsbodies – the butt of the bikers' jokes. Suddenly, though, they'd been promoted. They had all the swagger of the other men, but none of the expertise or experience to back it up.

Rivera had.

Spice's boys didn't stand a chance. Three weeks before, they'd been serving drinks to Spice as he bawled them out alongside Popeye, Pluto and Pugwash. Now, they were at war.

* * * * *

Both of the heavies were sitting in the cabin, drinking from a bottle they were passing between them. The commotion from above had stopped, and they assumed that all was as it had been before. Christie was at the other end of the room, hands fastened to the bed frame. She was staring at them, unblinking, searing contempt in her eyes. Neither of the men felt able to operate without Spice's say-so. As a result, they were uncertain – suspended in a kind of limbo; awaiting instruction.

As Rivera slipped into the room, Christie's eyes widened for an instant. He shook his head at her slightly, raising a finger to his lips. Silently, he crept up behind one of the men. He was talking loudly, recounting a violent incident. The ex-soldier rolled his eyes and ducked beneath the low beams and into the narrow confines below deck. The Heckler and Koch 45 Compact is a small weapon, but if it's wielded at the end of an arm, it packs a huge punch. Rivera brought its butt down on the head of the nearest man, sending him sprawling across the floor.

The other man rose, fumbling for his weapon. His face was a mask of incomprehension. The idea that the ex-soldier had suddenly traded positions with his master was impossible to compute.

'Leave it!' Rivera hissed.

The man kept moving.

Rivera shot him through the kneecap.

As he writhed around on the floor, he looked up at the armed man, aghast.

'I told you to leave it,' Rivera shrugged, his voice toneless. He shook his head, his voice rising a little in incredulity. 'When the fuck did society change into this kind of thing?' he enquired disdainfully. 'When someone tells you to do something, do it. When they say don't, don't.' He paused. 'And if they're holding a gun, then know it's not a bloody choice they're offering you.'

The first man was dragging himself to his feet. One hand grabbed at the edge of the table, while the other held the upturned bottle he'd been drinking from previously.

As he shakily straightened himself upright, Rivera looked at him venomously. 'I'm losing my fucking patience here.' He shook his head. 'Your skull must be caveman thick,' he announced.

'F-f-f-f-fuck you!' the woozy fighter slurred. He took a step across the room, the bottle held aloft.

Rivera shot him in the foot.

Grasping at his wound, the man rolled across the floor, smashing into his wounded colleague like an overweight domino.

*****

'He didn't...?' Rivera looked seriously at Christie as he loosened the ropes that bound her.

She shook her head quickly. 'No, but...'

From the floor, the groans of the two injured men sounded.

'So what's the situation?' Christie enquired, switching instantly into her police persona.

Rivera spoke swiftly. He wasted no words – all business. 'We've got a whole load of refugees. I suspect they're in the hold - they're the ones they were going to sell. There's an old captain who I think has been coerced into piloting the boat too. They were going to kill him, anyway. We've got Spice, and some woman called Safia. They're both - er - out of action, for the time being.'

Christie nodded grimly. 'This goes much further than I thought it did, you know?'

'Yeah?' Rivera replied. 'No kidding!'

'Where are they – the others?' she asked.

'Out here - I'll show you. But before you jump to any judgements, remember they were going to do the same to me and Lomas. And you. After...'

'I know,' she interrupted, a little breathlessly. 'But I'm a police officer, so...'

He nodded. As he followed her out, he stamped on each of the prone men's wounds, eliciting further yelps of pain. He then switched the lights in the cabin off. 'Might as well keep them guessing, no?' he shrugged. Christie nodded, and the pair stepped out into the darkness.

*****

'How am I going to explain this?' Christie demanded in horror. She looked at the bruised and battered captives as Rivera drew the tarpaulin aside.

'What?' Rivera shrugged. 'What goes around comes around.'

'I know,' the Detective Inspector nodded. 'But this is the kind of mistreatment of suspects that gets people let off charges.'

'This is what happened to my sister,' Lomas reported, standing up awkwardly, gesturing, the makeshift knife still in his hand. 'You know that, don't you? So don't go showing them any sympathy... please.'

Christie nodded, absent-mindedly reaching forward and lowering the blade to a safer angle. 'So what do we do? I need to take them in and...'

'And waste good concrete?' Lomas said bitterly.

Rivera smiled.

'I think they deserve everything they're going to get,' Lomas continued coldly.

Silence fell for a moment, broken only by the lapping of water against the hull. Spice moaned slightly. Safia glared with quiet defiance.

'I've got to take them in,' Christie explained. 'Keep it all above board. This is the kind of thing which'll need to go to trial.'

'What?' Lomas was incredulous. 'With Beatty and all those other corrupt cops? You know what they're like - they'll do anything to save their own skins. Spice will be out walking free if they have anything to do with it! Evidence will go missing. There'll be witness intimidation. Rigging of juries.'

At this, Spice came to. He raised his head and started trying to communicate in muffled shouts. Rivera levelled the gun at him, his finger whitening on the trigger. At the last moment, he changed his mind, lowering the weapon and punching him full in the face instead.

'We're not quite following police protocol here, you know?' The officer shook her head as she turned away from what she'd just seen.

'And why would you?' Lomas spat angrily.

Silence.

'We have to explain things,' Christie announced sadly. 'Outline the story.'

'Unless...' Rivera began.

Both of them turned to look at the ex-soldier.

'How's this?' He picked a cigarette out of the packet that had fallen on the deck and used Safia's Zippo to light it. 'Old Father Time at the wheel doesn't know whether he's coming or going. He won't even remember where he's been once he gets back to port - especially if you get him a case of rum.'

'Go on.' Christie frowned.

'You've intercepted a human cargo. Forty girls who were going to be sold into slavery. That's big news - like you said.' He paused. 'That's the kind of thing that'll get you promoted.'

'I don't care about that,' Christie shrugged. 'Anyway, we've still got two men who've been shot and who are rolling around on the floor...'

'*She* did it,' Rivera declared.

'What?' Christie narrowed her eyes.

'Safia,' Rivera explained. 'Tell anyone who asks that she fired the gun. You're not dealing with rational people here. So, why not say there was a power struggle? That they all flew off the handle?'

'But they'll do tests...'

'Doubtful,' Rivera interrupted her. 'She's an international people trafficker. You've just broken the chain. That's the story here. Nobody out there's going to believe she wouldn't be capable of firing a gun. You pin this end of the operation on her and the two goons and you've got your fall guys. No one will lose any sleep if they're off the streets.' He drew on his cigarette. 'Besides – it plays better for them to say she shot them. It makes her the perpetrator – they can just say they were doing a job. They won't get away with things, but it might lighten their sentences. You could – er – persuade them round to your way of thinking. If they claim it was just a charter boat and they were security, then it gets them off the people trafficking charge. That should be enough to make them keep their mouths shut.'

Lomas nodded. 'You've just saved a whole lot of people from a whole lot of pain, Lois Christie.'

Christie shrugged, any hint of satisfaction carefully disguised. 'So, that's Safia and the two stooges. We let the girls claim asylum and Sinbad, back there, walks free.' She nodded. 'I can see that working. But I'm still going to call this one in to the coastguard, though. I can't have any of the jokers at the station in Saltmarsh involved with this.' She sighed. 'They'll go into damage limitation mode.'

The wind fluttered at the heaped tarpaulin, rippling it slightly.

'What about Spice?' Rivera enquired.

Christie looked at the smaller brother for a moment before returning her gaze to Rivera. 'Who?'

'You know, the – ah...' Lomas paused, realisation dawning.

'My mistake,' Rivera added. 'There was never anyone on the boat with that name, was there?'

'Mr Lomas,' Christie began, gritting her teeth a little as she turned to the tall man. 'Perhaps you can help me carry Safia around to the front of the boat. I'm going to check on the girls. I think they could use some fresh air and travel sickness tablets. Don't you? I'll bring them up on deck in five minutes.' She turned to look at Rivera. 'Do you think there'll be enough room for them all?' She paused. 'I mean, can you clear some space by then?'

'Yes ma'am,' Rivera said solemnly, nodding his head in comprehension. 'Yes, indeed.'

Rivera turned back to Spice, his face expressionless.

Chapter 48.

Where the dock had been silent when the boat departed, the vessel returned to a hive of activity. The harbour was lit by floodlights and the flashing blues of police sirens. At a height of around a hundred feet, the coastguard's helicopter escorted the vessel. During the last mile of its journey, its accompanying floodlights picked out the horde of smuggled women who were now standing on the deck, clearly visible in the bright orange lifejackets Christie had distributed to them.

'I can't even imagine how much paperwork this lot will take...' the Detective Inspector sighed.

'You've changed your tune,' Rivera grinned. 'An hour ago you were going to end up on the seabed.' His expression darkened. 'And who knows what Spice and his boys would have done to you before that?'

'Who?' she frowned.

'Spice - the... nobody. Never mind.' A thin smile played across his face. 'Anyway, I reckon that you'll secretly relish all the paperwork, no?' He winked at her.

As the boat drew into the harbour, a multitude of official staff approached. The human cargo was carefully unloaded - the girls were ushered into waiting police vans - and Spice's two accomplices, along with Safia, were wheeled away, chained to stretchers.

'You'd make a good detective. You know that, Rivera?' Christie said, as the pair stood, each resting a foot on the side of the moored boat a short time later. Cordons had been set up behind which journalists shouted questions she was studiously ignoring. A couple of floodlights had been wheeled out onto the dock – they cast long, ghoulish shadows.

'I think that ship's sailed,' the ex-soldier replied, shrugging.

'Is that some kind of pun?' she asked, eyebrows raised.

'No,' he grinned. 'That would be way too clever for me. I'm just a wanderer. I travel around and live with my cat - that's all.'

'Shame.' She smiled a little sadly.

He shrugged. 'Stick to your guns, Christie. You're better than any of the other officers in this town.' He looked hard at her, squeezing her arm gently. 'Don't forget that. Alright?'

'Yeah,' she nodded.

His hand lingered on her arm. 'And if you still want dinner sometime...'

'You've got a bloody one-track mind, you know?' Christie smiled, while gently but definitely pulling her arm from Rivera's grip.

'Guilty as charged, Detective Inspector,' Rivera smiled.

Silence.

'I envy you a little, you know?' she began.

'What – for having a one-track mind?'

'No!' she chuckled.

'Why, then? Is it the fact I live hand-to-mouth on a military pension, or because my home is a 1970s campervan held together by rust?'

'I mean, the fact you don't answer to anyone. Me - I have to obey the law, but doing that and getting justice are two different things. You know that, don't you?'

'You're a hell of a good police officer, Christie.' Rivera dodged the question. 'That's all there is to it. You're dogged and determined, and you've got them all bang to rights. Illegal weapons. An international trafficker. A whole load of girls saved from prostitution and slavery. Even Spice is out of the picture.'

'And his brother.'

'What?' Rivera frowned. 'But...'

'I heard it over the radio a few minutes ago. An officer from the next district attended a call. Grizzly was found dead at the depot.'

'How?'

'Shot.'

'Suicide?'

'No,' Christie shook her head firmly. 'A double tap to the heart.'

'I thought all the bad guys were on the boat... or not on it any longer...?'

Christie shrugged. 'I think we disturbed something even bigger,' she replied. 'To be honest, I think Lomas' sister set a whole wasps' nest on fire. We're just clearing things up now. Dealing with the aftermath.' In the distance, the sound of a siren rang out as another emergency vehicle left the dock.

Rivera nodded. 'You should tell Lomas. Where is he?'

'Talking to the press. I think some of them knew his sister - I've already told him what he can and can't say. My guess is he'll embellish things a fair amount. With all that adrenalin pumping through him, he's talking quicker than anyone I've ever heard before. He'll have them hanging on his every word. The way he was telling it, he pretty much rescued all of them single-handedly.'

The ex-soldier smiled. 'He's sticking to the story, though. Right?'

'More or less,' she nodded.

Rivera turned towards Christie as he stepped down onto the stone of the seawall. His face was illuminated in pale blue; beyond him, the whirling lights of police cars danced. 'Who killed Grizzly, do you think?'

'I don't know,' she replied. 'But there might be someone else out there. My guess is that Safia has never come along on one of these trips before.'

'Did she tell you that?'

'No - she's saying nothing. She's conveniently forgotten how to speak English. *And* French. We're going to have to bring in a translator fluent in some kind of backstreet Arabic – they're pretty thin on the ground here in Devon. We'll end up making a deal, I think. But I want the story - trouble is, she's going to keep schtum until she's got guarantees. And then it would seem there's a killer on the loose. If they're still in town...'

Rivera scratched at the stubble on his chin and nodded. As he cast his eye out towards the horizon, he saw a faint lightening of the sky. 'So why was she on the boat? She's got a cushy number back on the other side of the Channel, I bet. I can't imagine she's short of a bob or two. Why the hell is she here?'

Christie sighed, fidgeting a little with the antennae of the radio she'd removed from the boat's cabin. 'I don't know. But I wonder about that thing up near Blackburn – where all those women were found dead in a layby.'

'You think?'

'Maybe. Either way, I think something went badly wrong before. I reckon that whatever it was might have been what brought Lomas' sister into the fray.'

'And you think that's it?'

'Well... with folk like her, it's never just about now. It's always about the bigger picture - longer term gains. More money. Greed. Expanding into new markets. This is just business to her. People are profits.' Christie's eyes darkened with suppressed rage. 'But she must be bloody ruthless.'

'So?'

'So, if she thought she could squeeze more money out of the whole thing, maybe she wanted rid of Spice and Grizzly. And I reckon she was smart enough to dupe them.'

'That's no great shakes!'

'Yeah, but I wouldn't be surprised if she wanted to take over this end of the business. Otherwise, why else would she be here? She seems to do everything else. So, why would you want two cavemen stealing your thunder - putting their hands in the cash register?'

'Makes sense,' Rivera nodded. 'And Grizzly's killer?'

'Yeah, that's trickier. My suspicion is that Safia paid someone to kill Spice and his brother.' Christie shrugged. 'Think about it – if they're out of the way, then she gets to re-make their operation in her image.'

'Won't they have skipped town by now then? The hit man, I mean.'

'Probably, but I'm not feeling too relaxed at the moment, even if they have.'

The ex-soldier nodded and began to walk away from the vessel along the seawall. He suddenly felt tired. The police would need to speak to him – that was certain. But, after that, he wondered if it might be time to leave town. Or at least to start thinking about it.

'Rivera.' The Detective Inspector's voice called out from the boat behind him.

He turned.

* * * * *

Christie didn't hear the shot until after Rivera had been flung from the seawall. She saw him rock slightly as he turned back towards her, and then he stumbled again. The echoing report rang out across the harbour, rolling across the still water a split-second afterwards.

The sound of a splash rose from below, as the man whose name she'd called a moment before landed in the water beyond the wall. Everything else felt strangely silent for a moment. Peaceful.

Back on the promenade, agitated shouts sounded. Officers took cover, pulling car doors open and crouching behind them.

'Shooter!' The radio Christie had removed from the boat and tuned to the police frequency crackled. She threw herself flat and rolled over towards the edge of the hull, trying to focus on where the shot had come from.

'Muzzle flash?' The voice over the radio sounded hopeful.

With all the illumination, picking out the pin-prick flash of a rifle would have been nigh on impossible. Hakeem had known that much. An amateur would fire again – maybe take out some of the lights to aid their getaway. In doing so, they'd reveal their position. Hakeem, though, was a professional. There was no second shot – he didn't need one.

Chapter 49.

When he'd reached town, Hakeem had ditched the Mercedes. He didn't think anyone would tie it to the death of Grizzly before he was long gone, but he never took chances if he didn't need to. The CCTV from the depot would show him, but the car wouldn't feature. The Mercedes was parked in a small wooded area - close enough to get to if he really needed it, but far enough away for him to operate incognito.

The sailing club building was perfect for the next stage of his plan. As far as he could make out, the soldier Safia had messaged about would likely be en route to the bottom of the sea. Why else would he have been in the container if not? If Safia hadn't seen him off already, Hakeem would take out the other brother once he stepped off the boat.

All Hakeem required for now was a place to monitor things from.

Once he'd confirmed the kills, the assassin could vanish again. His work would be done.

* * * * *

Hakeem looked around for lights in windows, but had seen nothing. The sailing club backed onto a car park. It had a derelict building on one side of it and a road on the other. Reasoning it was unlikely anyone would be monitoring it too closely, he made his way up the metal fire escape that was attached to the wall. Its staircase was a spiral that ran all the way down one side of the building. He still paused before climbing, and listened for two full minutes before judging the coast to be clear.

When he reached the top, Hakeem was met with a locked door. He thought about kicking it down, but wanted to avoid unnecessary noise. Instead, he removed the long bag from his shoulder and levered himself upwards, wedging his feet against the rail of the stair and reaching with his fingertips for the felt-covered edge of the flat roof. Once his hands found purchase, he dragged himself up and rolled towards the centre across the gravelled surface. Then he reached down and lifted up his bag. He was dressed in black. Invisible.

Built on to the top of the roof was a hut-like extension with a balcony. A large klaxon horn was fixed onto the railing; the balcony provided a perfect vantage point over the bay. Hakeem stepped over the iron latticework and tried the handle on the glass doors.

They opened.

Inside, the room was sparsely furnished. It was - he reasoned - clearly designed to monitor sailing races. A large telescope was positioned on a stand in the corner, and various nautical charts adorned the walls. As he looked through it and adjusted the focus, he could just make out the shape of a boat in the distance, its outline vaguely visible beyond the pinpricks of its rear lights. Other than that, the sea was dark.

Hakeem sat in a vacant chair and methodically assembled the International L115A3 rifle that he'd carried with him, sighted it, and leaned it against the wall. It was another of the gifts Safia had organised for his arrival in the country. Although he'd had plenty of practice with long-range firearms, such a rifle wasn't his regular weapon of choice. Hakeem preferred to be up close. Intimate. He liked to be on hand to hear his victims breathe their last. He leaned back. There was nothing for him to do but wait.

Hakeem was good at waiting.

* * * * *

The first indication the plan had changed again was the arrival of a procession of police cars. From within the unlit room, Hakeem was not worried about discovery. He reasoned that the brother - Spice - would have done all he could to avoid involving the police, so them arriving suggested a re-think.

Something had clearly gone wrong.

Word had got out.

A short time later, a coastguard helicopter swept over the bay. What had started out as a surreptitious night voyage was fast becoming a widespread operation. The helicopter made its way out to sea; the fishing vessel was no longer the only light over the water.

Hakeem waited and watched. Watched and waited. The increased activity didn't worry him unduly. At worst, he was looking at making two shots. The crowds and confusion would just make it easier for him to slip away. The soldier and the brother needed to die. Once that had happened, he would disappear. He nodded with satisfaction as searchlights were wheeled into position a short time later – they would blind any would-be onlookers to his escape.

* * * * *

For the last mile or so, the coastguard helicopter hovered above the returning boat, blazing its searchlights into the water around it. A lifeboat was also launched, and made its way out towards the larger vessel.

Hakeem looked out as a group of frightened ebony faces on board hove into view. Peering through the telescope, he watched as they were lifted into the waiting arms of the emergency services, and then loaded into parked vans.

He looked on as Safia was carried off on a stretcher. He hadn't seen her in the flesh for several years - she was paler now. The image of her lying there, helpless, shocked him. She'd never shown any vulnerability before. He'd always imagined she was invincible. An unfamiliar emotion arose within him; Hakeem found himself feeling rage - rage at whoever had reduced Safia to this broken state.

But he was nothing if not adaptable. She would bounce back, just like she always did. Just like *he* always did if he was ever tested. It was who they were. It was born of where they came from. He mastered his rage, knowing he could draw upon it later if needed.

Hakeem frowned, wondering again who the hell the soldier was? He then watched as two brutish men were helped off the dock - a burly paramedic on each side - bearing their weight. Both had leg injuries that had been heavily bandaged while they were still on board the vessel.

He stared as an olive-skinned woman stepped onto the dock. There was no sign of the brother - he checked against the photograph he'd removed from the depot. Instead, there were three men who climbed off the boat. The first was an old man who looked so decrepit as to be almost incapable of walking. He was wearing a captain's hat that made him look like a cartoon caricature. The second man was wearing spectacles. He was tall, gangly, and badly coordinated.

The third man was the soldier. It was instantly clear to Hakeem - there was something about the way he bore himself. Something that the sniper recognised. Even though the stranger was dressed in a suit. Even though the bottoms of his trousers were coated in a greyish powder. Even though he looked like a nonentity, something stirred within the assassin; a heightened sense of awareness - this was not someone to be underestimated. In Hakeem's universe, there were three types of men. Hunters. Prey. And Hakeem. And Hakeem feared nobody.

But this was clearly a killer. Looking through the scope simply confirmed it – this had been the man who'd been chauffeured to the depot earlier. The suit still didn't fit him right.

This was the man Safia wanted dead.

Hakeem took pride in his work. He always had. If he had a job to do, then he did it. In his business, people talked. And the line of credit Safia left open for him could just as easily be closed. The fact she'd been arrested didn't mean the organisation was dead - it would simply remould itself into something else. People like Hakeem were always in demand - as long as they got the job done.

And so he'd waited. Watched. And he thought to himself that the tables on board had very clearly turned. The soldier had been put onto the boat as an intended victim – that he was climbing out onto dry land unscathed surely meant the other brother was dead.

* * * * *

Peering through the telescope, he watched as the tall, thin man lumbered off to speak to the crowd of journalists pressed up against the police cordon. They'd appeared as if from nowhere - from the very moment the police lights started flashing. Like vultures. The sniper shrugged.

He'd watched as the geriatric sailor shuffled shambolically off in search of a drink. The waiting police had only spoken to him briefly before leaving him to his own devices.

Then, he'd looked on as the soldier had talked to the olive-skinned woman. Both of them lingered further out, alongside the mooring. Their feet rested on the edge of the boat. Their stances were almost flirtatious. It was a distance of 250 yards. An easy shot. He could have taken both of them, but killing was something he'd only really do these days for a significant amount of money. So, he opted to stick to the task he'd been given. Even if Safia was incarcerated, Hakeem would still get paid.

That was how things worked. And he had a reputation to uphold: a man who always got the job done. And at least now he had a target to sate his surge of rage.

He'd watched through his rifle sight as the man turned away from the woman and began to walk along the slippery stones of the seawall. His face was illuminated as an electric blue visage from the police lights, and - at that moment - he presented a perfect target.

Hakeem squeezed the trigger slowly as he had done thousands of times before. The rifle stock kicked dully against his shoulder. And he watched with satisfaction as the target tottered with the impact. The little matchstick man that turned to dust in his crosshairs was entirely at his mercy – it made him feel like God.

That his quarry fell off the wall was no matter. Either he would find the body or the police would do it for him.

But someone would find it. And whenever that happened, it would mean he could confirm the kill with a photograph. That was all he required.

The image would wing its way through a web of encryptions to the people who would settle the balance of his bill. And then he would depart. His exit strategy was always the first thing he planned – it was one of the reasons he'd remained alive so long.

Twenty seconds after he pulled the trigger, the alarm was raised. By then, Hakeem had already broken down the L115A3.

The usual chain of events kicked into action: panic reigned; police officers cowered, fearing follow-up shots; eyes were desperately cast around to locate his position; plans were hastily hatched.

Time was wasted.

Hakeem reckoned on a head start of two minutes.

He only needed one.

He'd already checked that the door locks opened on latches from the inside. So, he shouldered his bag and simply walked out of the building, vanishing into the night less than sixty seconds after the fatal shot had been discharged.

Panicked voices sounded from the seafront, but he'd already crossed the car park.

The darkness swallowed up his black-clad form.

Chapter 50.

It was the sea wall that saved Rivera.

The mossy seaweed that had grown on it over the centuries had soaked up a sheen of dew that would burn off with the dawn light. At that hour, though, the damp surface was like a sponge. The wall was slippery and uneven. And Rivera - normally as sure-footed as a mountain goat - felt the sole of his shoe slide for an instant as he turned in response to Christie's call. He shifted his position, automatically righting himself.

But it was enough to make him rock slightly.

His head dropped.

And so, when the round struck, it grazed his shoulder - in military terms, he was creased by the bullet. For a millisecond, he smiled at the ridiculousness of such a thought: the idea he was pedantic enough to correct himself about parlance at such a time was almost amusing. But then blood rushed to bruise the tissue beside where bullet had clipped bone. The pain was instant. Searing. And the impact, glancing though it may have been, was enough to send him plummeting over the edge. But Rivera knew that the shooter had missed anything vital. At least, he hoped they had.

Plunging towards the water, he sucked in a lungful of air and relaxed as much as he could, hoping for the best.

He was in luck.

His body wasn't broken by landing on rocks. Instead, he splashed through the sea's surface and sank deep into the water. The cold sharpened his senses, and thoughts raced through his mind. Dormant memories from training programmes completed under duress surged forward.

Adrenalin kicked his mind into overdrive, and his thoughts whirled. He reasoned the angle of the seawall would shield him from any follow-up fire if the shot had come from a seafront building, as he suspected. Knowing that Christie would raise the alarm, he guessed the police would swiftly seal off the area, so the shooter would make a break for it quickly. If any shots were to come, then they would come almost immediately.

So Rivera believed that he was as safe under water as anywhere else. He struck out, swimming with powerful strokes away from the seawall and towards the cliffs at the far side of town. His shoulder was numb and an aching sensation spread along his arm like a million pins and needles, but he knew he had to ignore it. To keep on moving.

Logic decreed that an injured man would make his way to shore. Rivera didn't like the odds that logic gave him, though, so he struck away, further out to sea, feeling the current helping him along. He knew it wouldn't be long until searchlights were directed on the area where he'd fallen. If the shooter moved along the coast and one of the phosphorescent beams picked him out as he surfaced, he'd be a sitting duck. Whoever shone a light on him hoping to save him might just as easily spell his demise.

His best hope for survival - he knew - was if the person hunting him thought he was dead.

* * * * *

It was only when his lungs were burning - fit to explode - that he finally broke the surface. Taking in great gulps of air, he dived again, kicking out and aiming for the rock island in line with the end of the promenade.

If nothing else, reaching it would shield him from the sniper's bullets.

The further he moved away from the seawall, the stronger the current grew. The River Salt was not sizeable, but it emptied out into the sea at the end of the harbour. It was enough to propel Rivera more and more quickly out beyond the sights of any rifle the shooter might be bringing to bear. The pace of the rip tide was so fast, though, that it took him by surprise. He realised he was at its mercy, and that if he struggled against it, it would likely go to work on him on behalf of whoever was attempting his assassination.

He swam parallel with the shore, emerging eventually into stiller waters. By this time, he'd rounded the far edge of the rock island. It was a human construction; great big boulders designed to shield the cliffs from winter storms, and so its surfaces were large and flat. He clambered up, swearing as he slipped and scraped his shoulder on the way out of the water.

Moving himself up higher, Rivera climbed until he was above the breaking waves. In this position, he was entirely shielded from the shore. He was, also, in almost complete darkness - the lights of the town couldn't reach him in his current position.

He waited. There was little more that he could do until dawn broke fully. That would give him the chance to take stock of his situation. The cold of the water, which had numbed his shoulder, was beginning to wear off. He grimaced, gingerly exploring the wound: it wasn't deadly, but it hurt like hell.

Chapter 51.

The Trinity chapel was the oldest church in Saltmarsh Cove. Centuries before, the population had consisted almost entirely of fishermen and their families. Their cottages were narrow terraced houses that clustered the streets a few hundred yards back from the beach. The land in front of them had been common land, there to act as a buffer against the sea. But once the Regency period had started, the town had become fashionable; the land between the terraces and the sea had become the preserve of big hotels. The wealthy land-holders who owned them lobbied for a sea wall to protect their investments. Along with this, sporting clubs, social organisations, and other public buildings sprang up. Anyone looking at a painting of the town from a century before would have recognised Trinity church, and not much else.

On his first reconnaissance drive through the town, Hakeem had earmarked the church tower as a possible place to keep watch over the seafront. At that point, he hadn't even located his targets. But Hakeem understood strategy. He knew about fields of fire. He also appreciated the value of holding the higher ground.

That was why he was there now. Beneath the eaves of the spire, there was an ancient pigeon loft. At the hour he'd arrived, the church had been deserted. Sprigs of flowers were wedged at the ends of pews to mark whichever festival had most recently been celebrated. The shooter swung open the main door - it had creaked, echoing and thundering as it shed dawn light through the hot, heavy air of the deserted church.

But it was no matter - there was no one there to hear it.

Hakeem then picked the lock to the tower. Its cogs and chambers were so large they made it a task almost easy enough for him to have done blindfolded. The steps leading upward were dusty - he locked the door behind him, knowing the chances of being disturbed were slim.

As he ascended, he listened to the echo of his footfall. He noted the way the stone had been worn in places. The air in the tower was warm; musty. He didn't expect to have to fight his way out, but he knew that - were anyone to try and surprise him - they would fail. And fail miserably. Halfway up, an old fire exit door led onto the roof. Hakeem checked that it opened and shielded his eyes against the dawn sunlight glinting on the lead covering. This – he reasoned – would be his escape route.

The pigeon loft was musty. It was choked with grime and reeked of guano. Most people would have found the aroma revolting. Many would have taken one look at the cramped space and departed. A few might have remained for a brief amount of time. But Hakeem was not like most people. Cramped quarters and unwelcoming scents didn't bother him. It wasn't just down to his iron discipline; growing up where he'd been raised, such things were simply a part of life.

So Hakeem watched and waited. Waited and watched.

* * * * *

The assassin had set up the same rifle he'd used the previous night. He positioned it so he had a field of fire that covered the whole sea front. The barrel did not protrude beyond the wooden frame built into the wall - he was all but invisible to anyone who might have cast a glance in his direction. There had been a few ancient sacks of rubble in the loft; Hakeem used these to build a mound on which he rested against to survey the scene. That way, he knew he could remain where he was for as long as he needed to.

The promenade stretched for a little under a kilometre. Hakeem had mapped this out with the Mercedes' Sat Nav when he'd first reconnoitred the town. He knew the rifle would be effective over double that distance from his position. The weapon he had was an International L115A3 – he had it on good authority that it could kill at nearly three times the distance he was likely to need it for. His plan was simple: watch and wait.

In the unlikely event that the soldier had survived last night's events, he would be injured as he made his way up the shore. He might even have the remnants of the incongruous lounge suit clinging to him to mark him out from the tourist fray.

Hakeem thought it much more likely that the first confirmation of the soldier's death would come from the police, though. The moment a body was discovered bobbing in the surf, the promenade would light up like a flashing blue beacon once again. Cordons would be hastily erected, and police would swoop on key areas.

So he watched and waited. Waited and watched.

His thinking was simple. If the soldier *had* survived, then he would have to come ashore. There was only one way to access the beach. He would have a fairly short time window. If – by some miracle – he was still in the water, then mid-morning would be the absolute limit of him being able to remain. The assassin couldn't see how he'd survive beyond that. Behind Hakeem, enormous cliffs stretched upwards, marking the western boundary of Saltmarsh Cove. Ahead of him, huge cliffs rose out of the sea at the eastern edge of the town. These were sheer and precarious; the sandstone from which they were hewn was brittle and unstable - climbing them would be suicide. The River Salt disgorged water before the cliffs began, and its currents were known to be strong and dangerous. The likelihood of any wounded man making his way alive out of the water beyond it was minimal.

In his mind, the sniper had drawn a line that stretched all the way from his tower to the souvenir stand situated at the far end of the promenade. If the soldier were to come ashore, then he would have to cross this line.

And Hakeem would be watching. And waiting.

* * * * *

As the sun lumbered across the sky to its zenith, it glittered on the water. Hordes of tourists descended upon the beach, dipping in and out of the sea. Their shouts and screams rose up to the pigeon loft. None of them would ever know how the briefest pull on the trigger could have despatched them; Hakeem swept the beach endlessly with long, slow, lazy arcs, watchful all the while.

Hakeem saw all via the brilliant resolution of his rifle scope. Every arrival was eyed, weighed, measured, and evaluated. Every departure noticed. He saw burned bodies; bronzed bodies; old; young; thin; fat; men; women. All of life's tapestry was represented on the beach.

But there was no sign of the soldier.

Beyond the sand banks, two coastguard helicopters patrolled, evidently looking for the body. They passed up and down the beach, listing lazily, the low drone of their engines a constant soundtrack. At times, they made sharp turns, and their engines were suddenly loud. But, for most of the time, they were simply a soporific background noise. Hakeem's concentration never wavered, but he still felt the creeping onset of fatigue. The assassin expected at some point to see one of the helicopters pause. For small boats to gather around a point in the water, coalescing around the orange hull of a lifeboat; ready to assist. He waited for a medic to be winched downwards towards the surface. All morning, he felt confident the alarm would be raised. Moving into the afternoon, though, he began to lose belief that a signal would ring out.

The soldier couldn't survive in the water that long. Not with a bullet wound.

* * * * *

ONE BAD APPLE

All plans have a cut-off point. It was mid-afternoon when Hakeem concluded that his had been reached. There was no way he'd missed the soldier - he was certain of that. But if the authorities were going to find the body, they'd have found it by now. The soldier would either have been swept far out to sea on the current, or he was sleeping with the fishes - another idiom he found tolerable – ready to rise again in a barnacle-encrusted, crab-chewed, seaweed-attired mess.

If, by some miracle, his quarry was somehow not dead, then he would have to be in town. Pondering this, Hakeem stood and slowly stretched. He could sit and wait, playing the part of the hunter forever. But he noticed kinks in muscles and cramps he didn't suffer from before. He couldn't see any way the soldier would still be alive, but he still couldn't take a chance on it. He gritted his teeth – if he found him, he vowed to carve him up in retribution for the extra time he'd wasted.

As he stood, a pigeon landed, fluttering on the edge of the wooden frame. It tilted its head, looking at the sniper in a confused fashion. Hakeem decided to use it as a yardstick: if it roosted, he would call it quits. If it departed, he'd continue the search.

The pigeon fluttered its wings, suddenly flying off again.

And so Hakeem crept down the stairs. When he emerged through the door at the foot of the tower, the chapel was empty, save for an old woman sat on a pew at the front. She was deep in prayer and didn't look round. He tip-toed across the stone floor behind her and moved into the shadows.

Looking around furtively, he stowed the bag containing his rifle in a recess beside the entrance to the crypt. It was camouflaged by the dappled light cast by a stained-glass window. Even with his cloak of invisibility, it wouldn't do to carry such a conspicuous weapon around the town.

Especially not the day after a shooting.

Especially not looking like he did.

* * * * *

Hakeem emerged at the west end of the promenade. He'd rolled up his sleeves and untucked his shirt, removing his tie and undoing his top buttons in the process. Pulling on a pair of sunglasses, he tried to adopt the carefree gait of a happy-go-lucky tourist. It was not a role he was accustomed to playing, but he forced himself to smile as warmly as he could.

Beneath his armpit, his Star 30M sat in its shoulder holster. The cold of its surface was always a comfort. Never more so than now – it sharpened his senses, reminding him to stay alert.

With every corner he turned, his ears pricked up; his eyes were arrows. He sniffed at the air, as if chasing down a wounded animal. The shooter cut through the colours of the town in full bloom and cast his mind back to what he'd seen the night before in the green and grey of his night scope.

Any of those targets who'd cantered before his crosshairs previously were dead. He had no reason to suspect that last night's victim was any different. But until he knew for sure, he would keep on looking. He needed proof.

After all, this wasn't just about pride. It was about money. And he wanted the soldier. Dead or alive.

Pacing the town, Hakeem returned to doing what he did best of all.

Hunting.

Years before, he'd been moved out of the desert by those who commanded him. They'd placed him in a series of cities to train new recruits how to destroy targets. He'd proven adept at his role, taking the brutality and cunning he'd learned on the battlefield, and employing it in urban environments. The plan had backfired, though; the idealist's eyes had been opened to the ways of the West. To money.

Not long after, Safia had called. And then his life had changed. Today, though, he'd shed his skin of modernity. He was back in Marseille; in Malmö; in Brussels; in Shumen. Hakeem was a bloodhound searching for a scent.

Chapter 52.

When the grey light of pre-dawn sought him out, Rivera sat, hunkered down on the rock island, shivering slightly. He massaged his damaged shoulder. Casting his eyes out to sea, he saw no boats. Satisfied that he couldn't be seen from the water, he inched himself up to the tip of the rock pile and looked towards the shore. He half expected a shot to come ricocheting off the stonework, but there was no motion save for the swell of the sea.

The river current had dragged him a decent distance east of the town. Before him stood the huge red sandstone cliffs that stretched up well over a hundred feet. In the gathering light of dawn, they appeared formidable and foreboding. Looking back, the town was only dimly visible. A few lights twinkled, but there were few other signs of life.

Rivera racked his brains, trying to remember his training. Trying to remember how snipers thought. How they felt. He also played out scenarios, trying to work out what had befallen him the previous night.

He reasoned that it must have been a contract killer who'd shot at him. Seeing no other explanation, he decided it must have been Spice and Grizzly that ordered the murder. But that made little sense. Surely he hadn't caused them enough problems to warrant such an action? And, anyway, they hadn't known who he was until a few days before.

Rivera then changed tack: what if Safia had ordered the hit? But, again, him beating up a few bikers was hardly enough to put her whole operation at risk. And surely she'd have delegated taking care of someone like him to her subordinates - or to Grizzly's neanderthals. She'd have been nowhere near. Added to that, she could hardly have ordered the hit from the police cell where now she would doubtless be incarcerated.

He wished he could call Christie, but his phone was somewhere on the seabed at this moment, good for nothing. The ex-soldier's mind drifted for a moment – he wondered if her attitude towards him had thawed a little. A shower of frigid sea spray snapped him back to his senses. He switched his thoughts back to the mind-set of the contract killer. More than anything, for a shooter to collect their payment, they needed proof of a kill. So, they'd want a body. Until proof arrived, they would likely try and stay in position, or remain as near to it as they could. If their target was still alive, they might get a second attempt to end their life.

Rivera looked back at the town once more and thought again. If the shots had come from the east end of the promenade, then picking another shooting position there would be foolhardy. That would be the area the police would be looking at most carefully. If it were him, he pondered, he'd pick somewhere at the other end of the beach. Somewhere high enough to give a view of someone staggering from the sea, bleeding and injured. Looking at the town's profile, there were three possible options: the top of The Cliffside Hotel; the scoreboard of the cricket club, or the church steeple.

A large wave broke upon the rock island behind him. Rivera looked at the current created by the river - where it had been a clear rip before, now it seemed to be more of a swirl.

The tide was turning.

He turned his thoughts to the shooter once again. Of the three options, the first was unlikely. Why choose a hotel? It would be busy - it wasn't like contract killers wanted to advertise their presence. If they were spotted, they'd have to fight their way out; there would be any number of possible witnesses. The second was a possibility. The scoreboard had a good view of the beach, and - unless a match was being played - the shooter would remain undisturbed. It was the third option that was best, though. It was the highest and - given the season and the heat - it would probably be the quietest. If he were sniping, the ex-soldier concluded, that would be the point he'd choose to shoot from.

Rivera weighed up his options. He reckoned the shooter would watch the beach. If he swam towards the shore from this distance, then he'd probably do so unseen. But that would be less and less likely the brighter the day got. From this distance, they'd be a hell of a sniper to pick him off, but it wasn't beyond the realm of possibility. If he thought *he* might be able to make the shot, then there were definitely people out there who would be able to do so.

No question.

He looked at the swirling water again. If he could get beyond it, then he would reach the river. He remembered the strength of the current last night, though. It would take an Olympian to traverse the rip, and Rivera was no Michael Phelps in the water. Even if he managed it, he wasn't likely to get up the shingle unharmed after that. It would be like an Omaha Beach re-enactment. The odds would be stacked against him. And then, there was the injury to his arm.

His only other option was up the cliffs. The ex-soldier sighed. Not only were they sheer, but the piles of rock from recent falls made it patently obvious how unstable they were. He wouldn't have been confident climbing up there with ropes and harnesses. As it was, he had no equipment. And his arm was throbbing in pain.

Rivera examined the wound once more. Though the bleeding had stopped, there was a deep gouge. Miraculously, the bullet seemed not to have injured him other than that, but the area was turning a deep purple colour as the bruising spread. He knew that this would hamper his climbing the worse it got.

Another wave broke on the rocks behind him. The tide was definitely coming into shore. Rivera – knowing time was off the essence - breathed deeply and sighed. Picking his way swiftly across the stone boulders, he climbed down to the water level and launched himself into the sea, pleading with the current to take him ashore.

* * * * *

The current was far stronger than Rivera had imagined it would be. He felt himself being whisked about on the waves like a discarded piece of driftwood. For every gain he felt himself making, an opposing current would clutch at his ankles, dragging him back the other way.

He grazed his knuckles on submerged rocks and then took in a great lungful of water. At first, he'd tried to go along with the current, but that plan didn't seem to be working. Instead, he resolved to plough on, swimming with as powerful a crawl as he could muster straight through the waves, heading directly for the cliffs.

The rock that smashed into his chin was the first indication he'd reached the shallows. Suddenly, he could stand. And then, hauling himself through the surf, he emerged onto the rocky beach and strode as quickly as he was able towards the foot of the cliff.

The day still wasn't fully light.

Rivera looked back towards the town, but saw with some relief he was now shielded from its view. He stared up at the cliffs. Where they'd looked like a solid mass of sandstone from the rock island, up close, he saw that wasn't the case. There were gullies and crevices of stone that traced upwards. Cracks in the surface would provide hand and footholds, and the branches of trees protruded in places. There was even a long length of what looked like electrical cable trailing down from one section. Clearly, a recent cliff fall had taken a shed or an outhouse, and that was all that remained. The angle, though, wasn't sheer. Yes, the cliff was incredibly steep, but the falls had happened unevenly.

He breathed deeply and began to look for handholds.

It had been a long time since Rivera had attempted such a climb. He'd been fitter then, and stronger. He'd also climbed as part of a team and had up-to-date military equipment.

However, he'd not been the specific target of a bullet for a while, either. That gave him a fresh sense of purpose. If he was going to disable his tormentor, then he would have to get into town and flush him out. And, if ascending the cliff was the only way to get there, then he had little choice.

Rivera began to climb.

* * * * *

After two near-falls, three partial slips, and one hair-raising moment where he'd had to simply cling to the rock face as loose debris poured down upon him, Rivera reached the top of the cliff edge. This was the most difficult part of the ascent. The rock here was held together with tufts of grass and tree roots. It was dry to the touch and crumbling; in places, there was nothing between the overhang and the beach down below.

Rivera managed to gain purchase on the trailing length of electrical cable. He looped it around his waist and then used a tree root to push himself upwards. It took a couple of attempts. The first handhold he chose turned out to be a clod of loose rock. It went plummeting downwards, while the ex-soldier swung back on the cord, smashing into the cliff face, bruising his cheek, his wounded shoulder shrieking in protest. The second attempt was nearly a carbon copy, but more earth and stone went tumbling on this occasion. It meant that a small wedge was created in the rock. Rivera was then able to use this to claw his way to safety.

Rolling over the top, he moved quickly away from the edge. He was at the end of a long garden that led up to a Georgian-style house in the distance. A wheelbarrow sat close by. Inside it, a jacket had been weighted down with a gardening fork. The ex-soldier crouched and stared at the house. There was no sign of anyone. Lowering himself down between two raised vegetable beds, he closed his eyes for a moment, exhausted. He hoped that whoever owned the house didn't have dogs.

* * * * *

The sun's heat woke him a couple of hours later. He arose, surprised. When he'd been in the military, he'd been trained to operate without sleep. Now, though, as a civilian, he'd lost that ability. Evidently, the night's activities had taken their toll – he had no recollection of closing his eyes.

Squinting, he raised his hand against the glare. Judging by the angle of the sun, he reasoned it to be mid-afternoon.

Rivera slowly pulled himself up, looking over the lip of the vegetable bed. He watched the house for the next fifteen minutes. Seeing no signs of activity, he walked towards the wheelbarrow and picked out the coat in the hope there might be a key in the pocket. There wasn't. What he did find, though, was a half-full pack of cigarettes and a box of matches. He lovingly passed the filter tip beneath his nose and breathed the tobacco aroma in deeply. The second match flared, and he lit up and inhaled; a glorious light-headedness passed over him. Two minutes later, he ground out the finished cigarette, and lit a second. Then, he replaced the pack and matches in the pocket of the coat.

As the ex-soldier approached the house, clothes were strung out on a washing line. They were dry to the touch. He lifted down a pair of men's jeans and a t-shirt, estimating that both would fit him – at least near enough.

After changing into his newly liberated wardrobe, Rivera ditched the remnants of Lomas' borrowed suit in a dustbin and tried the back door of the house.

It was locked.

The garden shed, though, was open. Rivera entered it and reached up, feeling around on the top of the door frame until his hand felt a key ring. Marvelling at how predictable people generally are, he took the key and unlocked the rear entrance of the house.

Once inside, he listened hard for a couple of minutes, alert to those indescribable dents in the air that denote the presence of another being. Satisfied, he entered the kitchen. He filled a pint glass from the draining board with water, downed it, and then repeated the action. He then looked through the cupboards, lifting out a two-litre bottle of water from a plastic packet. In another cupboard, he found a box of cereal bars and began to fill his pockets with them. Rooting around in the fridge, he removed a glass bottle of flavoured iced coffee from a stash, and drank it straight down. The sweet yet bitter taste restored some energy to his muscles and helped sweep the last of the tiredness from his brain.

In a room that was clearly used as a study, he dialled Lomas' number on the landline. The other man's phone had evidently been destroyed or lost at sea, though. The operator simply announced that the call could not be placed. As he listened to the recorded message, Rivera went through the desk drawers, removing a handful of banknotes from a pile. He peeled off £100 in £10 notes, pocketed it, and returned the rest. He found a bottle of painkillers in a bathroom cabinet and swilled down a handful. The ex-soldier then rubbed antiseptic onto his wound and dressed it as well as he was able.

The sleep had revived him and the caffeine was suddenly pulsing at his temples, buzzing through his brain. A plan was beginning to form. He cast his eyes over some of the framed photographs that hung on the wall. The inhabitants looked to be a male couple in their thirties. They were pictured on a variety of mountains and hillsides, and in a couple of group shots suggestive of walking tours. Their lives looked pleasant; comfortable. The house was large and well-kept. Rivera had hoped to locate something he might use as a weapon – he realised this was not the abode where such things would be found.

Out in the hallway, he took a rain poncho from a peg and then gratefully switched his broken shoes for a pair of boots that more or less fitted. He also put on a John Deere baseball cap, which he found on a sideboard, pulling it down low on his forehead. The old shoes went into the same dustbin as the suit. Checking his look in a pane of window glass, Rivera was satisfied he could pass for a tourist as long as people didn't look too hard.

He walked out through the property's front gate and started to make his way along the coastal path, and down into the town.

Chapter 53.

Hakeem's progress through Saltmarsh Cove had been slow and systematic. He'd planned a route in advance and, using a tourist map, followed it. To anyone watching, he hoped to appear exactly like a lost traveller. To further this pretence, he made a show of peering at buildings and scrutinising street signs. The only thing out of place was his attire, but people hadn't seemed to pay him much attention.

All the while, he was watching reflections in storefront windows, and casting his eyes over those people who passed him in the street. Searching for anyone familiar. The assassin's eyes flickered continually, taking in all that he saw.

He wandered through the park; past the cricket ground; alongside the bowls club; through the gardens bordering the library; between the theatre and the museum; down, beyond the stately homes and through the back alley behind the cinema. After a couple of hours, he was bored – fed up with relentlessly returning the smiles of cheerful octogenarians. He sat on a bench between two tennis courts, but then beat a hasty retreat when the groundsman joined him and began to explain how often he scarified the surfaces during the winter months.

Hakeem pressed on, navigating the busy streets; Saltmarsh Cove was alive. But it wasn't filled with the kind of people Hakeem was searching for. It wasn't until he rounded a corner between a confectioners and a dairy shop that he sighted a familiar figure. The gangly frame of the man who'd accompanied the soldier from the boat was sitting on a bench in the churchyard, eating a portion of chips from a polystyrene tray. He earnestly switched his attention between a copy of the local newspaper and the phone, which was perched on his knee.

He looked straight at Hakeem for a moment. The hit man froze. But then, he realised he wouldn't recognise him, anyway.

Hakeem ducked out of sight behind a tree. He removed his phone from his pocket, acting as if he was engaged in conversation. It was only when the tall man stood up awkwardly that he moved, too. As Lomas walked away towards the town, Hakeem set off in slow pursuit.

* * * * *

Eddie Lomas was almost feeling good. At least, he wasn't feeling quite as burdened with life as he had done for the past few weeks. He'd suspected for some time that he wouldn't find his sister - Spice's gleeful admission had left him cold, but had come as less of a shock than he'd thought it would. What surprised him more was that he felt no remorse at the villain's demise. Indeed, he found he'd been fully supportive of the rough justice Rivera had dished out.

He wondered where the ex-soldier was.

Rivera struck him as the kind of man who would vanish into the night and then reappear when it was least expected. He couldn't believe that he'd been killed. Yes, he'd turned back and seen the dark figure tumbling off the seawall. Yes, he'd watched the coastguard's helicopter sweeping the seafront and uncovering nothing. But he couldn't believe that his new acquaintance was dead.

Men like him didn't die. They couldn't be killed. Surely?

After all, he'd seen him fight. Lomas couldn't believe that bullets could harm someone like that.

As he sat on the bench outside one of Saltmarsh Cove's several churches, Christie's previous words about his sister came back to him: 'without a body - there's still hope. There's always hope.' So Lomas hoped beyond hope that Rivera was still out there. Somewhere.

He scrolled through his phone for news. There was nothing. He adjusted his glasses against the glare the sunlight made as it reflected off the newspaper on his lap. The glasses weren't really necessary - he'd put them on earlier because he thought they made him look intellectual. It was in a bid to impress Wendy Stratton - the journalist from *The Saltmarsh Herald* who'd taken a great interest in his story. Though the paper before him was nearly a week out of date, he'd scoured it, searching for her name in any of the by-lines. He was angling to compliment her on her writing.

Behind the tree at the corner of the churchyard, he'd seen a shadowy figure. Although the man was on his phone, Lomas swore he'd been scrutinising him. Ordinarily, he would have thought nothing of it. But ordinary didn't really apply to his life in the last few days. He knew Rivera had been shot, and he knew the coastguard had been searching the water. But nobody knew *who'd* shot him – Lomas couldn't get his head around the idea that he'd be a target too. But, these days, he found it difficult to know what to believe about anything.

He stood up, and then immediately paused, feeling a sharp pain. Then he clutched his side, realising he still had the rusted, makeshift knife tucked into the back of the waistband of his trousers. He'd been using it to regale Stratton; she'd even had the paper's photographer take pictures of him posing with it. After that, she'd given him her number.

* * * * *

Hakeem walked slowly after the gangly man. To the untrained eye, he would have appeared to be an unhurried window-shopper, looking at the various storefronts of the town. All the while, though, his eyes were locked on to the figure of Lomas. As he moved, he was continually calculating where he might turn next.

He felt the dull, cold ache of the pistol beneath his armpit and willed his quarry to move away from the main streets. After crossing a small park and making a show of looking at a local bulletin board, Hakeem saw his target turn and glance in his direction. People who've been trained to tail people, or to lose tails, have tactics to subtly confirm whether or not they're being followed. Lomas had had no such training.

He simply started running.

Hakeem knew that he'd been spotted. He also knew he had to strike quickly and took off in pursuit. None of the elderly pedestrians paid them any mind; they simply assumed the two men were running for a bus.

Had the other man had training, then he'd have known to head to the busiest street he could find. But, as it was, he panicked. Vaguely heading towards the crowds at the seafront, he took a shortcut that ran behind a hotel loading bay and an old people's home.

Lomas' gangling gait saw him lolloping along the back alley between the buildings. It was here that Hakeem caught up with him. Though the man in pursuit was much smaller than the man being chased, he was considerably faster. And much stronger.

He slammed Lomas into the wall, winding him.

* * * * *

'You talk. You live,' Hakeem announced, tonelessly. 'Maybe...'

Lomas gasped. At the end of the alley, the seafront was visible. It was the promenade that he'd been heading for. Throngs of people passed, their flip-flopped footfalls echoing off the high walls. Lomas felt his heart beating out of his chest. He could feel the veins in his temples throbbing. A thin sheen of sweat spread across his forehead.

'Your hands,' Hakeem began, pointing his pistol at the other man.

'What? Er - excuse me?'

'Tuck them into your belt behind you,' he ordered.

'Why?' Lomas frowned.

'You ask too many questions, my friend. If you're not careful, someone will cut your tongue out. Yes? Now - turn around slowly and show me that your hands are tucked into your belt.'

Lomas did as he was told. As he turned, he looked up and caught sight of a bee idly flitting from flower to flower in the creeper that cascaded down from the top of the wall. For an instant, its wing was caught in a strand of cobweb. But then, it struggled free.

'Since you must know,' the armed man began as Lomas turned back around, 'I don't carry handcuffs. So, this will have to do.' He paused. 'I'm sure you are as slow pulling your fists out as you are at running. I know I'll see any punch intended to hit me from miles away. Yes? But I take no chances.'

Lomas frowned, feeling his fingertip come into contact with the makeshift knife he'd still neglected to remove from inside his shirt. He'd been hoping to re-enact an embellished version of his escape for Stratton later on. As it was, his hand now closed around the corroded metal.

'Name?' Hakeem demanded.

'Lomas - Eddie. Eddie Lomas.'

The armed man nodded. 'The soldier - what's his name?'

Lomas shrugged.

Hakeem held the gun up. 'Must we really do this?' he frowned, bored, and then froze. A small child on a tricycle had turned into the alley. Hakeem lowered the gun and smiled broadly. Then, a parent arrived. As they talked into their phone, they took hold of the tricycle's handlebars and steered the child away, not noticing the two men standing by the wall. Hakeem raised the gun once more. 'Name?'

'Rivera.'

'First name?'

'He never told me...'

Hakeem closed his eyes and took a breath. When he opened them again, their cold hostility made Lomas flinch. 'You lie to me, then I'll shoot your balls off. And if you think I'm fucking around, you are mistaken, my friend. Understand?'

'Trent,' Lomas reported breathlessly. 'I only ever called him Rivera, but Trent was his first name – *is* his first name.'

Hakeem stood for a moment, pensive. 'Where was he staying?'

'He...' The armed man pushed at his chest with the muzzle of the pistol to hurry an answer, taking Lomas' breath. 'He was up on the campsite.'

'Which one?' Hakeem pushed the muzzle harder.

'The one up on the cliff. I don't know the name.'

'Vehicle?'

Lomas looked hard at the other man, his lip trembling a little. 'A Volkswagen camper. Silver. Old.'

Hakeem snorted. 'You are a weak man, my friend. A pussy. There is no fight in you. You are a man who is not really a man at all. You would just roll over, get fucked, and die. You don't deserve to live.' He raised the pistol.

* * * * *

The shout that came from the end of the alley wasn't particularly loud, but it was uttered with conviction. Hakeem paused, almost out of curiosity. His glance met that of Lomas, and he raised his eyebrows, almost as if sharing a joke with his captive.

'Police!' Detective Inspector Lois Christie was thirty yards away, holding a Sig Sauer P229 that was levelled at the armed man. 'Drop it, or I'll shoot,' she continued.

'Too many cop movies,' Hakeem hissed under his breath, lowering his weapon.

It was as the armed man turned his head to look towards Christie that Lomas moved. In one movement, with as much skill and force as he could muster, he removed the rusted sliver of metal and swept it towards Hakeem's head. As it made contact, it ripped a gash in his cheek that immediately spouted crimson.

The two men looked at one another. Hakeem's eyes widened in shock and disbelief; Lomas' expression was a mirror image, but underpinned by a sense of terror.

'Bastard!' Hakeem hissed.

As the captor raised his pistol again, Christie fired.

Her bullet struck Hakeem's trigger hand, knocking the pistol out of his grasp. It tumbled, bouncing onto the floor of the alley. He swore, hissing loudly.

A few screams sounded from the beachfront. Frightened tourists began to flee the scene. The morning had seen many of them head to the beach in morbid curiosity. Then, though, they'd been detached – safe from harm. Now, the danger of the town's situation was dawning upon them.

'Get down!' the officer screamed at Lomas. But he stood for a second, frozen in shock, staring in awe at the metal weapon he held in his hand.

'Down!' she screamed again, desperately.

This time, Lomas did as he was ordered, dropping to his knees and clutching his arms to his head as if to protect himself.

It was too late, though.

Hakeem was gone.

Chapter 54.

'Well, look what the bloody cat dragged in! Welcome back to Hooverville!' Fraser chuckled. 'You look terrible, chief. Here.' The man handed Rivera a fresh can of strong cider.

The ex-soldier looked at it for a moment, shrugged, and took it. Opening it, he drank a long draught and then took another.

'It'll cure you of what ails you, that will!' Fraser announced, nodding approvingly at the can. He paused. 'What *does* ail you, anyway?'

'I forgot to feed my cat,' Rivera shrugged.

'Yeah... that'll do it,' the other man nodded sagely. He paused for a moment. 'You find who you were looking for?'

'Well, yes and no,' Rivera shrugged.

'You're a puzzle you are!' Fraser grinned. 'Mind you – you should keep your head down until you work out what their MO is.'

The ex-soldier frowned. 'You're quite tactically minded for a bum!'

'Charming!' Fraser shook his head. 'I've lived a life, chief. Don't you worry about me.' He paused. 'You heard about Roy, right?'

'No. What?'

'Well... they say he hanged himself in his garage. But I don't buy that. I talked to him only hours before.'

'What do you reckon, then?' Rivera frowned.

Fraser shrugged.

The ex-soldier studied the other man, narrowing his eyes. 'What did you say you used to do?'

'I didn't,' Fraser announced bluntly. Then he laughed - a guttural wrench coming from his lungs. 'Your face is looking pretty colourful - what did you do? Walk into a door?'

'Honestly?' Rivera paused. 'I walked into a cliff.'

The other man frowned. 'Then you're a fool.' He paused. 'Listen. You look knackered. You need some place to kip?'

Rivera looked hard at him. 'No, thank you.'

'I'll keep an eye out,' the other man insisted. 'I don't drink so much that my eyes and ears don't work. Besides, this isn't the first time I've drawn sentry duty.'

'Iraq?' Rivera asked.

'No.'

'Bosnia?'

The homeless man grinned a little and shrugged. 'Time for you to piss off now, I reckon. You're like a kid who's playing for time now! If you're not going to lay down your weary burden here, then you're going to find somewhere else for your bed roll. Know what I mean?'

Chapter 55.

As Rivera entered the police station, Christie did a double-take. Then she smiled warmly, putting down the clipboard she'd been carrying. She frowned a little too, looking at the new arrival's strange get-up. She also noticed the bruising around his face.

'Did you miss me?' the ex-soldier enquired.

'Maybe a little bit,' the officer shrugged.

Rivera nodded. 'Updates?'

'Well,' Christie shrugged, 'I've got rid of most of the force – for now, at least. And I've replaced them with temporary staff – it's been sanctioned by the higher ups.' She paused. 'I guess the big news is that the shooter's still at large. At least if he's the one we're thinking of.'

'Yeah? He's not vanished then?'

'Negative. I don't think so – he came after Lomas today.' She paused. 'He's OK, but badly shaken. I've packed him off with Stratton – the journalist. I reckon there's a blossoming romance in the offing there.' She smiled a little. 'Oh, and I winged him – the guy. He looked to be of Middle Eastern descent. We're running various databases, but I can't imagine he advertises his services online. He'll likely keep himself pretty well hidden.'

Rivera nodded.

'And you? Dare I ask?'

He shook his head. 'Maybe tomorrow. For now, I have a favour to ask.'

'Shoot.'

The ex-soldier frowned.

'Too soon?'

'Something like that.' He shook his head. 'Can you stick me in the cells tonight, please?'

'On what charge?' The officer narrowed her eyes.

'I'm knackered. Dog tired. And I'm not sure Iris will be a good idea – especially if the sniper's still around. He's already tried to kill me once...'

'No can do,' Christie replied, bluntly.

'Really?'

'Yeah. Police procedure, I'm afraid.'

Rivera sighed.

She looked hard at him. 'You can come home with me, though.'

He frowned, smiling a little uncertainly. 'Yeah?'

'Yeah – I reckon.' She held her hands up as if weighing the situation. 'Onetime offer, though, so decide quickly before I change my mind.' She frowned for a moment, expectant. 'You coming then?'

'Yes, ma'am.'

* * * * *

Rivera rolled over, cocooned in delicious warmth. The scent of perfume was strong on the pillow. At the foot of the bed, Christie was pulling on her uniform. She looked at the prone figure and raised her eyebrows. He frowned, lifted the duvet, and – seeing he was undressed – stared back at her.

Silence. She fastened the buttons on her blouse and pulled on her jacket.

'Aren't you going to ask, then?' she enquired.

'What?' he frowned, groggy.

'What we got up to, lover boy?' She smiled, thinly.

'Er – did we...?'

'Oh yes,' she nodded. 'You were a real stud until...'

'Until what?' The ex-soldier sat up a little, leaning on his elbows. He looked at the time display on the radio alarm clock on the bedside table.

'Until you started snoring within three seconds of your head hitting the pillow.'

The ex-soldier leaned his head back, sighed, and stared up at the ceiling. 'How much of a rush are you in?' he enquired, raising his head once more.

'Too much for what you have in mind.' She paused, grinning. 'Swing by the station when you're up and about.'

Sighing, the ex-soldier nodded. Christie left the bedroom, and he heard her descending the stairs. He looked under the covers again, this time taking stock of the bruises, scrapes and other violations his body had endured. Before he faced the world, he knew he needed to spend some time patching his wounds as best he could.

But he'd heal. He was pretty certain of that much.

Chapter 56.

Rivera walked three times around the campsite before making his way to Iris. He looked around carefully, but saw no sign of an adversary. The hunter - if there was one - was either extremely good at hiding, or not present. The ex-soldier knew that the longer the contract killer stayed around town, the riskier his situation would be; he strongly suspected he'd have departed already. After all, for all he knew, his target was already dead.

Looking at the place with a sniper's eye, Rivera had sought out all the places he believed someone might shoot from were the shoe on the other foot.

There was nothing. Nobody. But then, why would there be?

He was a ghost. A dead man. Only Christie knew for certain he'd survived. And Fraser – but anyone listening to him would assume he was simply rambling in his usual, deranged fashion.

Reaching the campervan, he checked beneath it for any telltale signs of tampering. He peered at the sides, looking for any wires or charges, but couldn't see any. And so he opened it, sliding the door across and then climbing in.

There was no sign of Rosie. But everything else was exactly as it should have been. He lay back on the couch for a moment, listening. There was nothing – in his months on the road, he'd developed a strong sense of being able to sub-consciously read the world beyond her steel walls. He'd become like a submariner – able to spot subtle changes in engine rhythm even while sleeping deeply. But he sensed nothing.

He reached into a cupboard and withdrew a pouch of cat food. As he forked it out, he tapped the utensil against the side of the cat's tin bowl to see if it would bring her running. It didn't. He placed the empty tin and the fork on the work surface.

It was only when he turned back around that he realised his mistake.

He saw him.

Rivera had no idea where the man had hidden, but it was as if he'd simply appeared, rising from the ground like a malevolent spirit. In the split-second he had to view him before the taser was fired, he saw that one of his hands was bandaged. Other than that, he was attired far too smartly for a campsite: tailored suit; expensive watch; suede loafers. His adversary's expression was impassive, but his eyes blazed manically.

Rivera had nowhere to run to. He was trapped in the campervan's cabin. He began to launch himself away from the open door, but it was too late.

The next thing the ex-soldier knew, he was writhing on the floor beside his van as 50,000 volts passed along the wires and through the barbs that had punctured his t-shirt and were embedded in his flesh.

* * * * *

When he opened his eyes, Rivera felt himself being manhandled further into the campervan. He attempted to close a fist and tried to swing a punch at the man who'd tasered him, but he could summon no strength. Instead, his arm simply hung limply by his side. He looked up, feeling disembodied, unable to fathom quite what was happening. The other man's expression was fixed; the VW's interior seemed to scroll by on an endless loop until his head careered into the base of the bench seat.

The other man had dark skin and several days' beard growth, some of which covered a painful-looking and obviously recent wound to his face. A thick, expensive gold chain hung from his neck, and he seemed to be muttering to himself as he dragged Rivera towards the kitchenette.

'What?' the prone man gasped, eventually, jolted into wakefulness by the blow. 'What are you doing?'

'It's nothing personal,' the other man announced. 'Just business. You understand?'

Rivera squinted. Bars of shadow flitted across his eyes and his head pounded. 'Who are you?' When he moved his head, the periphery of his vision rotated in whirling spirals.

He turned to look down upon Rivera. A smile crossed his face. 'Where are my manners?' he grinned. 'It is important you know your killer, no?' He paused. 'My name is Hakeem.'

The ex-soldier sighed, feeling some of his strength slowly returning. He tasted blood where he'd bitten the inside of his cheek as he'd been electrocuted. His mouth had a metallic flavour, and his throat was sandpaper-dry. But he knew he had to keep his tormentor talking if he was to stand any chance of escape. His thoughts were stubbornly slow in their processing. He wondered where Lomas was. Whether Christie would come to his rescue. His confusion persisted, though – he kept expecting to see Fraser arrive. 'I...'

'...no questions,' the other man interrupted.

'I don't understand,' Rivera croaked.

'It is of no concern, my friend.' Hakeem stepped over the man on the ground and grasped again for a moment at the trigger of the taser. Rivera was once more jolted into blackness.

* * * * *

Rivera awoke spluttering, froth foaming at his mouth. He coughed, and his mouth filled with a brackish residue. The campervan reeked of petrol.

'Rise and shine then!' Hakeem spoke, an unlit cigarette wedged between his lips. His eyes betrayed a sense of mild amusement.

'Wh...?' Rivera began.

The other man had upended a jerrycan and was pouring petrol in great glugs all over Rivera's prone figure.

'You are a careless man, no?' Hakeem said. 'You left the gas on – at least that's what everyone will think.' The assassin stepped over to the stove and turned the gas taps of the hot plate on.

The effects of the taser were wearing off more quickly this time, but Rivera still felt all but paralysed. Musing to himself, he lay there, feeling strangely calm; he'd cheated death on myriad occasions, but he'd never expected his life to end like this. He pondered how he'd be remembered: soldier; traveller, or victim of a camping accident? The thought of the latter almost made him laugh. He saddened a little, thinking that few people would recall him anyway after his demise. He tried to raise his head, but his body seemingly refused to obey his commands.

Hakeem stepped back over him and paused on the threshold, turning around by the campervan's sliding door. He patted at his pockets, bringing out a lighter.

'Any last words?' he asked, the cigarette bobbing up and down as he spoke. 'Oh – I forgot. I don't give a shit!' He chuckled.

*****

Looking back, Rivera had known he was defeated. It was a humbling thought. Being out-fought was something he could accept, but being outsmarted like he had been was galling. He still didn't know where the other man could have hidden to surprise him like he had.

The shriek that wrenched him out of his unhappy reverie was ear-splitting. How the cat had managed to drag the enormous rat through Iris' open window was something that Rivera would never understand - it was an act that defied the laws of physics. She'd brought her owner sacrifices before, but this was on an entirely different scale – the rodent was as big as her.

As Rosie jumped down from the open window, she landed heavily. The still-breathing rat shook itself free and darted across the floor, screaming for all its worth.

It was this that distracted Hakeem. It was only for a split-second, but he turned sharply. As he did, he stepped into a pool of petrol, and his shoe - pricey but impractical - slipped. His automatic reaction was to put out his hand to steady himself. But he used his injured hand. In a clumsy grab, he missed the edge of the table and fell. As he careered through the air, his body twisted involuntarily. His bandaged hand flailed around uselessly and bore all his weight. The assassin was tough, but he wasn't so tough that the electric daggers of pain shooting up his arm didn't make him wince and yelp.

Rivera later remembered the moment as one of complete silence. The man turned, facing the ex-soldier - a look of furious incomprehension on his face. His good hand reached towards him, but the ex-soldier was alert enough to smash the taser into the skirting board where it cracked.

Slowly and shakily, Rivera dragged himself upright, using the edges of the units to support his weight. Gritting his teeth, he wrenched out the terminals of the taser from his chest, gasping at the smarting pain.

The two men spilled onto the dry ground outside the campervan. There was nobody around to witness them. Each of them moved with lumbering gaits, looking like punch-drunk prize-fighters. Hakeem's damaged arm hung down uselessly. He eyed his adversary with a hateful expression. There was no sense of fear, but he knew his arm would not improve. Rivera, in contrast, was beginning to recover from the jolt of the electric current, but he knew his recent exertions had left him in less than peak condition - the two men were well matched, and he had to act quickly. He aimed a kick at the wounded man's side. In an involuntary motion, the assassin raised his bad arm to block it. The impact sent an explosion of pain shooting through him; he reacted violently.

'Fuck you!' Hakeem grimaced.

'Fuck me?' Rivera snarled. He rarely lost his temper. But even he drew the line somewhere – the assassin had tried to kill him twice already. He smashed another kick into Hakeem's bad side. As the other man bent against the pain, he also prepared to strike in retaliation. But while the ex-soldier was physically compromised, his mind was increasingly alert. Anticipating Hakeem's move, he swept his legs away. The other man crumpled, and Rivera began to rain repeated blows down on his damaged arm once again. With each impact, Hakeem yelped, clutching desperately for invisible purchase at the air. It was vital – Rivera knew – that his assailant was given no time to recover.

The assassin rolled onto his back. Rivera smashed his fist into Hakeem's face. Beneath his knuckles, he felt the give of spongy tissue and bone. He threw another punch. The impact was greater. Three punches later, he felt something crack. The ex-soldier had some medical knowledge, but he was far from being a physician. The Army had moulded him into a killer; it had given him the ability to read the state of his opponent. As his fist impacted once more, he felt something give – this time it was something fundamental. Some unseen axis between blood, bone and being had shattered. Ordinarily, he'd have stopped. He might even have worried about witnesses – concerned about someone posting footage to YouTube.

But now Rivera was beyond caring.

He'd lost control in such an extreme way only once before. But then, he'd had a squad to pull him out of the fight. By the time he'd been wrenched away, the light of life had long gone out of the insurgent's eyes. The man's blood was seeping into the dust when his Corporal dragged the corpse into an abandoned hut. Shortly after, they torched it – along with the petrol-sodden body – and drove away. It wasn't something Rivera was proud of.

But every man has their breaking point.

Rivera grabbed Hakeem's collar and hauled the other man towards Iris. The assassin landed with his head half under the chassis and lay still.

* * * * *

The assassin's skull made a satisfying crunch as the campervan's wheels crushed it. Rivera's eyes were expressionless – it was as if he'd been taken over by an external force, and then suddenly conveyed back into consciousness.

He switched off the engine. Then, he stepped out of the cab and waited to return to himself.

After a couple of involuntary leg twitches, Hakeem lay still. Rivera held his fingers to the assassin's neck. At first, he felt the dying embers of a weak, irregular pulse, but it soon faded away into nothingness.

Rivera lowered himself towards a folding chair and then collapsed into it, heavily. Rosie, having consumed the food that had been left out for her, jumped up, settling herself onto his lap.

Chapter 57.

'I thought you said you don't go looking for trouble.' Christie frowned, suppressing a smile.

'I don't,' the ex-soldier replied. 'I guess it just kind of finds me.'

'So what happened here?' the officer asked.

'He started it,' Rivera announced bluntly.

Silence.

'You think he's the last of them?' Lomas enquired, frowning at the legs protruding from beneath the campervan.

'Yes,' Rivera nodded. 'My guess is that he was a lone wolf, anyway.' He looked directly at Lomas. 'I'm sorry about your sister.'

Lomas nodded.

A silence fell, threatened only by birdsong. Swallows swooped from the line of poplar trees bordering the campsite. As they fed on the wing, Christie stared uncomfortably at the floor.

'I doubt it'll be any consolation, but I think she was right about all of this,' Rivera continued. 'She just ended up in the middle of it.' He looked at Christie. 'And I think you'll have definitely managed to shut down an international operation by the time you're done. You'll be a celebrity on the force now!' he smiled.

'There'll be someone else who'll step into Safia's place, though,' the Detective Inspector shrugged, kicking a little at the stones on the pathway.

'Maybe,' Rivera nodded. 'But take the victory for now - you deserve it.' He paused. 'Anyway... we've kind of got a situation here...' He nodded down at Hakeem's corpse.

'That's why I didn't bring anyone else with me,' Christie explained. 'Eddie here will help me - and he won't say anything. It's a good job it's quiet round here.'

Rivera nodded. 'And the van?' He pointed towards the vehicle the pair had arrived in.

'What about it?' Lomas shrugged.

'Well, it's old and shit,' the ex-soldier replied.

'It's getting squished this afternoon,' Christie announced.

'Yeah?' Rivera raised his eyebrows.

'Yeah,' the officer nodded. 'But first it's going to transport our late friend here.'

The ex-soldier smiled uncertainly and folded his arms. 'You know how you said you want to try and keep things above board...?'

She sighed. 'Maybe I've learned something from you in that regard. Maybe you were right. Maybe justice and the law aren't always the same thing.'

The ex-soldier grinned. 'So what's the plan?'

'Hakeem never was,' Christie shrugged.

Rivera nodded. 'Enough said. Can't you pin it on... Bartle?'

'Beatty?' Christie shook her head. 'He's in a whole world of trouble right now, as it is. The higher ups took him away in handcuffs this morning. I've only got desk staff and a couple of officers drafted in from Dorset. No one's keeping an eye on me.'

'So?' Rivera raised his eyebrows.

'The Laine residence is currently a crime scene – authorised personnel only.'

Silence.

'Quicklime?' the ex-soldier enquired.

'Something like that,' the officer nodded.

'My kind of woman!' Rivera grinned.

'You wish...' Christie responded, her eyes locking with his for a moment.

Chapter 58.

After mopping up the petrol, Rivera left Iris' doors open. The smell would linger, but he reasoned he could live with that. He drove the campervan through the ford over the River Salt in a bid to rid the tyres of any remaining hint of Hakeem.

Leaving the VW, he then opted for a last walk into town before heading away. It was time for him to leave; for such a picturesque place, Saltmarsh Cove had too high a body count. He wanted to get away to somewhere less dangerous. Even the pull of Christie wasn't enough to keep him. He reasoned he was on a promise, but he also wondered if they'd shared too much for her to be just another conquest.

Walking the length of the promenade, he looked out towards the rock islands at the far edge of the town's boundary. He thought about how much closer they seemed from land compared with how they'd felt when he'd been in the water. Strolling along the high street, he stopped at an ATM and withdrew the maximum amount of cash it would allow. Pocketing this, he then wandered on towards The Cliffside Hotel.

Along the way, he noticed a board outside a newsagent carrying *The Herald's* latest headline: HEROINE POLICE OFFICER SAVES THE DAY! He smiled and peered at a copy of the paper. Scanning the story, he saw how the press had reported things and noted, with some relief, there was no mention of his involvement.

'Are you going to purchase that, sir?' the old lady behind the counter called out officiously. She peered angrily at him over a pair of bi-focal glasses, distracted from the roll of scratch cards she was working her way through.

'No, no - just looking, love,' he replied breezily.

* * * * *

Lomas opened the door to the hotel wearing a bright white bathrobe and disposable slippers. He had a face pack plastered on his visage, which made him look almost spectral.

Rivera grinned. 'What - are you powdering your nose?'

'No. I...' Lomas' reply was flustered.

'That thing... did you get it done?' the ex-soldier enquired.

'Yes – that's why I'm bloody dressed like this!' He shrugged. 'It's cathartic. My nerves won't take much more!'

'I can come back if you like?' Rivera smiled.

'Fancy a beer instead?' Lomas shrugged. 'I guess it's my round. We can talk about tits and fighting. And football.'

Rivera chuckled. 'I'll wait in the bar.'

* * * * *

'So you're heading out, then?' Lomas asked. The two men had half-drunk pints of lager resting on the wooden table before them. The bar was quiet. A bored barmaid scrolled through her phone as she waited for the smattering of slow-drinking customers seated before her to request refills.

'Yeah - it's time,' Rivera answered.

'Christie likes you, you know?'

'Yeah – I guess. But I'd be no good for her. Besides, she's too good a copper to waste time with me.'

Silence.

'You're a good man, Trent,' the other man announced. He raised his glass. 'Thanks for everything. I mean - I thought you were a bit of a prick when I first met you. And now...'

'You think I'm a bit less of a prick? Hopefully?'

'Yeah, pretty much,' Lomas nodded.

The ex-soldier smiled for a moment. Then his expression grew serious. 'I'm sorry again about your sister. I mean - I'm glad we nailed those guys, but I know it's not going to bring her back.'

Lomas sighed. 'I know. I used to think a lot about karma, and forgiving and forgetting.' He paused, picking distractedly at a beer mat. 'But I guess I might have learned a few things from you, you know?'

'Such as?'

'Forgiveness is weakness. Revenge is sweet. Stuff like that.'

The two men touched glasses.

'Safe travels,' said Lomas.

* * * * *

As Rivera parked Iris by the library, Fraser stood up from his chair and walked towards him, smiling. He gripped onto his regular bench, steadying himself; he'd evidently started early. The bruising had faded slightly.

'Nice ride you've got there, chief!' he beamed.

'She's alright, isn't she?' Rivera nodded, grinning.

'Yeah, I'll say.' He paused. 'You off?'

The ex-soldier nodded. 'Time to move on. You?'

He shrugged. 'I don't know. Maybe in the autumn? Maybe I'll follow the sun someplace?' He grinned. 'Besides, you've got rid of all the bad guys around here, haven't you? I figure I might as well stick around for a while. It'll be safer now!' The two men stood facing each other. Fraser idly flicked at the ring pull on his nearly empty can. His hair was greasy and matted, and his fingernails were rimed with dirt.

'Which unit were you in?' Rivera's question was blunt and wrong-footed Fraser. His face tightened for a moment, before he recovered his poise.

'Oh, what - you mean in the Army?'

Rivera nodded.

'Ancient history, chief. Those bodies were buried a long time ago. I used to stand on the terraces at Arsenal though - back in the Highbury days. You?'

'Fulham. For better or worse.'

'Well... worse much of the time, I should think?' The homeless man rubbed at his forearm.

Rivera peeled off £100 in fresh notes and handed them over.

'You don't need to, chief,' Fraser protested.

The ex-soldier shrugged. 'You can't take it with you, right?'

The homeless man nodded, reached out, and took the offering. 'Much obliged.'

* * * * *

Higher up on the cliff road, Rivera parked behind a screen of trees. He peered through the gateway of the house he'd visited before, but saw no movement. Walking hastily up to the door, he posted an envelope that contained the remainder of the cash he'd withdrawn on the high street.

On the front, he'd scrawled a short note, thanking the occupiers for the clothes, the snacks, and the use of their phone.

As he returned to Iris, he spotted a business card wedged beneath the rubber of the windscreen wiper. He hadn't noticed it before. It was another one of Christie's cards. But this one had a message on the reverse: CALL ME ANYTIME. MAYBE YOU'LL BE ABLE TO STAY AWAKE? LOIS.

Rivera paused for a moment, as if weighing the card in his hand.

He placed it in his pocket. Then, climbing into the T2, he started the engine, slipped into gear, and drove slowly up out of the valley.

Chapter 59.

Thank you so much for reading this novel. I hope you have enjoyed it. Should you have a spare 5 minutes and would like to leave a short review, I would be hugely grateful.

Please enjoy the first chapter of TWO'S COMPANY *over the next pages.*

Very best wishes.
Blake Valentine

Chapter 60.

The First Chapter of *TWO'S COMPANY* – the next novel in the TRENT RIVERA SERIES

* * * * *

TWO'S COMPANY
Trent Rivera's free-spirited lifestyle is a reaction to years in uniform. His only constants: a campervan; a cat, and the desire to atone for past sins.

When he secures work in the small village of Castlethwaite, the ex-soldier believes he's found the perfect place to wait out the winter and disappear from the world.

But Trent Rivera doesn't go looking for trouble. It finds him...

Behind its respectable façade, his new place of employment is not what it seems. Rivera senses evil and begins investigating, but finds himself in a race against time. For years his bosses have been operating in plain sight. They've covered their tracks well and have established escape routes that are ready for use at a moment's notice. Will the ex-soldier be able to uncover the crimes before those responsible disappear?

* * * * *

'That's enough,' the woman announced, her voice low.

'No – it needs to be deeper,' the man argued, mumbling. He gestured at the freshly dug hole with the barrel of his Holland & Holland shotgun. A pile of earth stood to one side of it, and the ghostly outlines of leafless trees were faintly visible in the moonlight.

'We haven't got bloody time,' the woman hissed back, her breath steaming in the cold night air. 'Let's just get this done with. The longer we delay, the riskier things get.' She huffed irritably. 'I haven't come this far to throw everything away now. We get rid of them, and then we vanish – just like we said.'

The man sighed, acceding.

Trent Rivera, sensing further disagreement brewing between the pair, stopped digging; his knuckles whitened a little on the handle of the shovel. The silence that descended was broken only by the dripping of moisture onto the mulch of the ground. Tendrils of fog rolled across the floor of the wooded glade, grasping at the trunks of trees and lying in ghostly wisps above the fallen leaves.

The vapour looked like smoke as it caught the beam of Rivera's head torch. Fog shrouded the hazy silhouettes of the two figures; as he cast occasional glances up from the bottom of the pit, the outlines of the two overseers were malevolent spectres against the bright gleam of the full moon. Another captive – a female - was standing against the backdrop of trees, her escape covered by the pair's weapons.

An owl hooted, and somewhere in the distance, a twig snapped. The sound echoed through the clearing, and then the eerie, dripping silence descended once more.

The captors froze for a moment. They exhaled simultaneously, looking warily at one another.

This – Rivera reasoned – was an opportunity. But from where he was at the foot of the hole, he knew he was at a distinct disadvantage.

They held the high ground.

They had a plan they'd carefully formulated. It wasn't their original plan; they'd had to adapt. But it was a plan, nonetheless.

And they were armed.

Rivera, meanwhile, was simply in the wrong place at the wrong time, improvising.

He was digging his own grave.

* * * * *

As Rivera looked up, the light from his head torch blinded the man for a split-second. He squinted, waving an irritated hand at the beam. 'Get that bloody light out of my eyes!' he hissed. His other hand retained a hold on the trigger guard of his weapon – the stock remained solidly wedged in the crook of his arm. The man was well-spoken; his tone towards Rivera was condescending.

'I'd better pass you the shovel then – no?' Rivera ventured, holding his hand up to cover the torchlight.

'What?' the man frowned.

'Well, if you're going to bury us, you're going to need it. Right?' Rivera shrugged and cast a glance at the outline of the man's accomplice. In the dim light she looked on, impassive. Beyond her, he heard the other captive weeping softly.

'He's right. Take the shovel,' the woman urged. 'Let's get this over with. I'm getting fed up with this fucking place.'

'I – er - very well,' the man nodded, taken aback at having to cede control. Hesitantly, he approached the lip of the hole and reached down to grab at the protruding handle. 'Wait!' the man called out suddenly, checking himself. 'No, no,' he chuckled. 'Not like that. Place the shovel on the ground and then stand back.'

Rivera grimaced inwardly. His plan had been simple: he'd wrench the handle, drag the man into the hole and then make things up as he went along. Whatever transpired, he vowed to get out alive. He promised himself that much. His opponents were two middle-aged teachers who'd grown overweight and complacent from years of sedentary living. He knew he could take them – guns or no guns. The only thing that had made him hesitate so far was putting the other prisoner in more danger.

But time was ticking now. The aces he'd assumed were up his sleeve hadn't materialised.

It seemed like time to roll the dice.

Only the older man wasn't as foolish as he'd assumed.

'What? Do you think I'd fall for a schoolboy trick like that?' the man tutted, before shaking his head and continuing in a superior tone. 'How disappointing! I'd have expected better from you.'

Rivera sighed, stepping away from the shovel and back into the centre of the hole. In his head, he was frantically running scenarios and their outcomes; he was ever watchful of the weapons, and ever mindful of how their crossfire might affect his situation. 'Can I just ask...?' he began.

At close quarters, the shotgun blast sounded like a cannon. Its sound ripped through the glade like a tsunami of sound, shattering the silence of the night. Loose earth from the freshly dug pile beside the pit stung at Rivera's eyes. And a split-second later, he felt a weight crushing down on him, twisting him; turning him; knocking him off balance.

His feet lost purchase on the slippery mud. The ground rushed up at him. His face collided hard with the compacted mud at the base of the hole.

Blackness.

About the Author

Blake Valentine is the author of the TRENT RIVERA MYSTERY SERIES. Prior to becoming a writer, he worked in the music industry as both performer and producer before moving into various roles in education. He has lived in Osaka, Japan and San Diego, California, and now resides on the south coast of England with his wife, 2 children, and a cat.

All books featuring Trent Rivera are available on Amazon and can be read for free on Kindle Unlimited. Please take a look at Blake's website for more information. News, updates and competitions are also featured on Facebook (www.facebook.com/blakevalentineauthor).

If you've enjoyed reading any of Blake's books and have 5 minutes to spare, then do please leave a short review online.

Read more at https://www.blakevalentine.com.

Printed in Great Britain
by Amazon